NEW YORK TIMES BESTSELLING AUTHOR

RAINE MILLER

writing as Brit DeMille

MR.
Hockey

MR.

Hockey

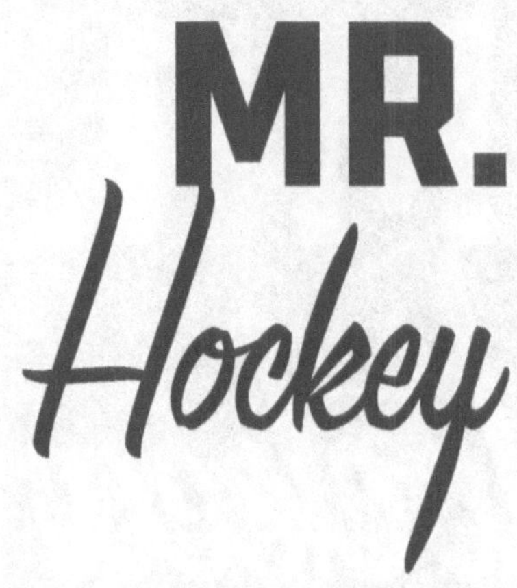

VEGAS
CRUSH

mikhail zelenka

left wing

MR.
Hockey

8

dedication

R. S.

*The first to wear #19
and my favorite winger forever.*

prologue

Mikhail

Fifteen years ago.

Ten o'clock on a school night, and I've been on the ice for three hours. *I'm so tired.* My dad has me working on a passing drill complicated for the Under 16s. *And I'm only ten.* I want to learn it, I do, but I'm tired, and the small dinner I ate before practice is long forgotten. So, when my stomach rumbles angrily, I try my hardest to hold back the anxious tears threatening to appear. *I just wanna—*

"Mikhail," Dad barks.

My head snaps up and I realize I've zoned out. I'm so tired. I really just want to go home and have my mom make me some hot chocolate.

"Where is your head, boy?" He stares at me, waiting for a response.

"I was thinking about hot chocolate. Dad, I think I've got this. Can we go home now?"

Asking to go home pretty much guarantees that I'll now be here until midnight. I cringe, mad that I let the words escape like that. I've already figured out the fewer words I say—*the fewer opportunities I give him to react*—the better it is for me.

"Get it right three times in a row and we can go home."

My shoulders slump in defeat. I haven't gotten it right one time *in a row*. Still, I square off, replaying the drill quickly in my head, giving my dad a nod that I'm ready to focus again.

We run the drill.

It does not go well.

Again.

And again.

And then, finally, something changes, and I get it.

I manage to nail it once, twice, and then a third time. My fist pumps in the air triumphantly as soon as it happens.

I did it. I look across at my dad, hoping for his excitement. All I see is a crease of his eyes.

"Clean up and meet me at the car."

This is how practices always go with him. *I don't know why I was expecting anything different.* A minute later, I'm alone on the ice, gathering loose pucks and cones. I drag everything to the supply closet and then sit, catching my breath as I loosen my skates and pull on my shoes. I throw all my gear in my bag and shoulder it, along with my hockey stick and pads, and shuffle out to the front door, waving to the tired front desk clerk, Mr. Stan, on my way out into the snowy, Detroit evening.

My dad has the car warmed up, which is nice, but he's totally cold and silent as we ride home. No "good job, son" for me. Which shouldn't be a surprise, but still, I'm disappointed.

So I slump in my seat and cross my arms, pouting on the lonely ride home.

My father, Jozem Zelenka.

Otherwise known as "The Great Zelenka."

He's a superstar in pro hockey. One of the leading scorers in NHL history. A future Hall of Famer without question. He retired about a year ago, on his thirty-ninth birthday. People made a big deal about how long he lasted in pro sports and how much of a legacy he left for hockey. People ask me every time I play if I'll be the next "Great Zelenka," if I will try to live up to my dad's records on the ice.

"Sit up straight, Mikhail," he scolds.

I scoot up in the seat, looking out the window. "Dad, can we stop and get McDonald's?"

"No. There is no nutritional value to that food. What a waste of money."

"We have plenty of money," I mutter.

"You have no money," he corrects. "I have money. Because I worked hard on the ice for a long time. Someday you will have your own money, and you can make your own decisions about how you spend it then."

"But I'm hungry," I whine. "Please, Dad. Just this one time?"

"No." His decision is final, and I have learned not to argue with my father. I never, ever win.

When we get home, my mother asks how practice

went. My father makes a comment about how bad my passing was and how we stayed late to work on it. He grabs the newspaper and walks out of the room, leaving me standing, slump-shouldered and defeated. She winks and says I can have some dessert before bed if I want.

This perks me up. I practically skip to the table, where my mom serves me a piece of chocolate cake. Just as I'm about to take the first bite, my father says from the living room, "You'll get fat if you eat that, Mikhail."

My mom gives me a conspiratorial look. I grin at her and then shovel that delicious chocolate cake into my mouth as fast as I can.

She shakes her head when she takes the plate to the sink. "Your sisters at least chewed theirs. Go take a bath."

I do as I'm told, but afterward, when I open the bathroom door, towel around my skinny waist, I hear my parents arguing downstairs. It's loud enough that I'm surprised my two sisters don't wake up. My mom is telling my dad that he's too hard on me. He says he's just giving me the best possible future as a pro hockey player. She says he should let me just be a kid, and he says that's not an option in sports anymore. Pro athletes start when they're practically babies.

As I get ready for bed, their argument moves on to other things, things I don't understand. It gets bigger and bigger until they're really yelling at each other and sound so angry.

My sister Iliana, two years younger than me, comes into my room and crawls into my bed, pulling one of my pillows over her head. "I don't like it when they yell so loud, Mikky," she says.

"I know. Neither do I, Illy." *I hate it.*

Normally, I'd kick her out of my room, but I won't. Not tonight.

I lie with my back to her, my own pillow drowning out the ugly sounds, wishing I was somehow capable of making it stop.

Sadly, I'd need some major superhero powers for that miracle to ever happen.

1
six christmas cookies

Mikhail

"It's pretty, right?" my mom, Maria, asks as I'm sprawled out on the huge living room sectional, taking in the sight of the Christmas tree we just decorated together.

The white lights sparkle against the ornaments our family has collected over the past couple of decades. My mom loves Christmas. She collects Santa figurines, nutcrackers, and every other kind of Christmas decoration you can find. The day after Thanksgiving, every year, she pulls boxes and boxes of the stuff out of the basement crawl space, carefully unwrapping each and every item, and placing it strategically around the house. It's like Santa's workshop, seriously. A Christmas wonderland.

We save the Christmas tree for two weeks before Christmas, though, because she insists on cutting our own. She doesn't want pine needles all over the place, so fourteen days before the holiday, we go to the tree farm and pick one out together. Usually, my sisters join us, but this year, it was just my mom and me.

"When are Iliana and Daniella coming home?"

"Iliana won't come until Christmas Eve," Mom says, a note of distaste in her tone. "Her new job doesn't offer much time off, apparently."

"Well, she's kind of low on seniority, so…" I shrug. My baby sister Iliana has a job at a big advertising agency in New York, and she works crazy hours, but she seems to like it.

"Daniella comes tomorrow," Mom says of my older sister.

"With Roman?" I ask hopefully.

"Roman is with his father for Christmas this year," she answers, with that same note of disapproval in her voice. My sister's baby daddy is on the *He Who Shall Not Be Named* list. They were engaged for a year before Daniella got pregnant, and then the moron bolted. He came back around after my nephew, Roman, was born, but my mom is never gonna forgive the fucker for bailing on my sister. *As she shouldn't.* Mom is silently badass in a way that needs no interpretation.

"Bummer," is all I say in response.

"You know what else is a bummer?" she asks, adjusting an angel in the display on an end table.

"What?"

"The fact that you play for a team that's all the way across the country. When will you transfer to Detroit?"

This makes me chuckle. "Um, never? I mean, it doesn't work like that with trades. And besides, Detroit suuuucks big time. The Crush keep winning.

Why would I want to get traded from an awesome team to a bad one?"

"Because you would be closer to your mama, of course," she says, grinning.

Frankly, the only reason I would ever even consider moving back to Detroit is for my mom. I have no desire to come home. I'm just fine with the two thousand miles between me and my hometown.

"Well, last I checked, you guys retired. Come out to Vegas more often. Come see a few games. We play like a million of 'em."

"I'd like to come out more. But it depends on Jozem. His schedule is more detailed than mine."

"What's he got going on? He hasn't worked for the past fifteen years."

My mom laughs and smacks me on the arm like I've told a funny joke. "He's still so in demand, Mikhail. He does a lot of speaking events and hockey clinics and camps."

"In demand, huh?" I roll my eyes, earning an elbow to the ribs. "Okay, whatever. The Great Zelenka is in high demand. Too busy to come out and watch his son play pro hockey."

It comes out more bitter than I mean it to, and honestly, I am a little bitter about it, but whatever. We don't question The Great Zelenka. He does what he wants, what he thinks is worth his time. He's hockey-frickin'-royalty, and I, most definitely, am not.

"Don't pout, Mikhail. You're too handsome for that."

"I'm not pouting." I say the words far too quickly. "It's whatever…"

She sighs, then changes the subject. "Anyone special in your life these days?"

"Oh boy," I say, mirroring her exasperated sigh.

"It's a serious question. I want to see you settle down, meet someone special."

"Mom, I *just* turned twenty-six. Please stop trying to marry me off already."

"Well, Iliana is so focused on work, and Daniella is...well, you know about Daniella."

I can't help laughing. This is how my mom handles any conversation about my older sister. *"You know about Daniella"* is code for *"your sister done messed up her life by having a baby out of wedlock with an idiot."* My mom is a devout Catholic woman, and the fact that my sister is twenty-eight, single, and had a baby with a man she did not marry is like too much for her to verbalize. She loves my sister, and she loves Roman to the ends of the earth, but she also loves her Catholic faith.

"What do either of my sisters' life choices have to do with my love life?" I try my best to change the subject.

"So you have a love life?" The expression on her face is open and genuinely hopeful.

"Not the kind I think you want for me," I say with a laugh.

"Oh, Mikhail," she says, her lips pursed. "I hope you're being careful."

This sets me into a fit of laughter and also gets me smacked on the arm again. My mom tells me to be serious. That *she's* serious. I finally have to ask, "Why do you want me to have a girlfriend so bad?"

"A wife, Mikhail. I want you to find a wife, and maybe someday give me grandchildren. And I can help with them because you'll get traded to Detroit and you'll move back home."

"By home, I assume you mean, like, nearby. Not, like, actually, home. To this house. With my fictional wife and children."

"Why not? We have so much space and you players travel so much...your wife would need help with the babies."

I roll my eyes for the second time in a few minutes. "Ma."

"You know, I'm going to have you do a chore for every time you roll your eyes at me, young man."

"Ma," I repeat, "no grown man comes home to live in the same house after he's married, unless he's a broke loser. And I'm not broke. I have plenty of money."

"Okay, but you haven't really answered me. You haven't met anyone out there in Las Vegas? Are you even dating at all?"

I lay my head back against the couch and let out a sigh, lifting a shoulder. "I did meet someone back in the summer. She was fun and funny, and I liked her, but she dumped me."

"Why would she ever dump someone like you?" My mom's look of shock and disbelief is slightly comforting.

"Well, apparently, for her, the relationship was purely physical," I say thoughtfully. "I wasn't in on that, though, so I thought we were, like, an actual couple. Silly me."

I rub my fingertips against my chest absently. Gia was a fling, I get that now, but I *did* like her. She's probably the only woman who I've let in enough to break my heart. *Not sure I'm in a hurry to do that again.* "I went over a week or so ago with a Christmas present and she looked at it like it was an alien with seven heads. She told me she didn't think we were on the same page about where the relationship was heading."

"Oh, well, I'm sorry," she says softly. "You thought it was getting serious?"

"Don't get ahead of yourself there, Ma." I nudge my shoulder against hers. "Not serious. But definitely...something. And she wasn't into it. Which is fine. I'm okay being single for a while."

"Were you in love with her?"

"Meh. Who knows? It's over now."

She leaves it at that, thankfully. We turn on the television and watch some mindless talent show, my mind still on Gia. It was meant to be a fun thing. A summer fling. A distraction during a boring summer. And it was that, for a while. The sex was great. She was funny and wild and had a mouth like a sailor. I definitely cared for her—obviously more than she cared for me. But love? Nah. I don't think so. And marriage? Having watched my parents bicker for decades, why would I want that? Mom is far too kind for someone as cruel as my father, and I can't help but wonder if I'd become more like him as I age. *Why would I want to put a woman I love through that?*

I'm deep in thought when my father comes back from whatever important event he had to attend tonight. He's in a dark suit, tall and broad shouldered, and still in great shape for a guy about to turn fifty-seven. He's got dark hair like me, slightly wavy and thick, just a few distinguished gray hairs at his temples. In comparison, my mom is on the shorter side. She's always been soft and curvy, her hair also dark, her face expressive and beautiful. My dad's face gives away nothing but annoyance and disappointment. I don't know if I've ever seen him smile. I sure can't remember it if and when he did.

Ever dutiful, my mom jumps up as he storms in, asking if he's hungry, reminding him she's got a casserole to heat up for him.

His eyes find me from where I'm sprawled out lazily on the sofa and narrow. "Did you eat casserole tonight?"

"Yeah, it's what Mom made," I say with a shrug. *Is this a trick question?*

"Have you been to the gym today?"

"Nope."

"What else have you eaten today?"

"Six Christmas cookies. A bowl of chili. Mom's casserole."

"That is not healthy. And you didn't work out?"

"Dad, I've been on a healthy diet since summer. I'm cheating a bit now, it's the holidays. The team has us on nutrition plans and workout plans, and I'm on vacation this week. It's no big deal."

My father shoves his hands in his pockets, his back ramrod straight. He never, ever relaxes. "When you get back, will you continue to allow Boris and Evan to have all the goals?" *Oh, for fuck's sake. This. Again.*

"Dad, I make plenty of goals. And by the way, I've been a starter at left wing since I was a rookie. At nineteen. And we've won the Cup twice since I've been there. I'm doing fine."

"Fine is not good enough," he says harshly. "You know this."

We stare at each other for a few uncomfortable seconds before he decides he's either made his point or won the nonexistent argument he thinks we're having, or whatever.

I've learned not to engage in these one-sided, futile conversations.

Finally, he turns and walks out of the room, leaving me alone with a twinkling Christmas tree with a zillion decorations and some dumbass show on the television.

2
right on time

"Give me a jab, cross, hook, cross, uppercut combo," my coach says as I dance around the one-hundred-pound bag.

I do the combo, but he steps behind me after the first go, pulling my gloved hands back by my ears.

"Pretend there are magnets in your cheeks and in your gloves. Those gloves go right back after each punch. Starting your punch there will give you more power, for one, but keeping your gloves up will help protect your face."

I nod and try the combo again, getting the bag to swing with the force of my punches. Wow, that's satisfying. I go again and again until it starts to feel natural.

"Good job!" he says. "That was good work. Did it feel good?"

I nod, grinning. I'm five three and a buck-fifteen. I've never been particularly athletic or strong or whatever, but boxing makes me feel like a total badass.

I honestly wish I'd learned it sooner, but this is good. As my grandmother used to say, things come into your life "right on time." I never really gave it much thought, but I guess she meant things happen just when they're supposed to. Boxing included.

It's noisy in the gym, which I'm glad about because it gives me a sense of anonymity, like no one is paying me any attention. Which would very much freak me out, making me more self-conscious than I already am.

"There's a lot of people in here, today," I say.

Theo, my trainer, looks around and nods. "Yeah. More than usual but it'll thin out. This is just the post-holiday New Year's resolution swell. Most will come for a few weeks and then give it up."

I snort at this. "I've never understood why people rush out to the gym just because it's a new year. So weird."

He shrugs. "Human nature. I ate too much during the holidays and I feel guilty, ergo I must show everyone on social media how committed I am to get back in shape."

Theo has me switch to round kicks for a while. I'm getting better at them, but I keep hitting on my shin instead of the top of my foot. "That's gonna leave a mark," I mutter after hitting on my shinbone one too many times.

"Yes, it will, but you'll get there." He gives me an encouraging grin.

The next stop is the speed bag. As we walk, Theo pulls off my gloves. I notice a tall, dark-haired guy in the ring sparring with another one of the trainers. Muscled and broad-shouldered with really good hair.

And tattoos from his neck down to his gloves.

Probably all the way down to his fingers, if the rest of him is any clue.

Beautiful ink, and a lot of it.

He moves gracefully, his feet fast and light as he dances around, jabbing and ducking. I watch for a minute or two, intrigued by him. It's hard to tell what he really looks like from this angle. He's wearing protective headgear and a mouth guard, neither of which makes anyone look particularly attractive. However, the full-body fitness, the artful ink, and the dark locks give me a feeling the face won't be a disappointment.

"Stop drooling and get to work. Thirty hits on each hand, then do a burpee in between."

Theo steps away to grab something from the office while I work. And by working, I mean making a total mess of my rhythm on the speed bag. Fundamentally, I know I need to keep my rhythm of movement and a one-two-three count between hits. But I keep losing it, hitting too hard. Hitting in the wrong spot. Forgetting the counts.

"Oof," Theo comments as he strides back over. "Did you forget everything you learned last time, or is that guy over there frying your brain right now?"

"Sorry." I frown and shake my head. "Can't get it together today, I guess."

"Take a water break, Reagan." He points me to the bench where my water is.

I follow his directions, my gaze going back to

linger on the big guy in the ring. "Do you know who he is?"

"Name's Mikhail," he says. "Plays hockey. Comes in to spar every once in a while."

I hum a sound and even I'm not sure what it means. Theo just raises an eyebrow and shakes his head before telling me my water break's over and to get back to the speed bag to finish up my workout.

WORKOUT FINISHED, I gather my stuff and shoulder my gym bag, heading outside into the mid-morning Las Vegas sun. Which is hot and getting hotter as the minutes tick by. I'm used to the desert heat now, but there was a time when I never thought I would. The gym is less than a ten-minute walk from my apartment building, so I never bother with calling a ride.

After one block, though, I feel the presence of someone behind me, my hackles rising. I hold my head high and square my shoulders, refusing to look weak. Eventually, I get the courage to look behind me and...*is that the guy from the gym, the one Theo said was Mikhail?*

Mikhail sounds like it could be a Russian name to me.

But he wasn't paying me any attention at all, so it can't be.

I attempt to calmly tell myself it's probably just a coincidence.

I take another glance as I quicken my pace. He's got earbuds in, and he's looking at his phone.

Not at me.

I try to keep my breathing under control and keep walking.

The past couple of years haven't been great. The last couple weeks? Even worse. I work at one of the bigger casinos—Tangiers—and there was some trouble with one of the high rollers recently. His people think I did something I did not, and now I watch out for creeping Russian goons everywhere I go.

Hence, the boxing lessons.

So yeah, maybe it's just a coincidence that a huge dude named Mikhail is following me down the street —call me paranoid or whatever—but I'm ready to pull out my pepper spray and give this guy a surprise. I've always been a shy, quiet girl. A wallflower. I've tried to stay out of the way, away from conflict. But lately, I've simply hit my limit. I'm tired of being used, pushed around, and being scared out of my wits. Aggression has never been my style. But now? Now, I'm ready to defend myself. *I refuse to be a victim.*

My pulse is pounding in my chest as I walk, trying not to look terrified, trying not to run. I do not want to answer the same questions I've already answered several times already. I do not want some strutting thug up in my face, touching me, threatening me. I'm so sick of it.

As I walk into the door of my apartment building, I let out the breath I've been holding, but when I turn around, that same guy with all the tats who was sparring at the gym, is walking in behind me. Into *my* building.

I spin around so fast I nearly give myself whiplash. His eyes go wide as I lash out. "Listen, creep, I told those guys I don't know anything. So stop following me and go back to your master like the good dog you are."

His face is totally open, shocked, mouth in an O, eyebrows up in the middle of his forehead. "Huh?" is all that comes out of him.

His shock rings truthful to me, but I've learned that some people are better actors than they are at being genuine humans; so even though my initial fright and anger have dissipated in this strange moment, I still say, "You've been following me for the past five blocks. You were in the gym, but I've never seen you there before. Then you happen to follow me all the way to my apartment building? I don't believe in coincidence these days. So, I want you to know you can go back to your boss and tell him I don't know anything and to leave me the hell *alone!*"

The guy's face has gone from shocked to incredulous. He's easily a foot taller than me. Also, very hot…just as I suspected when I was watching him sparring. I shake my head and silently scold myself. I should *not* be admiring the "hotness" of a guy who may just work for a crime lord.

"Lady," he says coolly, "I did just leave the gym and I did just walk here, but this is my apartment building. I live here."

The hell?

The elevator opens, and I step in. The big guy—

umm, "hockey player" per Theo—takes up the rest of the space as he pushes the button for the third floor at the same time that I reach out to push the button for five. We ride in tense silence after the door closes us in together. When the elevator doors open at three, he turns slightly and speaks, "Nice to meet you, I guess." Then he proceeds to step out and heads down the hallway with long, purposeful strides.

I hold the door open and peek my head out, watching the back of him retreat until he stops at a door, produces a key, and enters an apartment. I'm literally shaking as I step off two floors later for my own apartment. I never get aggressive like that, but I'm so tired of feeling terrified each time a man approaches me.

Grabbing a Vitamin Water from the fridge, I sink into my favorite armchair and think about the whole weird encounter. Theo said his name was Mikhail and he played hockey. Now that my paranoia has subsided, I can admit he didn't give off the same vibe as the other goons have lately. I probably overreacted. I credit the boxing for making me feel so badass, though. Which *was* the point of taking the lessons in the first place.

So I won't feel entirely helpless if (when) I'm threatened.

Because it's clear, they're not just going to leave you alone because you told them to.

Now I feel a little badly for lashing out at the guy if he indeed was just trying to get home after a workout. "Paranoid much?" I ask out loud with a bitter laugh. That Sodorov jerkwad...*I can't let him get to me.* What angers me the most is that *I* did nothing wrong, and yet, this creep feels it's okay to intimidate me.

Calm down, Reagan, you're okay. You're home safe.

After a few deep breaths and a quick pep talk, I call my mom. I need my anchor in the craziness that is my life—and thankfully, she doesn't know I desperately need a shower and stink. Surprisingly, she answers on the first ring, her voice chirpy and cheerful.

Immediately wary, I say, "Hey, Mamma, how's it going?"

My mom, Audrey, launches into a ten-minute story about how she met someone in her neighborhood who wants to start a community garden. She tells me all about how much she used to love gardening (she didn't) and how she can't wait to get out there and get her hands in the dirt. She can't wait to see food grow from her own work. It's simultaneously exhausting and exhilarating to hear her talk about this new project, because she puts as much energy into telling the story as she might put into the actual work.

I have no idea why she has this sudden interest in gardening, a hobby she's never engaged in, *ever*, in my whole life. In fact, she's always said how she couldn't even keep house plants alive. But this is my mother, and she seems happy for the moment, so I just let her talk.

She never really asks me how I am, but that's the norm. *I'd be more surprised if she did at this point.*

I don't tell her about Sodorov. I don't tell her about the near-constant dread I'm living with every day now. I don't tell her I'm hating my casino job but stuck working there anyway.

Stuck, truly...*because of her.* Her actions. Her decisions.

And I won't tell her, because she's my mom, and I'd do it all again if I had to. Instead, I let her talk herself out, finally saying goodnight, telling her I love her as I try to hold back tears.

"I love you, Bug," she says in her sweet voice, using the nickname she's had for me since I was a toddler.

I try to keep it together; I really do try. But I can feel a mini breakdown coming on as the pressure of the day and my spiraling emotions get the better of me.

When our call disconnects and I can hear the dial tone buzzing, I lose myself to the tears.

How did this become my life?

3
gotcha

Mikhail

Aiden yammers on and on about some girl he dated while he was at Yale. I think she must've really done a number on him because even though he spends most of his time talking about what a terrible person she is, it seems obvious he really cared about her.

"Another beer?" he asks, tilting his empty bottle toward mine.

I've spent the past eight months doing extra conditioning and improving my nutrition, which has included regulating my alcohol intake. I wasn't a big drinker before, but now I only allow myself a couple of indulgences a month, and I was overindulgent at home during the holidays. Alcohol is the worst way to waste calories, honestly.

Still, I had two full workouts today—one at the arena gym with Dale and one at the boxing gym—so I feel entitled to another beer. And some crazy lady accosted me in my apartment building, too.

"Yeah, one more won't kill me."

Aiden heads off to buy another round while I pick at the label on my beer bottle. When he comes back, he says, "So your trip home was obviously a rousing success."

I frown and tip the bottle back.

"How's The Great Zelenka?"

"*Na zdravi.*"I answer, holding up my beer. Aiden clinks it, and I add, "To your health."

"Went that well, huh?"

"I decline to comment."

Aiden snorts. "It must be hard, growing up with hockey royalty. Like, do you always feel you have something to live up to? Or like you're living in the shadow of everything he accomplished?"

My father was good on the ice, that much is true. In life, though? Meh. He does charity stuff and coaches little kids and shit, but he is not a perfect man. Not by a long shot. So, no, I don't feel the need to be anything like The Great Zelenka.

I don't say any of that to Aiden, of course. I just answer, "Please shut the fuck up. You're ruining my mood."

"I was just—"

I put up my hand. "Nope. I came here to have a good time, not be reminded of all the ways I'll never measure up to my father."

"Sor-ry," he murmurs, petulantly.

I quickly change the subject. "You know, I had the weirdest encounter today after boxing. I was just walking along, minding my own business, and as soon as I step through the doors of the building, this chick turns on me and starts accusing me of following her back from the gym, saying things to me like, 'I don't know anything and you can tell your boss that, too. Leave me the hell alone!'"

"What?" Aiden asks. "What the fuck?"

"Right. My reaction exactly, except I'm a gentleman and I didn't swear at her. So, I'm like, 'Look, lady, I live here, and I don't know what you're talking about.' Then, when I get off the elevator, she pokes her head out to watch me go to my apartment like she doesn't believe I actually live in the building."

"Wow. Bizarre, man. Was she hot, at least?"

I think back to our encounter. I didn't pay that much attention to her looks, come to think of it. I was so blindsided by her outburst that I sort of blotted out what she looked like. "She was petite. Short, dark hair. I mean, she might have been hot?" I shrug a shoulder. "Who knows. She was crazy."

"Hot, crazy chicks are my favorite," Aiden says, grinning.

"That seems obvious, considering the amount of time you spend pining over Lauren or whatever her name is."

He scoffs. "It's Lauree. And I am not pining. I'm going through the stages of grief after a breakup and this stage is molten-hot anger."

"Wow. How enlightened of you. I still think you're pining, and you make her sound *terrible,* so I have no idea why you're grieving."

We finish our beers and head out, but as we walk back toward my place, he points at one of the bigger casinos and says, "We should go blow some of our paychecks. Try our luck."

"Dude, no."

"I've lived here more than half a year and I've never been in one of the casinos," he says. "Come on. We'll just play like one round of roulette and a hand of cards, and we'll go."

"It's such a waste of money," I say, shoving my hands into my pockets. "No."

"Come on. Just two games. I promise."

I suck in a deep breath and roll my neck before letting out a reluctant groan of acceptance. "Fine. Two games."

As soon as we walk in, I see two women coming our way, phones in hand. "Are you Mikhail Zelenka?" they ask. "We're huge Crush fans. We watch almost every home game."

Both women are attractive, but puck bunnies have never been my scene. A few of my teammates would be all into this attention right now, but me? It might seem ridiculous, especially after Mom's insistence I need to *find my girl*, but one-night stands with girls only interested in me because of my status have simply lost their appeal. I actually like women and don't always only want to fuck.

"That's me and thanks for your support." I force myself to paste on a smile. "It's always nice to meet fans," I lie. "Have you met Aiden? This is his rookie year."

Aiden looks more than delighted to meet these women, who tell him they've seen him play, though I think they're lying just to make him feel good about himself. Or to get in his pants. Honestly, maybe both.

We take a couple of selfies with them, and they ask if we want to come back to one of their apartments, but I beg off, reminding Aiden that we had a plan to introduce him to the roulette wheel for the first time tonight. A round of drinks appears, the waitress telling us our drinks are "on the house" and thanking us for coming in to patronize their establishment, repping the Crush.

Aiden, new to all of this, beams as he eats up the celebrity attention with a spoon. I just nurse my—whatever this is, rum and Coke maybe?—and take Aiden to get our first round of chips.

"Dude, my advice? Pick an amount you're willing to lose and stick with it. If you win big, walk away happy. If you lose, don't let yourself go past your limit. It's supposed to be fun, but it can be a wicked drain on your wallet if you're not careful."

"Okay, Dad," Aiden drawls, making the bunnies giggle.

They each take one of his arms as he carries his chips over to the first roulette wheel he sees. I trail along behind, feeling a bit like a dad trying to keep my kid out of trouble.

He places his first bet as I bide my time looking at my phone. The wheel stops spinning, and Aiden chirps with victory. I look up, shocked he would hit something on his first spin. I'm even more shocked when I catch the eye of the roulette operator.

It's *her*.

The crazy girl from earlier today, and it's so

shocking that I let out a loud bark of a laugh. This, obviously, gets her attention, and she looks more closely, eyes narrowing, only to glower at me. Yep, she recognizes me.

Aiden wins another round, hooting like he's just become a gazillionaire or something. I try not to look directly at crazy girl, but I can't help stealing glances as I pretend to look at my phone. She *is* pretty, not gonna lie. I'm six two, but I've always had a thing for petite women, and this one is maybe a foot shorter than I am. Her hair, which was pulled up under a headband earlier, is cut sleek and straight to her shoulders. Her skin is creamy, but her cheeks flush pink every time we make eye contact. It's a funny juxtaposition, considering she's wearing a scowl like her life depended on it.

After a couple of rounds, I tell Aiden I need to piss and head off toward wherever just to get away from the awkwardness. It's so strange. I've run into this girl twice in the same day, when I've seen her zero-point-never in all the years I've been living in that building.

I mean, maybe *she's* the creep. Maybe she's the one working for some seedy Russian weirdo or whatever it was she accused me of earlier today. I heard some wackadoodle story about Boris and his financial advisors from Russia a couple years back, like he tried to leave them and go work with his now-girlfriend Talia, so they kidnapped her or some crazy shit. Maybe this girl works for them, and they target hockey players.

Not likely, I know.

When I make it back to the roulette table, Aiden is

gone. I find him at the blackjack table, so I sit down and play through a few bets with him, winning a decent amount of money in the process. The table is not far from where crazy roulette girl is working, and I still can't help my eyes from sliding to the side to take an occasional peek.

I've managed to stick with just the one drink while we've been here, but Aiden has had many more than that, so as the clock hits one in the morning, I try talking him into heading home for the night.

"Dude, don't be such a grandma. I'm winning so far."

"Then take your winnings and cash out before you lose your shirt."

"Blah, blah, blah, you old woman. Stop telling me what to do." He's sloppy now, in a frat-boy way I find completely unamusing. "You go home if you're so ready to go, Mik."

Unfortunately, he turns back to the table just in time to miss my epic eye roll in response. Of course, I'm not going to leave my drunk-ass teammate alone in a casino where he could really do himself some financial damage. He's a rookie player with a shitty contract. He doesn't make the ridiculous bank you make when you've proven yourself in the league.

Still, he milks the fact that he's a pro athlete for all it's worth with the ladies, the two blondes we met when we arrived, having moved on to higher rollers and several other women now in their place. They take selfies in between bets, giggling and drinking and getting louder and louder with each passing minute.

Maybe I'm just in a shitty mood. Or maybe I *am*

being a grandma tonight. Either way, I really don't want to be here. The only thing keeping my interest is my curiosity about the dark-haired beauty at the roulette table.

And it looks like I'm not the only one interested.

I haven't missed her eyeballing me when she's thought I haven't been paying attention.

Gotcha.

4
saddest space in nevada

Reagan

I hate this stupid, starched, tight-necked uniform. Stupid white shirt making me sweat like a pig. Stupid black bow tie choking me. Stupid casino job and stupid Russian hockey dude stalking me.

Yeah, I see you staring at me like a creeper. In my head, I keep thinking of all the things I'd like to say to the hulking monster with the good hair as I work through my shift, my feet aching inside my sensible, black dress shoes.

I can't decide whether I'm glad for the distraction or if it's annoying. Maybe it's a little of both? Regardless, he *is* really pretty to look at.

With his lazy pompadour and his perfect lips and his deep blue sea-colored eyes.

With his tatted-up athlete's body looking like he's carved in stone instead of a mere mortal made of flesh and bone.

With what I'm betting are some serious washboard

abs hiding beneath that long-sleeved T-shirt he's wearing for nobody's benefit.

See? This is not good. I'm obviously conflicted in how I feel about Mikhail-the-maybe-creeper showing up twice in one day.

Is he hot? Affirmative. Is he mysteriously aloof and stealthy? Also, affirmative. Is he working for a Las Vegas crime lord on the side of his hockey gig? Unknown.

This is all very confusing and distracting. Also, I need no men in my life right now. As evidenced by the last man I dated who got me into the ditch out of which I'm currently trying to crawl.

Also, I really hate this job, and this fact is what consumes my thoughts for much of each shift I work. I came to Vegas for college, majored in hotel and tourism, and then couldn't find a job in hotel and tourism that paid more than the casino. I still hope to move over to event planning for the Tangiers, but for now, this pays the bills. And there *are some bills*, unfortunately. Bills that keep me up at night and cause me to break out in a cold sweat.

It's not that I mind working the casino games. Sometimes, the people are funny. Sometimes, crazy things happen. Sometimes, people win big and really deserve it. Sometimes, people lose big and really deserve it, too. If I were a writer, I could write a whole book about the characters I see in this place. Some are sad and make my heart hurt. Some are happy and funny, and I bask in being their friend for the evening. Does that make me pathetic? *No, Reagan, it's called loneliness.*

Truly, it's been a while since I've had friends. Early in college, really. But then things went sideways in my life, and it was all I could do to hang on, let alone make time for real relationships. So yeah, sometimes this job makes me feel like a human for a minute. A real person and not this ghost I've become. I go to work. I go home. I go to the gym. Lather, rinse, repeat.

And sometimes I get the shakedown from Russian crime dudes in between all of that.

It's not what I expected for my life when I came to Vegas as a starry-eyed freshman who'd never left the state of Ohio. By graduation, though, my view of the future was much more in line with reality.

As my shift nears its end, I notice my hottie stalker, Mikhail, manhandling his very drunk friend. The friend is loud and grinning despite barely being able to stand. They gather up their chips and head over to the cashier's window to check out. My late-night replacement comes, and I slip away, back to the employee lounge, hoping that's the last I'll see of Mikhail.

Our lounge is decidedly less glamorous than the front of the house. It's really just a medium-sized room with a few tables, some chairs, and a wall of lockers. There are two vending machines, as well as an iPad, where we swipe our badges to clock in and out. The walls are a drab taupe, and the only adornments are a few framed photos of some of the casino's most famous performers. It's a far cry from the overstimulating, opulent environment of the floor.

Because it's the saddest space in Nevada, I try not to spend too much time in here. So I grab my backpack, clock out, head for the back door, and then into the alleyway that fills the space between the casino and its adjoined hotel. My apartment is only a few blocks from work, so I usually walk. Tonight, I feel oddly anxious as I make my way up the dark alley and out to the brightly lit Strip. Something claws away in my stomach. Hunger? *Fear?*

Determined not to let nerves rule me, I grab a slice of pizza about the size of my head from the walk-up pizza window on the way home. It's covered in grease and cheese, and I shove the goodness in my face the second it comes my way. The first bite is hot and gooey and burns my tongue, but it would not be an overstatement to say that pizza is one of the great loves of my life. Feeling slightly better after my small fix, I step off the curb with my building in sight.

Just as I make the final last steps before being home free, the hairs on my neck stand on end. I'm grabbed by rough hands, pulled into the alleyway, and shoved against the wall, my pizza falling from my hand as I try to throw whatever punch or kick that'll get me free. But the guy has me thoroughly pinned, one strong hand pressing against my windpipe.

"Each struggle takes more of your air." He sneers in a heavily accented voice.

Breathe, breathe, I think, looking around wildly. Oh fuck. *Can anyone see me?* Stay calm. *Get a description.* Reluctantly, I force my eyes back to my attacker. *It's not Mikhail.* Definitely one of Sodorov's goons. He's wearing a brown suit. A tie. If he didn't have the long scar on his cheek, he'd look like an executive. His breath is acrid, and one of his front teeth is chipped as he gives me a predator's smile.

I know better than to scream, but I do spit at him, the mark landing on his chin and earning me a knee to the gut. Air whooshes out of me in a rush. I'd double over if not for the fact I'm still being held by a meaty hand, the worst kind of flesh collar pinning me to the wall.

"Mister Sodorov requests your presence," he says close to my ear. "Now you're going to come with me, and you're going to behave yourself."

"Now, why would I agree to that?" I squeak, my voice hoarse. "I've answered all your questions. I don't know anything about Sodorov's missing money. I told him already."

"He thinks you're lying. Video doesn't lie, little girl. And you're a little slut who has reason to take an extra cut. We know it's you, so fess up, tell us where you've hidden the money, and we'll keep your punishment manageable. Maybe a finger or two. Maybe just a night with the guys at the house."

My stomach turns violently at the threat, tears welling instantly in my eyes, quickly overflowing to streak down my face. I'm so pissed that I'm crying right now. I want to look strong and capable, and here I am, immobile, ready to throw up, and crying like some kid that just fell off a bike. "You have the wrong person," I manage to plead. "Please! Just let me go—"

The force holding me up against the wall and the restriction to my airway suddenly evaporates, along with my attacker. I heave in much-needed breaths, desperate to stop the dizziness.

And then I notice *how* I'm free.

The goon is on the ground.

With Mikhail on top of him, a brutal beatdown in progress.

He's snarling in a language I don't recognize as he punches the enemy again and again, the sound of fist against flesh enough to turn my stomach a second time. Sodorov's lackey manages to scoot away and get to his feet, wiping the blood from his lip before running down the alley and into the night.

My feet won't move. I know I should run, get to my apartment, and lock the door. But all I can do is stare into space. A handsome face comes into view. Mikhail. Not a stalker but my rescuer. He's saying something to me but, there's a rush in my ears, my own heartbeat, and I can't hear him. Not at first.

The volume suddenly returns in a rush. "Are you hurt?" He's asking me a question. I take a deep breath as he asks again, "Are you okay?"

"I-I th-think so." I focus on his face and nod, breathing in the wonderful night air, filling my depleted lungs with glorious oxygen.

"Let me walk you to your apartment? Should we call the police?"

"No police...please!"

He puts up his hands. "Okay. Fine. I'll get you home, then."

Nodding, I follow him to where his drunk friend is sitting against the building around the corner, eyes heavy-lidded, half-eaten hot dog about to fall out of his hand.

"Aiden!" He kicks the bottom of the guy's shoe. "Wake the fuck up, man."

Aiden stirs, blinking slowly as the world comes back into focus. He grins and shoves the rest of the hotdog into his mouth as he stands clumsily, using the wall for support.

Mikhail shakes his head and rolls his eyes, but while his reaction seems so totally normal, I can see how his chest rises and falls, how he rubs at the top of his hand, now scuffed and raw from the fight.

He saved me...

"Mister Sodorov requests your presence...Video doesn't lie...And you're a little slut who has reason to take an extra cut. Tell us where you've hidden the money, and we'll keep your punishment manageable. Maybe a finger or two. Maybe just a night with the guys at the house.

I could have been taken...*fuck.*

We don't talk as we head inside nor as we step into the elevator. Aiden leans heavily on Mikhail, still obliviously drunk, grinning. Mikhail hits the number three button and explains, "Let me get him situated in my apartment first?"

I nod again, following behind them as they head down the hall, Mikhail unlocking his door and leading Aiden inside. I step only a foot inside his apartment, too scared to remain alone in the hallway, watching blankly as Aiden is told to lie down on the couch. A moment later, Mikhail is back, asking, "Ready?"

I nod for the third time, grateful not to have to speak. *My throat's far too sore anyway...*

Back in the elevator and up two more floors, still

silent. It's not until we get to my own apartment door that I'm able to articulate a "thank you."

He waits at my door, his eyes scanning the space. "I'm just downstairs if you need anything."

I give him a fourth nod, the only response I appear capable of making right now.

"What's your name?"

"Reagan. Reagan Marlowe."

"Mikhail Zelenka." He holds out his hand. I take it, thinking in the moment how weird and normal it is to shake the hand that just threw punches to rescue you. To learn his full name. To realize he just saved me from something terrible, or quite possibly, my life. I'm too scared to even contemplate that last one.

I can't stop the rush of understanding that comes to me with such force, I *know* it's the truth as he steps back and pulls my door closed.

Mikhail Zelenka is my own personal guardian angel, and I owe him...*I owe him my life.*

5
blu-rays forever

Mikhail

Sports Center highlights roll out from the TV as Aiden snores on my couch, completely oblivious to the utter insanity taking place while he was passed out on the sidewalk with his half-eaten hot dog.

Holy hell, I just beat a man. I pulled him away from a woman half his size, and I beat him to a pulp. It felt a bit dreamlike. As if I came upon the scene and just turned into an animal.

My hand is swollen and cut in a few places, and I've got an ice pack on it as I stare blankly at the television screen. Aiden mumbles incoherently in his alcohol-addled slumber, and I glance over at him just to make sure he's okay. He's gonna be feeling that in the morning and probably a good half of tomorrow.

I don't miss that. And I especially don't miss the morning after the rager from the night before. I'm only four years older than him, but it might as well be a decade. I'm just not interested in that lifestyle anymore. Aiden's still a college kid in a lot of ways; less than a year out from campus bar crawls and frat parties. Of course, I never had those experiences since I didn't go to college. The first few years I played in the league, though, I partied a bit. I did the clubs and the women, but in the back of my mind, always niggling, was my dad's voice. The voice telling me I needed to be better, work harder, get stronger than everyone else. Aiden's relationship with his parents is much different, I think. They're proud of him. He's just happy to be playing in the NHL. The pressure doesn't seem quite so great for him as it felt when I started out professionally at nineteen.

Christ, I feel so much older now. How will I feel when I'm thirty if I feel like this now? But I made it. Did I hate every moment of my dad's harsh words and criticism? Fuck, yes. Do I feel I could have made it to this level without him? The jury is out on that one.

I rub my eyes with my free hand, wondering how I'll explain the busted-up hand to my coaching staff. Flexing it open and closed, I steel myself for playing through it. I don't think it's broken or anything. Nothing a little Ibuprofen can't fix.

And what about Reagan? She said she wasn't hurt, but that guy had his hand around her neck, choking her. Her outburst earlier in the day makes sense now. No wonder she was paranoid and thought I was dangerous. *Fuck, she's really in danger. What trouble has she gotten herself into?*

My mind is a jumble, wondering who the fuck this tiny woman has gotten herself mixed up with. The guy choking her was underworld, if I had to guess. Could it be related to her casino job? Maybe, but he didn't look like he was on any kind of legit payroll. Also, I keep going back and forth between thinking I should've offered to let her stay here with me. But isn't that just weird? Because I don't know her.

When I was a kid, I was really into superhero comics. Name the superhero, and I can, to this day, tell you their powers, their backstories, and where they fall in the multiverse. Yep, total nerd like that. I have my bookshelves lined with all the comics I've collected over the years, all organized by number and series. I also have all the movies, in their Blu-ray cases—which I started collecting long before everything went digital, so there's no way I can stop now.

My sister Daniella tells me I have a "superhero complex," which she thinks stems from living in the comic-book universe every minute that I wasn't in school or on the ice as a kid. I was quiet growing up. Popular, mainly because I played hockey and my dad was a god on the ice, but quiet. I wasn't the best at school, and I had a bit of a temper, especially when I thought people were getting bullied or harassed. Daniella and Iliana were both really pretty girls—are still really pretty—and I felt very protective of them both as we were growing up. But my sisters never had the same level of pressure on them that I did. Our dad treated them like princesses, while I was the one stuck on the ice until late at night, practicing and practicing until I got it "right," whatever that meant to my dad at a given moment. I was never jealous of them for escaping our father's scrutiny though, and I could've been.

Over the years, I imagined myself standing up to him, being bigger and stronger than him. Like a superhero, I guess. So, it's no big surprise that I've found myself in more than one situation where I've jumped into danger.

When I first got to Vegas, I was walking along the Strip, slightly tipsy after scoring one of my first game winning goals in an NHL game, and I came across this guy harassing a woman on the street. He had his car door open, one foot on the street. He was balding and overweight and sweaty, and I imagined he was propositioning a sex worker. She wasn't having whatever he was offering, and when she tried to turn away, he grabbed her arm and attempted to forcibly pull her into his car.

I saw red. There's no other way to put it. Before I could even consider my actions, I was there, pulling the guy off her, fists swinging. I'm pretty sure I punched his tooth out of his mouth before he jumped in the car and sped away.

Guy deserved it. I don't feel bad about it, just like I don't feel bad about what I did tonight. I saw the terror on Reagan's face. I know I did the right thing.

But did I do the right thing by leaving her alone in her apartment? I blow out a loud breath as my knee bounces up and down with some strange mix of energy and anxiety. Maybe I should run up and check on her. Of course, it's like three in the morning now. Maybe even later than that. Should I just try to get some shut-eye now and check in with her tomorrow?

When I stand, it's more like getting shot from a cannon. I'm almost out the door, decision made, when there's a soft knock on the other side. Without checking the peephole, I swing it open, knowing it'll be her.

And it is her.

Reagan's hair is wet, and she's changed into sweatpants and a T-shirt. A sizable bruise is blooming on her forearm, and a red stain rings her neck from where that fucker held her to the wall.

I point to her neck, then her arm. "I thought you said you were okay."

"It's just a bruise. I'm fine." She bites her lip. "I just wanted to thank you again. I don't—I'm not sure what would've happened if you hadn't come along."

I'm ready to shrug it off. No big deal. But then she adds, "I'm sorry I thought you were one of them earlier."

Her chin quivers, and tears well in her eyes, overflowing, big tears streaming down her sad face. She's so small, just a tiny thing. She doesn't even come up to my chin, and everything inside of me wants nothing more than to shield her, to protect her.

"Do you want to talk about it? Come inside?" I hold out an arm to welcome her in.

She steps into my apartment.

And then she steps into my arms.

6
my weird life

Reagan

Mikhail is rock-solid, holding me in his arms as I cry into his T-shirt. And it's at this moment that I notice I haven't been hugged in a long time. Not like this, where it's easy to feel warm and cared for. *Protected.*

I'd probably not let go of him but my stomach growls at the same time his drunk friend from the casino, I think Aiden is his name, mumbles incoherently from the couch in his sleep. Mikhail laughs and shakes his head at the utter insanity of the situation. For whatever reason, this makes me want to cry even more. "I'm sorry." I sniffle. "I didn't get to eat my pizza."

"Come into the kitchen and just ignore him. He's out for the count." He shakes his head again and gestures to his kitchen table. "Let me find you something to eat."

Rifling through his fridge, he peeks over the open door and says, "I don't have any pizza, unfortunately.

I've been on this new nutrition program. Well, it's not new, I guess. But anyway, I don't really have stuff like that around because if I have it, I'll just eat it, and—"

He clamps his mouth shut, like he realizes he's babbling, before dipping back down out of view behind the open door of the refrigerator. Weirdly, I can't keep from grinning through my tears.

"Do you like chili? I made it in this, uh, cooking class I go to sometimes."

"Chili's great. Thanks for feeding me."

He heats up a bowl of chili, fills a glass of filtered water, sets both down in front of me before returning with a spoon and a napkin.

For a moment, I just stare at the food he's laid out for me and take a deep breath, hoping I don't lose it all over again. Because I'm sitting in a stranger's apartment in the middle of the night—the same stranger I accused of stalking me earlier—sobbing and eating his food after being accosted in a dark alleyway on my way home from work.

My life is so weird.

We're both quiet as I try a few bites of the chili he made. "It's good." I speak only to distract from the silent awkwardness that's settled around us.

"Who was that guy?" Mikhail asks, all tightly bound, his hands in fists on the table. My water vibrates in its glass with the force of his knee bouncing up and down.

My mouth opens, but nothing comes out right away. How do I explain? And what will he think of me if he knows? No, I'm not ready. "First, tell me about you. Your name is Mikhail, which sounded Russian to me. And you showed up out of nowhere today when I've never seen you one time since I've been living in this building or going to the gym."

He chews on his thumbnail as he appraises me. I take another bite just to disengage from his intense gaze. "Well," he says slowly, "I'm not Russian. I'm American. From Detroit."

For some reason, this makes me blush. I feel like an ignorant hick. "Sorry."

He grins. "My dad, however, was born in the Czech Republic. My mom is Canadian but of Czech descent, so I grew up with both Czech and English spoken in the home. I've lived in Detroit for my whole life up until I moved here to play hockey."

"You play hockey, that's right. My trainer at the gym mentioned it when we saw you sparring."

"I play for the Crush. I got agented when I was still in high school and came to Vegas as a rookie. The first year playing for their AHL affiliate team before earning a spot on the NHL roster a few weeks before my twentieth birthday. Been here ever since." He tilts his head at me and smiles slightly. "I thought the same thing, earlier, by the way. That it was weird I ran into you twice in one day when I'd never seen you before. I've lived in this building for four years."

"Two for me. I moved in here the year I graduated UNLV. I still feel like I might have, um, noticed you before now though." I feel the flush of heat fill my cheeks because he's doing a really good job of making me blush.

His lips quirk as he looks down at the table. "Well, I travel a lot during the hockey season. Most days I'm up early for practice or meetings. I go home to Detroit on breaks." A quick shrug, like he's not sure what else to say.

But no matter, everything Mikhail just said rings true. He saved me tonight, and there's no reason to think he's anyone other than who he says he is. He seems serious, well, kind of, but he's also kind. A bit boyish and cute, but not at all in an immature way. I don't have many people in my corner, and I suddenly want him to like me. Not to think of me as some crazy person living this wacko life with a ton of baggage.

I do have a lot of baggage, but I still want him to know the person I really am inside. The girl I was before the last two and a half years happened. The Reagan who was proud of her life choices and had hope for the future.

I steer the conversation in a new direction, hoping he'll go with it. "You know, I didn't grow up too far from you in Columbus, Ohio. I hated the weather, so I only looked at schools in warmer climates. I always wanted to be an event planner, so I picked UNLV, thinking I'd get some swank job in one of the fancy hotels."

"Makes sense," he says with inquisitive blue eyes searching mine, assessing, no doubt, the strange situation of an even stranger girl in his apartment at three in the morning scraping the last bite of chili from her now empty bowl. *How did I get here again? And why am I so awkward?*

I push my bowl away, embarrassed I scarfed the entire thing down like a starved stray. Chewing on my bottom lip, I try to assess just how much of this story

I'm going to tell him. I doubt he wants all the details, especially given the time. And he probably wants me out of his apartment…"I started working in the casino my junior year of college. I worked two jobs because I needed to make extra money. My first job there was as a cocktail waitress, but it wasn't my favorite. Near the end of my senior year, I asked for something different, and my manager asked if I wanted to become a croupier."

"I'm sorry," Mikhail interrupts. "What's a croupier?"

"Oh, that's the fancy name for the casino game operators. You have to go to school for it. The casino paid for my training, which was cool, but I had to do it while I was finishing my degree at UNLV and working a ton of hours. It was exhausting. I ran blackjack for a while. I actually just started on roulette a few weeks ago."

Suddenly, the adrenaline of the night wears off, a huge yawn overtaking my face despite my best efforts to make it as ladylike as possible. I shove away from the table, grab my bowl and glass, and walking them to the sink.

"I guess I'd better get some rest. You should get some rest."

I'm to the door before I turn back. "Thanks for the food, it was delicious. And for what you did tonight. I think—I think you really might have saved my life."

Mikhail is up and in front of me in a few short strides. He's so much bigger than I am—big enough that I might normally feel intimidated. But he doesn't intimidate me. Instead, he makes me feel oddly sheltered, and safe for the first time in a long, long while. Feelings I haven't experienced much lately. I hate that I have to leave here right now, because the thought of going back to my cold, dark apartment alone is a miserable one.

"Will you be okay, Reagan?" he asks quietly as I step out into the hallway.

I nod, hoping he doesn't see the trembling of my hands or sense the unevenness of my breath. "Thanks again, Mikhail, for *everything* you've done for me tonight," I say with a nod before heading down the hall toward the elevators.

It's not until I'm inside with the doors shut that the dread and the fear take over once again.

7
buckaroo?

Mikhail

We're at home and still playing like total shit.

The Crush have had a good season, yes, but it hasn't been perfect. Certainly hasn't had the magic of our previous winning seasons. We feel like a good team but not a great one.

Our new GM came last summer and started making changes like it was nobody's business. Honestly, it's not in a player's best interest to get involved in management decisions. We make good money to play the game. We have to figure out how to fit into any environment as players, how to match up with any coaching style. My dad always stressed that when I was growing up. He'd pull me from teams just to make me learn to adapt because pro players in the league get traded often. And frankly, this new style is a lot more like how other teams play. Guys don't get three full periods of play on other teams. Players sub in and out constantly.

This team has been different from the first day I came here. The first-string players get most of the playing time. They know each other like peanut butter knows jelly. There is trust and kinship between them that doesn't really extend to other players on the team. And I can see where that could be a colossal mistake— except for one impressive fact.

It has worked. We've won a lot. We've won the Cup...twice since I've been with this team.

It's a double-edged sword, right? We need strength in the other lines, throughout the team. But we also want to capitalize on the mojo we've built on the front line.

I've played maybe ten minutes of the first two periods, and we've been sloppy all game. Sloppy passing, sloppy shooting. I'm royally pissed about the whole thing by the time I get on the ice in the third period. Our full first-string is back out there together, and we have a single-point lead over New Jersey. Play is fast and furious, ice showers flying as we duck and move, working to play keep-away from the other team.

The puck is all over the place. One, two, pass. Fake. Pass. A New Jersey defender scoops and sends it, but it's a bad pass, and I end up with it just as someone comes flying at me, chucking me right into the glass with a loud bang. The crowd groans in response, and I shove the guy off with a guttural sound of my own. Skating free, I see Boris stop another of New Jersey's passes. He eyes the goal and makes to shoot, but just before stick-touches-puck to send it, I see his eyes shoot to me. He fakes the shot, the puck flying my way. I take it up toward goal; the goalie moves in my direction, but I sneak behind the net and shoot the puck in behind his back.

The horn buzzes. Goal!

Boom. That's what I'm talking about.

We make it through the remainder of the period with the constant subs that we've become accustomed to this season, but no one else manages to connect for another score.

Post-game, I'm getting a ton of pats on the back, but I'm in a funk, and all I can do is nod my thanks. Evan, still in full gear, strides over and says, "Why the long face, buckaroo?"

I give him a raised eyebrow in response. "Buckaroo?"

He shrugs. "Just trying it out. No good?"

"If I were three, it might be good." I laugh. "It's clear you're spending a lot of time with young children, Cap."

"Thass cuss he hass tho damn many," Tyler says through brushing his teeth.

"I like making babies, what can I say? Bugger off if you've got a problem with it," our team captain barks, grinning like a schoolboy.

I just shake my head, ignoring them both. Evan tries again. "Seriously, you made a top-notch shot tonight. Like, expect to see it on ESPN's weekly round-up level good. Why aren't you smiling?"

"When does he ever smile?" Tyler says, mouth now free of toothpaste. "Serious as a heart attack, our Zelly."

"Piss off, Locksey," Evan says to Tyler in his British/Ukraine/USA mashup of an accent. His euphemisms are always straight up British though and usually fucking hilarious. But today, I'm still salty about the new line rotations.

"If you really want to know, I'm annoyed about the constant in and out. I like our lineup. It works. Why mess with what's good?"

He lifts a shoulder. "Every team out there plays like this. And management's not wrong that our bench was becoming brittle with no playing time. One of us goes out, who's there to pick up the slack? Plus, we were getting predictable."

"Well, now, we're nowhere near predictable, even for each other. It's fine to switch out when we're several goals up, but not when it's tight."

"Not getting enough minutes, young Zelenka?" Georg taunts. "Daddy gonna go talk to Coach about getting you more ice time?"

"Like you can speak on controlling fathers," Evan says, rolling his eyes.

Tyler barks a laugh. He just got engaged to Kolochev's sister over Christmas, so I'm sure he knows more than enough about how controlling Georg's dad, a well-known Russian hockey coach, can be.

"It's whatever." I grab my shower kit. "I'm being a baby. Everyone else loves this new plan. I'll go fuck myself."

Evan pats me on the back. "What we've built here is great, but it won't last forever. We've got to build a lasting legacy."

That statement stays with me as I clean up and dress to head home. He's not wrong. I mean, we all want to leave our own individual marks on the sport, right? But what we're doing with each year we win is to build a legacy that Vegas can be proud of, and I understand the need to make sure the talent is there to make that happen.

Doesn't mean I have to like it.

I like having Viktor at my back. I like having Boris breathing ice-dragon fire at center. I know how they play, how to anticipate what they'll do. I don't know fuck-all about these other kids, and the unpredictability affects everything.

Aiden elbows me out of my thoughts. "Want to go out? Get lit? Celebrate your kick-ass goal-making trickery?"

"Nah. I'm good. I'm pissy. Not good company."

"How's that different from any other day?" Aiden laughs.

"Fuck off." I say it half-heartedly so he doesn't take it personally.

"All right, fucking off now...so, I'll catch you on the flipside. Enjoy your brooding. Text me if you change your mind."

THE COOKING CLASS Aiden and I did last summer was surprisingly useful. I learned how relatively easy it is to cook my own healthy food, which is primarily all in the prep, but I learned that too. The team's nutritionist, Devon, ran the classes before she had to take a pause to finish "cooking" the twin babies our new GM, Grant Gerard, also her husband, are anxiously awaiting in a couple months.

Tonight, I used my new culinary skills to grill some chicken teriyaki kebabs on the new indoor grill. It was the first time I'd used it, and it worked beautifully. I tossed a salad together to complete the meal. I gather up my plate and head to the couch, ready to throw on a movie and enjoy my dinner. Just as I get the Blu-ray loaded, a frantic knocking at the door has me on my feet. Opening up without checking the peephole again, because again, I have a strong feeling who it might be.

My "feeling" is confirmed when Reagan tumbles inside, out of breath, her dark brown eyes wide with fear.

I shut the door behind her as she slides down the wall, head between her legs. "I'm sorry." She takes a few big gulps of air. "I didn't know where else to go and I didn't want to go home."

"It's okay." I crouch down in front of her. "Are you hurt?"

"No. No. I worked from noon to eight and then someone was running late, so I said I'd stay. But when they showed up to relieve me and I walked outside, there were *two* of Sodorov's lackeys posted in the alleyway. I booked it back through the casino and out the front door. Ran all the way here. I don't think they saw me, but I don't know for sure. And if I didn't exit through the back where they expected me, I'm scared they might come here looking for me."

"But you don't think you were followed?"

She cries. "I don't know! I don't know. I feel like I'm going crazy. And I'm sure they know where I live by now, so I didn't want to go there. I'm totally paranoid every moment of every day and it's just too much for me to deal..." She trails off, sobbing.

I hold out my hand and haul her to her feet, walking her to the couch. We sit without talking while I wait for her to catch her breath. I can't imagine how terrifying it must be to feel so endangered. *And I'm honestly glad she came to me. Trusted me enough as a safe place to land.* Minutes go by, but eventually, my curiosity gets the best of me. "So, you never did tell me what that situation the other night was about. Who is Sodorov? And why are his guys after you, Reagan?"

She sighs heavily. "Sodorov's a regular at the casino. A high roller. Mostly plays at the blackjack table, and only maybe once or twice at my table. We never interacted at all, really, but everyone knows who the high rollers are. You're expected to know, to take care of them."

"And I take it he's Russian?"

A few small nods with just the saddest look on her face really gets to me. I want to help her, but how can I if she won't tell me what the fuck is going on with the Russians chasing after her? "I know plenty of Russians who aren't creeps." When she looks up at me with a confused expression, I add, "You said you thought I was one of them and that my name sounded Russian. I'm not, but I know Russians and they're not creeps or thugs."

She just looks confused again, and I don't know why I'm babbling stupid nonsensical shit like this.

Well, I kinda do know why. It seems to happen whenever Reagan Marlowe is around. She fills me with this weird, nervous energy. "Sorry," I mumble, running a hand through my hair. "Please continue."

"So one night, there was this big commotion on the floor. Sodorov was screaming and yelling at the casino managers, at the cashier, at the blackjack operators. And then every single employee got brought in and questioned. Apparently, someone swindled him out of millions via his house account. Just wiped him clean. And, you know, a guy like that has all kinds of money all over the place, right, so a couple million probably barely makes a dent."

"I don't know about that, Reagan. People who have money tend to know where every cent of it is. They keep track. So, someone at the casino stole it or what?"

"We still don't know," she says, looking me straight in the eye with absolutely no visible tell she could be lying. I'm inclined to take her at her word, but then again, I don't know her, and she could be feeding me a line of crap.

"But they think it was you?"

Another nod. "A week or two went by and everything seemed to have settled down. Sodorov hadn't been in. There was all this hush-hush talk about how they wanted to call in the FBI to investigate but he refused and said he'd hire his own investigators."

"Didn't want the Feds involved." If Sodorov is indeed underworld, then that's a given.

"Definitely not. I don't think gambling is, like, his worst hobby. So one night after my shift, I head out the employee door to go home. The second I stepped outside, I got snatched. Hood over my head, shoved in the back of a van or something. I ended up in some high-rise penthouse, tied up and sitting on this massive leather couch. They asked me more questions and then it got really weird. At first, it was like a good cop, bad cop thing? They'd threaten me, then try being nice. And I really had no idea what they were talking about."

"So, the place is near here, then? Or on the Strip?"

"Not the Strip. And I didn't get the impression it was Sodorov's main place of business, either. It was fancy—big windows looking out on the city? Like a party place, maybe? They made up this whole story about how I siphoned money out of his account slowly and sent it to some hidden bank overseas. Their accusations were insane. I was like, 'I have no access to computers at Tangiers. I am not a hacker. I would have absolutely no clue how to do whatever it is you're accusing me of.'"

"So why do they think it was you?"

"They said it was someone who looked like me, a woman with a petite build and short dark hair, on camera in the finance office—*but it wasn't me*, Mikhail. I don't have security access to *any* of the offices. There are super strict protocols about handling money and chips in any casino by law. But Sodorov's people didn't believe me. They roughed me up a bit and said they've been patient, but they're dead serious about getting Henri Sodorov's money back. Then they took off my restraints and sent me out the door. Said I had a few days to think about it and come clean. That the next time they came for me they wouldn't be so nice." She sucks in another deep breath and speaks in a shaky voice, "The *n-next time* was when you saved me on my way home from work in that alleyway."

Christ on the cross, this is so fucked up.

I'm sitting beside this woman who looks like a little pixie, sharp-jawed and wide-eyed. She's beautiful and mysterious, and I feel oddly nervous and protective around her. And fuck me, but she could be a criminal. She could be totally grifting me right now. I'm a pro hockey player with a decent bit of money of my own. Maybe this whole story is meant to make me feel sorry for her, to let her get close.

And maybe everything she's telling me *is* the truth. Maybe she has stumbled onto the radar of a group of Vegas underworld mobbed-up Russians through no fault of her own.

Organized crime can be found in any gambling city on the globe. That's an indisputable fact. It's been thriving in Las Vegas for nearly a century, maybe even longer.

I want to believe her. And what's more? I want to *help* her.

But will I end up in just as much trouble as Reagan?

8
chaos theory

Reagan

This hockey player does not need my drama.

I finish telling my story and I can tell that this is way out of Mikhail's depth. *He must doubt that I'm telling the truth, too. Who wouldn't?* I've clearly interrupted his dinner, yet he didn't complain, which I do appreciate. But he does not need me, some stranger, pulling him into my dramatic world.

Scary-as-fuck-drama.

Taking a deep gulp of air, I try to steady myself. But I'm terribly uncomfortable in my casino uniform. White shirt. Black bow tie. Black pants. "I need to change." I pull at the bow tie as if it might choke me at any moment. Honestly, the thought of going back out into the hallway, to maybe face yet another assault by Sodorov's henchmen, terrifies me.

"I can walk you up, just to make sure you get in okay. If you'd like?"

Relief forces an audible exhale out of me. "That would be great. Thanks."

He stands and holds out a hand to help me up. I take it, trying to convince myself the flip of my stomach when I touch him is just misplaced gratitude. He's a good guy. He's helped me. He continues to help me. That's all.

Unfortunately, by the time we reach my apartment, the relief I felt just moments ago evaporates as soon as we see the state of my door.

The lock has been jimmied, judging from all the scratches and marks. Mikhail steps in front of me and tries the handle. To my horror, it opens easily.

And I *never* leave it unlocked—especially lately.

He looks back at me, then both ways down the hallway before pushing the door the rest of the way open.

It's quiet as we step inside. I swear I can hear both of our hearts beating in the eerie silence. Stuff is strewn all over the place. Papers on the floor, drawers hanging open. *Oh, God.* These people were *inside my home*.

Limply, I stand, taking in the chaos. Feeling the chaos. Becoming one with the chaos in the span of a single moment.

This situation feels like a tunnel, a long, dark tunnel where no light ever appears. I can feel my tears start to stream down my cheeks as my chest constricts. It's hard to breathe. How will I ever feel safe in this apartment again, knowing someone can so easily bust in?

"What do you think they were looking for?" Mikhail asks as he returns from my bedroom area. "They're gone now."

"I don't know. If I had to guess, maybe proof I took Henri Sodorov's money?" I look around and sigh helplessly, repeating myself, "I don't know."

As if that somehow helps me out of this mess. *Riiight.*

I can feel myself going into shut-down mode, and the effort of answering coherently to questions must be weighed with my ability to keep breathing.

He's got his cell phone in his hand. "Should we call the cops?"

"No!" I say a tad too sharply. "No. I think involving the cops will only make it worse for me."

He chews on the corner of his lip. Runs a hand through his hair, both things I'm starting to recognize as nervous habits. And what does that say about me? Pretty much that I've stressed this poor guy out enough times in our very short acquaintance to spot his nervous habits of chewing on his bottom lip and dragging his hands through his really good hair. Both of which look incredibly hot whenever he does either. Not that I should be taking notes or anything, but impossible not to admire.

Not good. For me or for him. And I really need to put a stop to this. My problems are not Mikhail Zelenka's problems. "You don't have to stay involved in this though. This mess has nothing to do with you, Mikhail. I'll figure it out." I probably won't. Of course, I won't, but at least I've given him an out. He should take it and get away as fast as he can.

Shoving his hands in his pockets, Mikhail blows out a long breath. "Reagan, I confess, I don't really know what to do here. I don't feel great about just leaving you in an apartment that was just vandalized. I guess...maybe grab some stuff and come stay at my place for a few days while you think things through?"

I look around at the mess of my apartment and realize that I don't want to stay here. *I can't stay here.* Not right now. But where can I go? Most of my friends from college have scattered, and there's no one at work I'd feel comfortable staying with. *Should I actually consider Mikhail's offer?* Surely, he's only offering out of obligation. *What other choice do you have, Reagan?* None. And that's the saddest part of this. I have no one. "Okay," I mumble quietly. I take another deeply relieved breath. "Okay."

After quickly packing a bag, I call the emergency maintenance line and ask them to change out my locks.

"I NEVER ATE MY DINNER, do you mind? I'm just gonna heat this up for a minute and make some tea. Can I get you anything?" Mikhail asks after taking my bag and leading me to his couch.

Guilt washes over me yet again for disrupting this man's life as I sit, leaning my head back on the couch and staring up at his ceiling. "I'm so sorry for interrupting your meal." I shake my head in disgust at myself. "I already ate, but I'll take some tea if you're making some," I lie. I didn't eat, but honestly, I don't think I could right now. "Please, have your dinner." He flashes me a quick nod combined with the sexy bottom lip chew he's got down to perfection and heads for his kitchen.

I can hear him using the microwave and then the clink of utensils as he eats, I imagine, standing at the counter for efficiency. After he finishes his food, I hear him busying himself with the tasks of organizing hot water, mugs, and tea bags. I have no idea how much time passes while he's doing all these things. It doesn't matter. I haven't changed my position since he let me back into his apartment. I'm still stiff-backed with my head on the back of his couch, staring up at his ceiling, racking my brain for some magic solution to the fresh hell I've landed myself in.

He sits down next to me a while later, handing me a steaming mug of tea that smells comforting and amazing. I cup it with both hands, savoring the warmth. "Thank you. This is lovely," I say, trying to give him as big of a smile as I'm capable of, which probably isn't much, but I do try.

"Do you have any friends here that you could stay with for a while? How much longer do you have on your lease?"

I can tell he's processing choices, problem-solving. He's got a hot mess of a girl in his apartment, and he's a decent guy, and he doesn't know what to do. I would be doing the same. I'd be counting the seconds until I could rid myself of this unwanted visitor.

"I work a lot, so I don't really have close friends here in Vegas, just acquaintances. Being on the floor, I don't get the chance to really talk to my coworkers much. And my college friends all went their separate directions after graduation." *I lost contact with all my friends before I graduated*, but I don't say that part out loud.

He nods a few times. Reflects. Sips his tea. "Can you go home for a while? Lie low for a bit? Maybe start fresh?"

"No." I shake my head. I can't say more, won't say more. He already thinks I'm damaged goods. He does not need to know about my family situation, about the reasons I won't go back home.

We sit in silence for a while, both of us deep in thought, drinking tea together. Eventually, the choke of my bow tie reminds me that I went to my apartment with intention to shower and change. I unclip the tie at the back of my neck and pull it off, unbuttoning the top button of my shirt.

"Do you mind if I take a shower?"

"No, of course not," he answers, quickly standing.

I take my bag as he leads me to the bathroom and hands me a clean towel. I thank him and shut the door, that tight feeling of panic in my chest and throat returning the instant I'm alone. As the water heats, I undress, focusing on one tiny task at a time. But the second I step under the calming, hot water, the tears I didn't realize I was holding in, let loose.

My body slides down, my back slick against the wall, with my head in my hands, I sob and sob and sob. *What am I going to do? If I leave, they'll come after me. It'll look like I'm running, like I'm guilty. And I am not guilty. Not of stealing.*

I left Ohio to get a fresh start. I went to college with

a plan. But now, in so many ways, that plan has gone off the rails in a cataclysmic disaster.

I'm stuck here in a dreadful situation I could've never even imagined…running literally for my life.

And if not for Mikhail, I could be dead already.

9
pietrangelo's pizzeria

Mikhail

I hear the water start and sit at my kitchen table, googling Reagan Marlowe. She doesn't have much of a social media profile. A LinkedIn with a cute, professional photo that was probably taken as part of some college course requirement. Not much to speak of, otherwise. No Facebook. No Insta. Nothing random out there floating around.

But something isn't right. Why would these criminals be all over this girl if she didn't do something to royally piss them off? Guys like that don't come after randoms, not unless there's a connection somehow. And they really roughed her up. Possibly would have killed her if I hadn't come along. She's so tiny and scared, though, and I want to believe she's innocent. Still, I can't shake the feeling that there's something I'm missing, something she's not telling me. Maybe several "somethings."

But it's obvious I can't just send her out there to fend for herself. That feels all kinds of wrong to me, and I'll have to just follow my gut on this one. I would want to maim any man who wouldn't do the same if this was one of my sisters in a similar predicament.

When Reagan finally emerges, she's in a sweatshirt and joggers, her dark hair still wet, her cheeks flushed. But I can tell she's been crying, even as she attempts a smile.

"Feeling a little better?" I ask hopefully.

"I am, thank you. Hot water therapy can be a miracle worker sometimes, you know?" She brings a hand to her stomach. "Thanks again for letting me stay here."

"No worries. It's no big deal, and I'm glad the shower helped," I say, just as her stomach growls loudly, a lot like the last time she was here in my apartment—needing food. "You told me you had dinner, Reagan," I scold with a tilt of my head.

"Um...when I said I ate at work, I might've been talking about lunch though." She shakes her head shyly. "I couldn't eat when I first got here anyway."

"Okay, but you still need to eat something for dinner," I argue. Jesus, she's so small already she can't afford to be missing meals. "You should have said something."

"You got me. I haven't had any dinner tonight." She laughs lightly. "You're kind of a mother hen, you know?"

I shrug off her comment. It's nothing I haven't heard before from my sisters. "So, let's order you something. Pizza, is it?" I toggle my phone at her.

"Sure, that would be great, but I'm doing the ordering and the paying." She pulls out her phone.

"You've done enough just by letting me stay here with you."

"Okay, whatever you want," I say as she takes a seat on the couch. When she sits, it's right next to me. Like a lot closer than I would expect. I don't mind, though because, as she taps away on a delivery app, I'm surrounded by her scent. Her hair smells really good. *What is that? Oranges?*

I turn on the television, pulling up a streaming service. We flip through different movie options and decide on the Lara Croft *Tomb Raider* reboot from 2018. We talk about what a badass video game character Lara was and how she didn't quite make the transition to film in the same badass way she was in the game. Reagan makes a joke about how she'd probably come up to Lara's navel. It's a good distraction but not enough to make things less awkward for me. Because I'm still focused on the smell of her clean, wet hair and how close she's sitting next to me.

When a knock sounds and Reagan about jumps out of her skin, I tell her, "It's okay. I'll get it." I pause the movie, thankful for something else to focus on besides her proximity.

It's Aiden, surprisingly home early after a night out celebrating a home win. I know he's just stopping by to shoot the shit like we often do, but I tell him I have a guest. He gives me a thumbs-up and a cocky head nod before heading off to his own place a few floors up. We were roommates for a bit in the summer while he was waiting for an apartment to become available in the building. He knows the drill about overnight guests. Aiden's cool but he'll want to play twenty questions at practice tomorrow. Something along the lines of: *Who'd you bang? How'd you meet? How'd she do? Gimme a rating one to ten. Or was it Gia back for a li'l more o'that Zelenka D?*

Yup. All those questions and probably others will be on the docket tomorrow. Which is stupid on his part because he knows I won't kiss and tell. I'm just not wired for it. I've always been tight-lipped about my personal life, casting a wide net of privacy over all things related to my family, relationships, or my dating habits with those I may have, on occasion, hooked up with in the past—

"I have a delivery for Reagan Marlow." Called to the door for a second time in as many minutes, I can thankfully step off the Aiden train. This time, it's Reagan's pizza from one of the best in Vegas—*Pietrangelo's Pizzeria.* I tip the delivery guy, who looks to be in his sixties, a little extra for his efforts. Gotta respect the hustle of so many who work in Las Vegas doing all kinds of jobs in the city to make ends meet. "Thanks, man." He pauses and tilts his head. "You're number nineteen on the Crush, aren't you?"

I give him a quick nod. I don't like to make a big deal out in public with fans, but I never lie to them. That's just a dick move on the part of the athletes who try it.

"Thought so. No worries, man, I'll forget this address by the time I'm back out in my car. You have a nice night and thanks for the tip." He salutes and heads off into the night like a seasoned pro used to interacting with athletes, news media, and celebrities.

Probably happens all the time in his line of work in this town.

Reagan joins me at the kitchen table as I'm grabbing plates and drinks. "So what's life like for a pro hockey player? What's Mikhail Zelenka's life like when he's not rescuing damsels in distress?"

I feel my cheeks burn. "I don't love talking about myself," I say as I sit down at the table across from her —for my second meal of the evening. My eyes flit to hers and she seems genuinely interested, not just making conversation, which makes it even more awkward for me.

"I've met a couple of other hockey players at the casino, and they've very much enjoyed talking about themselves. They tell their whole life stories."

This makes me chuckle. "Well, I can probably guess which ones you've met."

"But what about you? What's your story?"

"I, uh, grew up in a hockey family. My dad played for a long time. He's considered one of the Greats in the NHL. I started playing young, loved the game, and went straight to the pros after high school." I shrug, not sure what else to say.

"That's normal? To go straight to pro hockey? Don't they have juniors and a bunch of levels before the pros to play through?"

"It just depends. I played in juniors all through school. Some guys play in college first. I wasn't so great with school stuff. I got some college offers, but I couldn't stand the thought of four more years of classes, so I signed with the Crush's AHL affiliate, the Henderson Havoc, right out of high school. I didn't expect to make it to the NHL right away, but I actually earned a starting position in my first season. I got called up to meet the Crush on the road in Detroit, where I was born and raised, of all places. Their starting winger had sustained what turned out to be a career-ending injury, so a spot in the lineup opened for me to slot into. I did well in my NHL debut. I made three assists that night including the game winner in overtime. They kept me in the lineup for the rest of that season and I was a starter the following season when we won the Cup."

"Wow, so you're, like, following in your father's footsteps, then."

I grunt a sound of dissent. "I'm not looking to be what my dad was."

There's a bit of an awkward silence after that. I hope I haven't shown my "daddy issues" card. I shove a slice of pizza at my face to stop myself from talking anymore.

Reagan just smiles softly. "Well, see? You can talk about yourself a little."

"Doesn't mean I like to," I answer, staring at the table and thinking about all the extra reps I'll be doing tomorrow at practice to cancel out eating my delicious late-night snack from Pietrangelo's.

"Do you like hockey?" she asks.

"I love the game, yes."

"Good. People should do what they love." Her dark brown eyes have flecks of gold in them that I can't help noticing. They're very expressive and... beautiful...like the rest of her.

"And you don't love working the casino games?" I

ask, suddenly interested in knowing more about her as well.

"No, I do not. I mean, I don't hate it, but it's not what I envisioned for myself. None of this is."

"Why not get another job, then?" I ask gently, remembering all the crazy she's been through lately.

"Oh, I've tried. I've interviewed and I've gotten offers, but they all want me to come in at a crap salary. I have debts to pay, student loans, and other stuff. I can make more money on the floor. I just...I can't afford to take a pay cut."

She might still be a little bit hysterical on second thought. The night has been hard on her, and I guess I can't blame her. I try to change the subject to easier topics. "Did you like college, at UNLV was it?"

Picking at her second slice of pizza, she sighs. "I did. I liked living away from home and in a dorm. Making my own way. My first two years were really great." A shadow of a frown appears as she shoves a glob of cheese into her mouth, clearly not sharing all her story about the last two years of college, which also, clearly, were not *really great.*

"I never went to college," I say absently. "Have I told you that already?"

"Yeah, like, five minutes ago." She grins at me. And I like seeing the sight of a smile on her pretty face so much that I can't look away.

"Sorry." I feel my cheeks flush as I break eye contact. What is it about this woman that makes me feel so off-kilter? "I, uh, wasn't good in school, you know? Teachers always said I had my head in the clouds, daydreamed too much."

"The daydreamers are usually the smartest ones, you know. The ones who get lost in the cracks because people mistake their creativity for apathy."

"Yeah, maybe. I don't think that was me. I really did hate school." I meet her gaze and find myself grinning this time. "Usually, I was sneaking comic books into my desk and not paying attention to class. Then I would cheat off the smart kids that sat near me because I hadn't paid attention. Total dumb jock move."

Reagan smiles. "A pro athlete with a superhero complex. I get it now. You just show up to save people in distress like you have some Spidey sense or something?"

"I've been known to jump into a situation or two," I admit. "But I think any decent person would help if they could."

"I don't know about that," Reagan argues. "You'd be surprised at how many people turn the other way. Rather than be uncomfortable or whatever, they pretend they didn't see anything. It's pretty disheartening. But you, sir? You are reigniting my faith in humanity."

"Well, I'm glad I'm able to help. With your faith in humanity."

"You've helped with more than that." She reaches over and takes my hand in hers, and there it is, an electric zing of chemistry between us. "Thank you, Mikhail."

I clear my throat and ask if she's going to have more pizza. She says no, and I get up, busying myself with putting the pizza box in the fridge and washing the plates.

Reagan appears at my side, taking the plates and drying them, putting them back in the cabinet. "Are you a shy guy, Mikhail?"

"I'm, uh…" I don't know how to answer that. "No, I'm not shy, I don't think so."

"Just not a big talker? Were you an only child, trapped alone with your comic books and superhero fantasies to keep you company?"

I chuckle, shaking my head. "No. I have two sisters. They did most of the talking in our house. We Zelenka men are more action-oriented, I guess."

"Are you close with them? Your sisters?"

"Somewhat. We were close when we were younger, but our lives went in different directions. My little sister is in New York with a great job. My older sister has a son and a drama of a love life."

"And you're the famous hockey hunk, the bright star of the family." *Famous hockey hunk?*

Is Reagan attracted to me? I'm not blind, so I know women find me attractive, but I honestly hadn't thought Reagan would see me like that. Not after how we first met. It's been a minute since I've had sex, so I'm horny as fuck. Not that I'd take advantage of this pixie cutie.

Just answer her question, dumbass.

"Nah. Just a hockey player. I manage to disappoint my father every game." I turn away from her as I say it, hoping she won't ask me any more questions about my family.

Dishes done, we head back to the couch to pick up

with *Tomb Raider* again, sitting in companionable silence, something I'm *much* more comfortable with. It's strangely nice. The few times Gia and I hung out, there was little talking. Well, actually, *she* talked *at* me quite a bit. About everything under the sun. Interesting turn of events when she wanted out the minute she caught a whiff of my developing feelings for her.

I've always been fine being alone though.

Still, I'm oddly comfortable with Reagan, just sitting here next to her, breathing in the scent of her hair, and feeling easy in her company.

And I worry that feeling comfortable with this strange, beautiful girl might just be trouble waiting to happen.

10
walk of shame

Reagan

The movie ends, and I've been yawning for the back half of it. Mikhail gets up and tells me to make myself at home in his guest room, assuring me he's changed the bedding since Aiden used it last summer. "I keep hoping one of my sisters or my parents will come to Vegas, so I'll be motivated to fix this space for guests. It's kind of a bare-bones-bachelor-pad look at the moment."

"Oh my gosh, don't apologize for the décor, please. I'm the one intruding here. Bringing my drama."

"Yeah, well, we all have stuff sometimes." Lifting one muscled arm to drag his hand artfully through his hair, he makes a very pretty picture towering over me. "Let me know if you need anything. I'll just be...in my room across the hall. Obviously."

He blushes in a way I find incredibly endearing. For a guy as hot as he is, as alpha as he looks, he sure is a shy boy.

"Thanks, Mikhail." I pull him impulsively into an awkward hug. "For everything."

For saving me, again.

For being my hero.

For becoming a new friend.

For being someone I can trust.

He returns my hug, his big body surprisingly hard and soft at the same time. But then I feel him tensing, as if catching himself. There's a quick moment when I think he might kiss me, but it's gone as quickly as it came. He pulls away and takes a step back before saying, "Good night, Reagan."

I get settled for sleep in the guest room, ditching my sweatpants before sliding under soft sheets that smell clean, while reminding me I'm alone in a strange bed. But sleep feels far away for me. Despite yawning for the last forty-five minutes, I can't make my mind slow down enough to lull myself into sleep. I toss and turn, my thoughts a torrent, an emotional storm keeping me from the rest my body so badly needs.

At first, it's just the whole night replaying itself. The fear of being followed. The panic. The shock of seeing my apartment upended. The reality of what that means. I do not feel safe. *Because I am not safe.* Anywhere.

But it's not just those thoughts that replay over and over. It's the shy smile of a man who, I'm guessing, doesn't share said smile all that often. Mikhail, who showed up when I needed someone to show up, to save me. Who didn't send me away, didn't run for the hills when a stranger needed help.

And he doesn't feel like such a stranger, now, does he?

And I'm a fraud. He's good and talented and successful. And I'm well, I'm nobody. And while I did not steal from Sodorov, there are things I haven't had the courage to tell Mikhail yet. There are reasons Sodorov might think it *was* me.

I feel badly about this sin of omission. I'm not lying, not really, but I'm also not telling the whole truth. And he deserves the truth, but I'm just not ready to share it yet. Still, I feel like I'm putting him in danger, taking advantage of him. I hate myself for it.

Shaking the thoughts away, I find myself just thinking about his dimpled cheek. The lopsided smile he breaks out only occasionally. The amazing head of hair that he swipes his hands through when he's nervous.

This guy is something else, for sure.

He keeps a clean apartment. For a single athlete, I'd expect a straight-up bachelor pad, but this place is well-kept and very tidy. Mikhail takes care of his personal space as well as he obviously takes care of his body.

Oh yeah, Mikhail Zelenka is quite the male specimen. Incredibly sexy in a tall, dark, and handsome, seriously mysterious kind of way.

Just to push away all the random voices in my head, I keep thinking of Mikhail, especially the way his T-shirts cling to his tattooed pecs and biceps, showcasing his muscular body.

Yep, guilty as charged with the crime of checking

him out, for sure. I may be in crisis mode, but my eyes still work just fine.

My fingers snake their way down beneath my underwear. I touch myself in the darkness of a bed that is not my own. I do it gently at first, building up some pressure before slipping two fingers inside to drag back and forth across my clit. Despite the ache that grows, I can't get myself there. My mind is too jumbled and stressed.

Without really thinking, I throw the covers aside, my feet hitting the floor. His room is only steps away, and his door is slightly ajar. When I peek in and see that he is also awake, I can make out his eyes staring back at me in the dark.

Is it possible he was thinking of me just now in the way I was thinking of him?

Before I lose my nerve, I pull my T-shirt over my head and take the last few steps to stand beside his bed. Except for the soft boy shorts I wore as pajamas, I'm as good as naked.

His mouth opens slightly, like he might say something, but his eyes are wide, hungry. I take his hand and place it on my breast. He touches me, his fingertips graze across my nipple, hardening it and giving me goosebumps.

I push his hand down into my panties, letting him feel how wet I am already.

"Fuck, you're wet," he growls.

"Mmm." That's all I can say. His fingers feel amazing.

He drags them along my clit and presses two inside

me. His strokes are firm as he moves his fingers slowly in and out of me. *It's so, so much better than I could ever do for myself.*

"Fuuuck…Reagan."

"Yes. Please…" Sighing, I push my hips toward him, wanting him to touch me all over, to make me come so I can forget all this noise and fear and chaos screaming in my head for just a moment. *Lose myself in more of what he's doing right now—*

But he doesn't.

He takes his fingers away first, and then his hand is gone altogether. "I'm not going to take advantage of you here like this."

"You wouldn't be—"

"I would," he says quickly. "You're scared and alone and you think you owe me something for helping you. But you don't. I'm helping you, no strings attached."

"I know that. You've been nothing but kind but—" My voice is raspy, thick with need. "I just…couldn't stop thinking about you."

"Reagan," he groans. And then a heartbeat of a pause widens the distance between us to at least a hundred miles. "I'm not going to be one more random guy trying to use you…or whatever. You're beautiful and I'm attracted to you, okay? But this—this does not feel right to me right now…tonight."

I wish a hole would appear so I could gladly jump in and disappear, erasing the last few minutes from the history of time. I back away, my cheeks heating with embarrassment and humiliation. I grab my shirt from the floor and slip it over my head as I flee his room, shutting the door behind me.

For the third time in twenty-four hours, tears are burning in my eyes. This is so not like me. I grab the few things I brought from my apartment and bundle them back into the duffel. I can't stay here now after what I just did. I don't know how I'll ever face him again without bursting into flames on the spot. What the hell is wrong with me?

I slip out of Mikhail's apartment, making the lonely walk of shame to the elevator that will morph into fear when I get to my apartment. Have Sodorov's men come back? Will they before this night is over? Tomorrow or the next day after that? I know the building super hasn't changed my locks yet because he said he couldn't do it until tomorrow at the earliest, so I don't have a choice. I guess I can barricade the door with furniture for the night.

I step inside my trashed apartment, walking past the disarray to get the baseball bat I keep in my room. I return to wedge it against the doorknob at an angle and slide the chain lock into place. I drag over my coffee table and turn it on its side as an extra barrier. I'll deal with sorting out the mess and putting things back in order tomorrow.

When I slip into bed, my head is aching. I'm so angry...*and mortified.* Angry about Sodorov. About what just happened with Mikhail. I just made an absolute ass out of myself by flashing my tits and initiating a finger bang with a guy who only sees me as a needy obligation. *Why is this my fucking life?* Being rejected by a nice guy.

If I'm honest, my misery is also about feeling so stuck. I *cannot* move forward. And I hate it.

I feel trapped.

I *am* trapped.

11
king zelenka

Mikhail

Two weeks later.
Columbus, Ohio

"That Caulfield is about as dumb as a box of nails," my father says, launching into a play-by-play of the moment one of our third-string players missed an easy pass from me, allowing a Columbus player to make off with the puck. Straight into our net. Cal didn't even have time to adjust, and that's saying a lot because our goalie, Cal, rarely misses a damn thing when it comes to the trajectory of that biscuit. "Why did you even load the pass like that? You should have just taken the shot."

I lift a shoulder and grunt. "We've been asked to be more trusting of our fellow players. I was trying to do my part."

My father snorts. "Well, that was stupid of you, then. He's barely worth the shit contract they've got him on now."

"He'll probably go back to the taxi squad after last night's play," I answer, refusing to take the bait on his personal jab toward me.

"He'll probably ride out his contract and then find himself in need of new employment. What's he on?" my dad demands, as if I'm responsible for knowing the contract details of every teammate.

"I dunno. Three-year, entry level? He gets very little playing time. I almost forgot his name." I didn't forget. It's Jamie Caulfield, and he's okay for a kid experiencing his first starts of his NHL career. Everybody starts somewhere, and *everybody makes mistakes* when they first come into the big league. But my dad doesn't want to hear that, so it's useless to try even defending a player like Caulfield.

"Well, he's a joke. This whole new approach thing is also a big, fat joke. When you have a championship team and a championship front line, you do not throw your chump players into the mix at random."

"They'll weed it out soon enough. They've made coaching changes, administration changes. It's only a matter of time. They want bench strength, and they want everyone else sharp."

"In theory, I get this. If I were the GM and coaching staff in Austin or Salt Lake City, I might be making some changes like that myself. But not in Las Vegas. I simply would not take out my top players unless I was up by three goals in the third period."

"I don't love it, either. If Evan had been on left wing, there wouldn't have been an extra goal by Columbus. But it is what it is, and we won, so whatever. Caulfield can seize his opportunity or eat a shit sandwich for all I care."

My mother giggles at this for some reason. Nervous energy, maybe? It's always a tense scene when my father starts analyzing my every move after a game.

"Are there retirements on the horizon?" he asks. "Is that why they're doing this? Trying to see who the next generation winners are?"

"Probably." I shrug. "I mean, there are always rumors swirling around."

"Who?" He sneers with a laugh. "Kazmeirowicz? Kolochev? Demoskev? They're not that old. They have several years of top play left in them. And people love them. They shit gold."

I shrug again because while the statement is true, it's also a dig at me. In Jozem Zelenka's eyes, Mikhail Zelenka does not shit gold. Mikhail Zelenka is the marginally-okay player who happens to bear his family name, and who will never, ever live up to his great expectations—*aka* his own illustrious career in the greatest game of hockey.

"Well, they're all in peak physical shape, making the best money they'll ever make in their careers. No way are those cows heading off to pasture any time soon. But they'll sure as hell walk once their contracts are up if they get short shrift on the ice for much longer."

"It's not my job to question the management decisions or the contracting or the lineup. It's my job to go out and perform as best I can every single game." My dad opens his mouth to argue, but I add, "And that is what I do. Every single game. And when my contract is up at the end of the season, they either extend me with a fair deal or I'll be on the left wing somewhere else. Nic told me I have nothing to worry about." My new agent, Nic Marchessault, who also happens to rep our GM, assured me he's got it handled, and I have a raise coming to me next year, whether it's with Vegas or another team. I trust him. But my dad is not a fan of my agent, or my coaches, or anyone else who decides how much I play, or where, or for how much money. It's fucking exhausting listening to him bitch about stuff beyond my control.

He raises an eyebrow and leans forward, a smirk on his face. "Grow a pair of balls."

My mom smacks him on the arm. "Shush, Jozem. What is wrong with you?"

"I want my son to have the best opportunity to play," he answers. "What do you mean, what's wrong with me?"

"You're being a nag." I catch her eye, and she grins slightly. I hold back my returning grin, as I know it'll only piss my dad off even more. My mom usually doesn't break rank like that. He's probably raging, but he won't show it while we're sitting in some hipster breakfast joint in Columbus, Ohio.

"I'm thinking about my son," he says, folding his arms over his chest as I poke my fork into my now-cold scrambled eggs. "I may go talk to the owner about this. It's ridiculous."

"Pop, it's not kindergarten. You can't go yell at the coach to give me more ice time like you did when I was a kid."

"Well, it worked, didn't it?"

I roll my eyes. "Sure it did. When I was five. And because you were The Great Zelenka and you donated a shit-ton of money to the club and the facilities. You essentially used your reputation and money to buy me the ice time."

"It was worth it," he says harshly. "That extra ice time meant you were ready to go straight into pro hockey after high school."

I notice that he does not include the fact that I not only went straight to the pros, but that I also started in the NHL by the end of my first year. *It's a big deal.* He may have been one of the Greats, but he was not an NHL starter in his first year. *And he'll never give me credit for that accomplishment.* Praise is not in his wheelhouse. *And yet I turn up and somehow expect more from him. Every fucking time.* I'm done with this conversation, so I stand up and lean over to kiss my mom on the cheek.

"I have to get to the airport. Thanks for coming last night. Thanks for breakfast this morning."

My mom tells me to call her when I land, and I nod before saluting my father, who just sits there scowling.

Two hours later, I'm on the plane, noise-canceling headphones on, ignoring Aiden's jabber about some puck bunny he met while he was out with the team last night. I could have gone, but I was feeling out of sorts after the goal loss with Caulfield. Instead, I used the gym at the hotel and worked out until I could barely hold my phone, then stumbled to the shower, and then to my bed. Lights out after that. I woke up to the sound of my alarm buzzing and realized I was about to be late for breakfast to meet my parents who'd flown in from Detroit for the game.

An elbow to the ribs has me pulling off my headphones so I can tell Aiden to settle the fuck down. "It's like sitting with a toddler with you. Can't you just sit fuckin' still?"

"Damn," he singsongs. "Someone's pissier than usual. What's the problem, Prince Zelenka?"

I let out a huff. "Command breakfast with King Zelenka."

"Enough said." A few seconds pass before he speaks again. "What's the latest with crazy casino chick? Are you two still banging?"

I sigh, because there are so many ways to speak to Aiden's questions, but I'm not much of a sharer of my personal details as a rule. There's really no reason to spill my guts about Reagan with Aiden, but still, I want to correct some of his assumptions. "First of all, we're not." I give him a pointed look, letting him know that line of questioning is a dead end. "And second, she's not crazy, even though I thought so at first. Now that I know more about her situation, I feel like she might be mixed up in something shady, and it's probably for the best I'm not involved."

"Meh. I think you should go with the flow, see where adventure takes you. Be her hero or whatever," Aiden says with a shrug before putting his ear pods back in.

I don't admit to him that I do kind of like being Reagan's hero. I like that I saved her in that alley. I like that she came to me when her place got broken into. I get the impression she doesn't have a lot of people who have her back, and while I think there's a lot more to her story than what she's told me, my heart doesn't tell me she's a bad person. In fact, I get the feeling she's a good person who's been in the wrong place at the wrong time for a while.

When I woke up the next morning, after turning her away the night before, it was no surprise she was gone. I mean, no one feels good when they propose sex and get shut down. Still, as much as I wanted her, I knew it wasn't right. She wasn't offering herself for the right reasons. I wanted to go up to her apartment and talk to her, explain myself better, but I didn't. Instead, I took my frustration straight to the gym, where I punched it out until it was time to clock in with the team for a two-week road trip around the Eastern Seaboard. Got on the plane and slept straight through until we landed in Toronto.

I haven't seen her, obviously, since I've been traveling with the team, but I haven't had *any* contact with Reagan at all. And that doesn't feel right, either. While we were in Columbus, it reminded me she said she grew up here. Did she ever go to a hockey game at the home arena? Was she into any sports as a kid? She's very fit, and I know this because I got a real good look at her banging body. Those tits of hers were perfection. The vision of her standing beside my bed after ditching her shirt is sealed in my memory. Gorgeous breasts that fit in my hand, and so soft and round, tipped with dark pink nipples I *needed* in my mouth but didn't have the pleasure of experiencing. I'd love another chance to show her how much I could appreciate her offer if it were under better circumstances. So, *I know* exactly how well Reagan takes care of herself. Was she always into fitness? What about her family? Are they still in Columbus?

I know none of those things about Reagan.

But even so, I haven't stopped thinking about her. Regardless of the strange way she came into my life, I really do feel right about my role as her protector. Maintenance better have done what I demanded, too. I told them I'd pay double to give her a stronger door. Better lock. A security camera. Hoping it made her feel safer. *Somewhat. I've hated not knowing if she's okay. If she's been safe getting home from the casino.*

As Columbus disappears below the clouds, and Aiden falls asleep with his head on my shoulder, I think about how much I want to see a certain mysterious, dark-haired beauty when I get home.

Also...I might really like this girl.

12
a shrugger

Reagan

Raul, my boss, is checking his cell phone while I'm trying to talk to him.

"Raul." I wave my hand in front of him. "This is important."

"Mmm," he grunts, still not looking up.

"Sodorov still won't leave me alone. I still don't feel safe, especially since they broke into my apartment." Not that Raul was particularly concerned when I told him about this two weeks ago. He knows that they roughed me up in the alley. He saw my neck the next day. *And yet...* The man's a brick wall, and I'm so sick of it. "They try to follow me to and from my building. Can't you do something?"

He looks up and tilts his head. "Have you called the police? Made a report?"

"No."

He lifts his shoulders. "Well, then, I don't see how I can help you if you're not willing to make a report."

"You know who these guys are," I say harshly under my breath. "Calling the police will only make things worse. These guys are above the law, and you know it. If I call the police, they'll come back with something twice as bad for me."

He opens his mouth, and I know exactly what he's going to say before he says it. "Well, it *does* look like you in the video, Reagan, you have to admit. I mean, isn't that why they're so focused on you?"

"I admit she does look like me, but you know it wasn't me. I don't have access to those offices, my fingerprints weren't found there. And besides, if I'd stolen millions from someone's house account, do you really think I'd be hanging around, still working the same job, still living in the same apartment?"

"I mean, I guess," he says while smoothing his dark, slicked-back hair. "I've seen stupider criminals come through here."

"Well, I'm not one of them. Do you have any other leads? Maybe if they knew the casino had leads, they'd back off."

"I can't really comment on that, Reagan."

"Isn't there anything Tangiers can do to protect me? I shouldn't have to live this way. I didn't do anything wrong."

"Look, I'll see what I can do, but I can't guarantee anything. Don't you have some other issues with any of those guys? Isn't that what I heard?"

My cheeks feel like they've been set on fire. Damn, how does he know this?

"It has absolutely *nothing* to do with Henri Sodorov, though. I've barely met the guy."

He gives me a look. "Drama breeds drama, girl. You should keep your head down. Stay away from the drama. Blend into the background for a while."

"Wow, thanks for the sage advice, Raul. Perhaps I could avoid the drama of being beaten, having my apartment broken into, and having strange men following me if the casino I work for would tell its high-roller underworld client to back the hell off and leave its employees alone."

My hands shake as I turn and head out for my floor shift. Raul is a terrible manager, to begin with, and this only solidifies that he is among the worst people I have ever worked with in my entire life.

Maybe I should just quit. Go hide out somewhere; try to start over in a new city somewhere far from here.

The casino is busy tonight, and I'm grateful for the distraction from my thoughts about Raul and my job and this Sodorov drama. There's a loud guy in a huge cowboy hat playing tonight. Introduced himself as Wild Bill, no joke. He jabbers on and on, two women in sparkly, beaded dresses hanging on his elbows, laughing at everything he says like he's just the funniest guy since forever. It's entertaining, at least, and makes my shift go by more quickly.

At one point, I look up and scan the room when someone familiar catches my eye. A tall, dark, and handsome guy all alone in the casino would be enough to catch anyone's eye, but he's striking in other ways, too. His carved, muscled body, his arm sleeve tats, his great hair. Even more so because *I know this hot guy* sitting alone in the casino.

Mikhail Zelenka is sitting at the bar in my section, nursing a beer.

And he's watching me.

When he realizes I see him, he nods. That single acknowledgement sends a flutter through my belly, and at the same time, it fills me with an overwhelming sense of relief. *Is he here for me? Why is he here? To make me feel safe?* I don't know the reason he's here, especially after how we left things when I fled his apartment in the depths of horrified embarrassment. I haven't seen him in a couple weeks, obviously, with his team on a multi-city road trip in Canada and the East Coast.

How did I know this?

Because I started watching Vegas Crush hockey games. More specifically, a certain player with the number nineteen on his back. While off work, I'd tune into a game, and if I was working, I soon discovered that all Crush games conveniently play on TV screens throughout the casino whether they're at home or on the road, so it was easy to keep up with his whereabouts. He played a game in Columbus last night.

So, I really have no idea if Mikhail's here to make me feel safe or not, but he makes me feel it anyway. Knowing him the little I do, I also know he'd step in to protect me if someone was trying to hurt me. He's done it before, and I'm certain he'd do it again.

The comfort of knowing he's here helps me relax in a way I haven't for weeks. I laugh and joke and do a much better job than I've been doing of late, encouraging bets and keeping the clientele happy. Raul even comes over and tells me what a nice job I'm doing tonight. I glare at him in response because, well, he deserves it, but secretly, I'm pleased at the compliment.

When my shift ends, I close things out and walk over to where Mikhail is waiting. "Fancy meeting you here."

He picks at the label on his beer, his leg shaking maybe a tad...nervously? "It's been a while. I just wanted to check in and make sure you were okay."

"Oh, yeah, all right," I say, nodding and trying my best to cover. My words drop like a lead weight between us, which pretty much matches the way my stomach drops along with it. Because suddenly, I'm not as thrilled as I was before, knowing he just came by to make sure I was okay. I didn't realize until just this moment how much I wanted him to come by because he wanted to actually *see me*.

"But also," he tacks on, "I thought maybe I could buy you a drink?" He arches a brow at me hopefully.

I bite my bottom lip and consider his invitation. A surprise, yes, but a good surprise. I have a dress in my locker I keep here in case I pick up shifts as a hostess in the casino's posh restaurant. Mikhail is in dark jeans and a gray button-down. I'll probably look way overdressed, but I can't sit out here with him in my casino uniform.

"Give me a minute to change?" I ask, making the decision to do this with him.

The hint of a smile that appears on his face boosts

my confidence, but it's his reply that really does the trick. "I'll be here waiting. What will you have? So, it'll be here when you come back." Such a serious guy, but I do like it. *On him.* Yes, indeed, Mikhail Zelenka has the brooding male vibe down to per-fec-tion.

"A vodka cranberry sounds lovely," I tell him before heading back to the employee lounge to attempt a transformation.

Ten minutes later, I'm in a short black dress and strappy black heels as I dig through my bag for makeup. I cobble together some red lip pencil, a kohl eye pencil, and a mascara that miraculously still works. I haven't worn makeup in forever, but for tonight at least, I want Mikhail to see me as someone other than a damaged girl who needs saving. I want to look good. And for him to think I'm sexy—someone desirable he won't want to turn away for a second time *if we ever get to that point again.*

When I walk back out, I watch his dark blue eyes widen as he shifts in his seat. He stands as I approach him, towering over me as he pulls out a bar stool for me to sit. "You clean up well." He gives me a wink and it's freaking adorable. "A little black dress and everything. I'm feeling underdressed now with you glamming it up."

"It's just an outfit I keep here. I work as a hostess in the steakhouse sometimes for extra money, so I come prepared."

"You wear it well."

I smile at him, relishing his compliments as I pick up my vodka cranberry. He offers his beer bottle to clink with my glass. "Cheers, Reagan, we made it through another day."

"Did you have a bad day?" I'm intrigued by his presence here, seeking me out in my place of work, and hoping like hell that he'll tell me why at some point tonight.

"Not bad, necessarily," he says with a shrug. His leg bounces nervously again. I long to reach out and put my hand on his thigh to calm him but I don't dare. "I've been on the road for games the last two weeks. We finished in Columbus, your hometown."

I know. "Is that why you thought to come check on me?"

"Not completely," he answers with no elaboration whatsoever. "My parents came to Columbus to see me. We had breakfast together this morning. Well, more like they had breakfast while I sat in front of my food listening to my dad bitch for an hour."

"I'm sorry." It's the only thing I can think to say to him. Sharing his personal thoughts has me suddenly feeling shy, when he's never made me feel that way before. Mikhail's been pretty easy to open up to. *Except for that one time I tried to get him to fuck me and he turned me down.*

"It's fine," he says with another shrug. "It's no different than any other day. How are you? Any sign of those guys lately?"

How do I answer this question? I take a big drink from my glass before attempting to explain. "I'm terrified," I admit after a tense moment of quiet, "but I do have extra locks on the door. Maintenance was far more obliging than I expected. They even put up one of those little security cameras, and still, I'll spot them lurking around sometimes." *At least they haven't touched me. Nor have they tried to break in again. Thank God.* "It feels like a ticking time bomb with no clock on it to me. You know? I just don't know when the next thing might happen."

"I feel…" Mikhail stops before he finishes his thought. He turns the beer bottle around and around in a circle on the bar. "I feel like shit for leaving Vegas and not checking in on you first."

A surprised laugh bubbles up and out of me. Mikhail frowns slightly and looks down at his drink, so I put my hand on his bicep. "No, I'm not laughing at you. I'm—it's just that you don't have to feel guilty or protective or whatever, Mikhail. You've helped me so much, and I'm just a random stranger who crashed in on you, and quite rudely, you'll recall. You can go live your life. Please, you don't have to worry about me."

"But I do, all the same," he says, slowly lifting those stunning, deep blue eyes of his to look at me.

Taking a deep breath, I sit up straight in my chair and toss back the remainder of my drink, holding up a finger at William, the bartender, for another. "Let's change the subject. Enough of my drama. How's the hockey season going?"

His eyebrows rise while his face contorts in a way that does not indicate that things are great. "It's weird," he says after a moment.

"How so?"

"They're trying some new lineups, breaking up our comfort zones, trying to give other guys more playing time. And, you know, it's normal to do that. Most teams make switches all throughout the game. But with our starters, we have such great chemistry, and we dominate out there. We trust each other and we win because of that. So, historically, we've gotten the most minutes and didn't sub out very often."

"Until now."

"Yeah."

"And you're annoyed you're not getting as much playing time?"

"Well, our focus on the front line is what's won us the Cup in the past." He shrugs.

I lean over and bump my shoulder against his. "You're a shrugger, you know that?"

He shrugs again and grins. "Sorry," he mumbles, his leg starting to bounce again.

This time, I put my hand on his upper thigh. It sends a jolt through my body to touch him, to feel the strength and muscle there. The idea of Mikhail naked is suddenly the only thing on my mind. Somehow, though, I manage to clear my head enough to speak. "You bounce a lot too. Your leg. Like you're nervous."

"I'm not nervous," he says too quickly. He looks anywhere but at me, finally settling on William, who nods at him and brings him another bottle of beer.

"I caught the game on the telly the other night," William says to Mikhail, his British accent ringing out over the bar. "You guys aren't playing as you have in past seasons."

"You're telling me." Mikhail heaves a huge sigh.

"Well, a win's a win, I s'pose," William says. "But it'd be a right kick in the arse to lose what you've built there. This town's all aflutter for you boys. Don't go mucking it up now."

"I just work there," Mikhail says with a laugh as he pulls the bottle to his lips.

As William salutes and heads off to help another customer, I say, "You and I live such different lives, you know? I mean, he just walked up to you and knew who you were. This pro athlete, famous guy that people know on sight. They want to talk to you, want to take selfies with you. And I'm just a nobody—well, my life is nothing like any of that."

Mikhail's face goes dark as he rolls his beer bottle between his palms. It's a few moments before he speaks. "Everyone has problems, you know."

"Sure," I say, though I keep to myself the fact that I'd bet my right hand that his problems aren't nearly on the same level as mine. Money and privilege and status are powerful like that. "What are yours?"

He gives a dark, humorless laugh. "I suppose my daddy issues aren't nearly on par with you having a crime lord on your ass."

"Well, I suppose it depends on perspective."

"How so?" He looks over at me and cocks a sexy brow.

"Well, if your dad is like a pedophile or if he beat the crap out of you, then maybe your daddy issues really do trump my situation with the crime lord."

"He's not, and he didn't."

I nod, feeling like I've hit a nerve. Still, I stick with my original assertion. Mikhail and I are from different planets. He's been groomed to be right where he's at right now. And he's pissed that he doesn't get playing time, but I'd also bet it has very little impact on whatever big-ass paycheck he gets. He could probably afford a much nicer apartment than he has. He's probably got a financial manager, tucking his money away for a rainy day.

Me? *It is a rainy day.* It has been rainy for a very long time, and the skies don't seem to be ready to clear any time soon. Mikhail has no idea what my life is like. Which is why, even though I may or may not have imagined him naked on more than one occasion, nothing will ever happen between us. I know that. Despite my many troubles, I am a realist.

Still, it's fun to pretend. He's here to make sure I'm safe. He's handsome and strong and kind. I feel cute in this dress. And I don't see any of Sodorov's goons lurking about. So why not have a little fun for a few hours tonight?

"So, see that guy over there?" I say, changing the subject again as I try to discreetly nod at a rotund man working on one of the digital slot machines.

"The guy with his ass crack hanging out?" He chuckles. "I see him, though I'd rather not have."

"His name is Brick. No joke. He's, like, thirty... moved here from Kentucky or West Virginia. I guess he had a high school girlfriend come out here for college and he followed her out, only to get dumped. He's nice enough, but he talks all the time about how much he hates it here, wants to go back home, and blah, blah, blah. So, one day he was doing maintenance on one of the older machines—the ones with the levers—and this attractive woman walks up to him asking about the way the machines work. Are they rigged or are they really random? She's all flirty, like she's trying to seduce him into telling her some kind of deep secret, and he's getting redder and redder. Finally, he tells her he needs to get back to work, and she says to come find her if he remembers anything important. She kisses him on the cheek, and he turns around, bends down, and out slips a huge, loud fart as she starts to walk away."

Mikhail's mouth hangs open. "That is...I don't know where I thought your story was going, but I'm pretty sure, in my mind, it didn't involve farting."

"I know, right?" I smack him on the leg, just an excuse to touch him again. "Poor guy."

"I'm sure you see all kinds of characters in a place like this," he muses, his posture more relaxed now that we've moved away from the serious subjects.

"That is true. One night we had a woman at the blackjack table who had to be one hundred years old. I'm not even exaggerating. She was, like, less than five feet tall and she was wearing, I swear, every piece of jewelry she owned. Like, sixteen necklaces, multiple rings on every finger. She had both arms full of bracelets. She kept telling everyone this was her last hurrah, and she was going to meet God tonight. She told people she was getting drunk and gambling all her money away and then she was going to go get a hot call girl to give her oral because she'd always been curious about women."

Mikhail nearly spits his beer out at this. He cracks up, his face splitting into a real, bona fide smile. And, my God, it is the most beautiful thing I have ever seen.

If I wasn't crushing on Mikhail Zelenka already, I certainly would be now.

His smile makes me smile, which makes me giggle, which turns into a whole fit of laughter and a few more stories from my time working here at the casino.

"You know," I say, a third drink and as many stories later, "I might have said I hate this place on more than one occasion, but there have been some funny things happen here. Some sweet things, too. I've seen a couple of people get engaged. I saw a woman give birth. She was like nine months pregnant and on a hot streak and her water broke. She told her husband she had plenty of time, still, but she ended up going into active labor in the rotunda out front. She had a little girl and named her Isla. Totally crazy."

"Only in Vegas," Mikhail says. He smiles at me before bopping his fingertip against the end of my nose. I suspect he's a bit drunk. I know I am. "I like seeing you laugh and smile."

Something warm pools in my lower belly, the way he looks at me. I meet his gaze, but my eyes move quickly to his lips, which look supremely kissable at the moment.

"I don't do it very often," I say. It comes out kind of breathless. "Smile, I mean. It's been kind of a shitshow for a while. But I'm having fun with you. You remind me that there are good people out there."

He opens his mouth, and there's a long moment that stretches between us where I think he might kiss me. I want him to kiss me. Instead, he looks at the tab, pulls out some cash. "Can I walk you home, Reagan?"

Not what I was expecting, but again, I can be a realist. "Sure, Mikhail. That would be nice."

I get off my stool and wobble a bit on my heels. He holds his hand out to steady me and I take it. He doesn't let go as we walk through to the front door, out onto the bustling sidewalk foot traffic, all while still holding my hand.

I shiver, the night air a little chillier than usual, and then something wonderful happens when Mikhail drops my hand to wrap an arm around my shoulders, pulling me against his warm, sexy body as we walk.

It feels so good having him close, our bodies aligned to each other, even though I only come up to his shoulder.

"You a little tipsy?" he asks, a lopsided grin making him look rakish and naughty and totally like TROUBLE in warranted all shouty caps.

"I am. You?"

"Yeah," he says, smiling like he's had a taste of freedom. He pinches his fingers together. "Just a bit. It's been a hot minute since I've had that much to drink. My nutrition plan and all that."

"Lightweight," I say with a hiccup.

"That's the pot calling the kettle metal, or whatever the saying is."

This makes us both laugh uproariously as we walk. "Put the kettle to the metal," I say in response so that we laugh even harder.

"Don't metal with my kettle," he answers, grinning. At this point, my eyes are watering from laughing so hard. I haven't felt like this in a long time—safe and free and, well...happy.

Before we know it, we're at the apartment building. It's not until we stand, awaiting the elevator, that he asks, "Do you want to go home? Or would you like to come to my place?"

There is no expectation or implication in his tone. In fact, he seems a bit shy about asking. But when he looks down at me, I see how his eyes darken as he zeros in on my lips, and I know that he wants just what I want.

13
the altar of reagan

Mikhail

My heart beats wildly in my chest. Reagan was right when she mentioned it back at the casino. I *am* nervous. About how she'll respond to whether I crossed a line by asking her to my place. I've turned her away before. She could flip the tables on me now and I'd deserve it. She probably should turn me away, to be honest. We've both been drinking.

Still, she's so beautiful right now, with her dark hair shiny and sleek, her lips bright red, and her eyes glittering with humor. She has an amazing smile. When she directs one at me, something strange happens inside my chest. I don't know what it is I'm feeling, either. I just know I've never felt it before with any—

"Sure." At first, I'm not sure what she means. It must show on my face because she adds, "I'll come to your place."

As we ride the elevator to my floor, she looks up at

me with a rueful smile. "My place still gives me the heebs." Now I'm wondering if she's just coming to my apartment to feel safe. Maybe she missed the meaning of my question?

I want her.

Standing next to her, I tower over her petite frame. I want to pick her up so badly. I want to press her up against the wall of this elevator, hit the button, stop our ascent, and kiss her until she's fucking blind with wanting me too.

But I won't take advantage of her. I need Reagan to feel safe with me. So I shove my hands in my pockets and look down, trying to hide how anxious I am.

When we make it inside my apartment, I toss my keys on the table and ask if she wants anything. I'm not prepared when I turn back around to find her right there. I feel my eyebrows rise as she literally throws her arms around my neck and launches herself at me. I catch her though, and then her legs wrap around my hips as I take her weight, holding her easily in my arms. We stare at each other for a beat, her looking up at me with her dark, sexy eyes, telling me exactly what she wants to do here.

I crash my lips down on hers and take her mouth as she rakes her fingers through my hair. *Fuck, it feels good, having her in my arms.*

A little off balance, my hands take a tight grip on her equally tight ass as I frog-march us over to the nearest wall for stability. I press her against it so I can press myself up against her. My cock goes rock-hard as we deepen the kissing, our tongues tangling together wildly. She moans when I move to kiss her neck, her back arching deeply, making her tits thrust up closer toward my mouth.

Thank God.

I kiss her clavicle and then down the vee of her neckline to the tops of those spectacular tits of hers. My memory works real well—I can remember just exactly how spectacular they are. I need one in my mouth, but this wall isn't gonna work. So, with a groan of frustration, I pull her from the wall and move her to the couch.

I need more of a surface to rest her on than the fucking wall to accomplish all the things I want to do with her.

As I set her down on my couch, she quickly reaches down to the hem of her little black dress to pull it over her head. She immediately puts her hands behind her back to unhook her lacy black bra. I think I stop breathing as I watch her slowly draw one strap down her slender arm, then repeat the action on the other side before sending that pretty lace bra to the floor with a determined flick of her wrist.

Reagan is a fucking vision sitting on my couch, her perfect tits on display for me a second time with nothing else on her banging body except for some tiny black panties and her matching high heels.

My lips are on her breasts in an instant. I fall to my knees to access them, my tongue working against her tight, dark pink nipples, first one and then the other. I feel like I'm worshipping at the altar of Reagan, and my hands, initially braced against her calves, so shapely in her high heels, move up to the back of her thighs, willing her legs to part for me.

They do. With only the thin barrier of her underwear between my fingers and her pussy, I'm almost to my goal.

I determinedly push two fingers beneath the silky black fabric to find her warm and wet for me. I think I groan, but it's totally animal, involuntary, as I drag them over and then back and forth through her slick arousal. My cock hardens even more, knowing she wants me. She's wet for *me*.

I look up and find her eyes heavy-lidded, and dreamy. "Are you sure? We can stop. I don't...I don't want you to feel like you have to do this. We're both a little drunk and—"

"Don't be stupid. Please don't push me away again. I want this. I want you, Mikhail." I breathe in and out deeply while staring down at her spread open so beautifully for me to take. Then, just one word, "Please." It comes out of her pretty mouth in a desperate plea.

I can't deny her.

I don't want to deny her.

Ever again.

I sink two fingers into her cunt, dragging them in and out as she immediately starts to come, a long cry of pleasure erupting from the back of her throat in a sexy song that sends me into another realm.

I can't get enough of this erotic creature.

Like I need to legit ask her the question: *"What planet did you just fly in from...because I've never seen anyone on this earth as sexy as you are right fucking now...in my whole life."*

I *need* her pussy on my mouth or I feel like I could die here.

No, scratch that, I'm dead already.

I'm done thinking when I pull away her tiny black panties and dive right on in. I lick, suck, finger and stroke...at the *altar-of-Reagan's-beautiful-fucking-pussy*.

Her hips grind against my face and her fingers rake through my hair as she works herself closer.

She loves it. Wants it.

When I make her come again, she cries out, her hips going rigid as she clenches around my fingers.

I look up and our eyes meet as she's orgasming.

It's the hottest thing I've ever seen.

She *is* the hottest fucking thing on the earth right now.

This intensity...*this level of insane attraction*...it's all new territory for me.

And I can't look away.

I'd have to be dead for that to happen.

14
sexy af snow white

Mikhail

As the aftershocks subside, she backs away and holds out a hand to help me to my feet, only to push me immediately down to sit on the couch. She pulls at my zipper, tugging at my pants to get them down. I undress awkwardly, struggling to get my shirt over my head as we both giggle like two teens trying to avoid being caught by our parents.

She stares at my cock once I'm bare, her eyes wide. "Stroke yourself." She licks her bottom lip and then bites down on it as she says it.

Fuuuck.

I do as I'm told, running my hand up and down my cock as she crawls back up on the couch, positioning herself above me. She watches for a moment before replacing my hand with her own. My eyes practically roll back in my head at the feel of her hands on my skin.

When she licks the head, I nearly come. She takes me into her mouth slowly, going just a little deeper with each movement of her head. It's an elegant torture of the very best kind. I want her balls-deep down on me. I want to shove my dick down the back of her throat. But I don't. I let her go at her own pace as I enjoy the build of what is sure to be an explosive orgasm.

I watch as her head moves, her red lips wide around my rock-hard cock. I don't want to come in her mouth, but when she finally opens the back of her throat to let me in, her hands on my balls, I can't help the inevitable.

The explosion, when it comes, is so fucking good as I let go with a powerful release down her throat. Reagan takes it all, swallowing all my cum, milking me dry as she sucks and licks and then runs her teeth lightly along my shaft. I'm in orgasm heaven as it rolls through my whole body.

SHE'S HALF-LYING, half-sitting, while sprawled on top of me, skin on skin. I stroke over her hair, her shoulders, and her back. "I need a minute, or ten," I say with a laugh.

"That was..." she starts, "phewwww."

"I assume that means it was okay?"

She giggles. "Um, yeah."

We're quiet for a long time, her head on my chest.

"You know, this can just be a safe space for you," I say after a while. "It doesn't have to—we don't have to—"

"Get out of your own head, please."

"I just don't want to be one more negative thing in your life," I admit.

"Negative things don't make you see stars when you come. Negative things don't make you feel wanted and beautiful."

"You *are* beautiful, but I made you see stars?"

"Yes, but don't get cocky about it," she teases with a little flex of her hips against mine.

I snicker at this. "I think I already did."

She smacks my arm playfully. "You know what I mean."

"I'll always try to protect you, though. No matter what happens between us."

She's quiet for a long time. Long enough that I wonder if she's fallen asleep. But then she says, "You're like my own, personal superhero. I need to give you a name."

Nothing gets a superhero nerd amped up more than being called a superhero. It makes me hard, not gonna lie. And when Reagan reaches out to stroke my cock, her words repeat again and again until I can't take it any longer.

"I need to see you," I growl like an animal.

She's so light I'm able to stand with one quick movement while taking her with me. I carry her to my room, to my bed, and lay her out.

She's open for me, arms over her head, her legs splayed apart. A feast for my eyes as I take in every inch of her. Perfectly round full breasts with their dusky tipped nipples budded up and waiting for more from my mouth. Her slim waist and hips and the long, toned legs I want wrapped around my neck. Down to her pretty feet with toes painted dark red peeking through the front of the heels she's still wearing. Then back to her wet pussy, bare but for the smallest little strip—just all of her is fucking sexy and beautiful.

To her face, with her wide, dark eyes and creamy skin, cheeks flushed as she looks up at me, waiting patiently. Her lips match her toes, dark red like a poisoned apple. Her hair looks almost black against the white comforter. I'm struck with the thought I know I'll never forget.

Reagan Marlowe looks like a sexy as fuck, Snow White.

She lets me take my fill of looking. "Are you liking what you see?" She asks this while looking like a naughty princess lying in my bed, waiting patiently to be fucked. *By me.*

I scoff in response to the question, as if it doesn't deserve an answer. My cock going hard tells her everything she needs to know. Even more so when she dips a finger down to stroke her slippery clit, her hips raising in response to the attention. I groan and nod at her, stroking my cock as we engage in this eye-fucking session of wonderfulness. I want to be the one stroking her clit. I'm gonna make her come. *Again.*

Still, I want to take my time with her beautiful body, to savor her slowly for the special feast she is. So, I kiss her first. Deeply and thoroughly. With my tongue thrusting slowly in her mouth, I add one of my fingers to join with hers, pressing down on her clit as she moans in my mouth.

Devouring her mouth, makes me want to do the same thing to her pussy. *Also, again.*

So, I move down between her legs and take up my position to start fucking her with my tongue as she writhes and moans, her lovely cunt against my face, crying out for more. *Fuck, fuck, fuck yes.* If more is what she wants, then I need to be the one giving it to her.

I push two fingers inside of her as I continue to lick and suck. I bite her inner thigh and she comes instantly, her hips pushing up off the bed, her body going rigid as I feel her pussy tighten around my fingers.

"Your cock," she breathes, nearly delirious. "I want your cock."

"Are you sure?"

"Please. God, yes...*please.*"

After grabbing a condom from the drawer, I roll it down my length. My cock is so hard I don't know how I'll last with how much I want inside her. I hover above her, my fingers slipping inside her for another touch. She begs me again, her hands pulling my ass to bring me closer. "Please, Mikhail. Please!"

I position the tip of my cock at her entrance, checking one more time to make sure this is what she wants, that it's okay, that she knows this isn't a condition of my caring about her well-being. "Reagan? This okay?"

"Shut up." She pulls me forward, her hands still on my ass, her hips lifting as I push my cock deep inside her.

Fuck me, it's good.

Reagan cries out, stopping me for a moment, so I put my lips to her forehead, giving her time to adjust.

When she starts to move again, I move. Slowly, at first, but then with more momentum. She feels so fucking good. A thought I hear myself saying out loud, over and over and over, between deep kisses.

It's too soon when I feel close to coming again, so I slip out of her and roll to my back, pulling her on top of me. Straddling me, she takes me in deep, her eyes rolling back in her head as she starts to move. I sit up to give myself access to her gorgeous tits, sucking them into my mouth, rolling her nipples with my tongue. My hands cup her ass cheeks as she rides me hard, her breath literally stopping as she orgasms, her pussy contracting around my cock in little clenches that wind me up further.

It feels like it lasts forever, her release. I'm mesmerized by the way she seems to disappear from the world, her eyes going to some other place. When she blinks back to consciousness, she grins at me with a satisfied glaze to her smile. "*That* was amazing."

I flip her over again, this time to her hands and knees, her ass bared as I take her from behind. This is the deepest yet and she groans as I take her roughly, picking up the pace, fucking her hard until she cries out, another orgasm from her pumping my own release free. We ride each other's waves until I'm spent. Sweating and breathing heavily, we fall into the soft bed, my arms around her, her back to my chest, my cock still twitching against her as she reaches down and deals with removing her shoes. Which looked so fuckin' sexy on her pretty feet while I was fucking her.

God.

There are no words for this, for the way I feel right now. I'd kill anyone who tried to hurt this woman.

It's not love—no, definitely not that.

It's just a connection I feel. A sense of responsibility, a need to keep her safe, a desire to be near her. I'm attracted to her, yes, for sure. But it's a confusing set of feelings for me to process because I really don't know her that well. I still don't know her whole story, or how far I should run if she's not who she says she is.

As Reagan's breathing evens out, I realize she's fallen fast asleep.

My naughty Snow White looks gorgeous asleep in my bed after mutually fucking our brains out in only the best way possible. Sex with her is intense and amazing, and I have big plans to do *all of this* all over again tomorrow morning.

I deal with the condom and then settle back against her, put one of my arms into a comfortable position over her, easily following her to dreamland while breathing in the flowery scent of her hair.

15
who's the guy?

Reagan

I blink awake, confused about waking up in an unfamiliar room. It's dark and hard to see, but there's definitely a warm, solid body draped over mine while other parts of me feel chilled.

I'm in a strange bed. Also, very naked.

And without even a sheet covering my very naked body, the early morning chill I'm feeling makes more sense.

I wriggle loose and turn to my other side to find Mikhail in the bed with me. But he's still asleep. Also, incredibly beautiful and kissable.

Ohhh.

Yeah, that really happened. The realization warms my body instantly. Yep, last night was mind-blowing.

And not just the sex was mind-blowing.

Mikhail Zelenka blew my mind off the planet.

He was protective of me. Careful. He was powerful and commanding, but he asked and made sure I really wanted to go down this road with him. And I did. I very much wanted to be with him.

I am in no way disappointed.

He really is a specimen, totally fit—every muscle toned, not an ounce of body fat on his frame, combined with the good looks, he's off-the-chain hot.

I'm still processing that he wanted *me*. Mikhail would probably have no problem getting any woman he wanted. Somehow, though, I sense he doesn't engage in random hookups. He doesn't strike me as the kind of man who takes sex for granted or uses women that way. Even though he was a beast in bed, he always remained a gentleman. Which was a whole turn-on, all on its own.

I'm kind of embarrassed I fell asleep like that, right after having the best sex I've had in my life (not that I've had a ton to compare it to). I guess if he was bothered by my sleeping over, he wouldn't have been cuddled up to me fast asleep and looking so peaceful.

I slip out of the bed and tiptoe into the bathroom, taking a human moment and cleaning myself up before doing a tour of the apartment to find my clothing—what little there was of it. I slip my dress over my head, not worrying about anything else since I'll just be going up two floors to my own apartment. I throw my shoes, bra, and underwear in my bag, and see my phone is lit up with text message notifications.

I sit on Mikhail's couch, pulling a throw blanket over my shoulders while I check to make sure the messages aren't important.

Only one is from my mother. The other three?

They're from *him*.

Cold dread mixes with a stomach-flip of anxiety. It stops my breath for a moment, seeing "Peter Pellton" on my phone. *Why? Why is he contacting me again?*

I blow out a loud, long breath and walk back into Mikhail's bedroom. Still sleeping deeply, he's now moved onto his back, his long, naked form sprawled out for my viewing enjoyment. His body is truly a work of art, especially with the inked sleeves covering his arms and shoulders, there's still real estate lower on his chest for future tats I'm guessing. Ripped abs clearly visible even while at rest. His chest is smooth, but he does have a little happy trail that starts below his belly button. Leading the way down to his magnificent cock. Speaking of which, it's long and thick while perched on those ripped abs of his as he sleeps. Just the thought of what he did with it last night makes a deep ache zing between my legs.

I want him—badly.

I want to ignore the texts on my phone, crawl on top of him, and ride him until I come again. And I almost do, to be honest. But when it comes right down to it, I also need to be honest with myself about the situation with this beautiful man I admire so much.

I like him. He's gorgeous and very generous in bed. Kind of serious, kind of moody. But I like him. And because I like him, I need to stay far away from him. I need to go away and leave him to his professional hockey player life because he sure as hell does not need the mess that is my life mixed up into his.

So, I grab my things and slip out, leaving my hockey god superhero to his much-needed sleep as if I were never even here.

IT'S six in the morning, but Peter's text just came through an hour ago, so I'd bet he's awake now. Calling him is something I've been avoiding like the plague for a while, but I know I can't keep ignoring him. So, I hit the green button and hold my breath.

"Reggy," he says, using the pet name I hate so much. "You're up early."

"So are you."

"Oh, just the same-old insomnia as usual. What's your excuse?"

"What do you want? You sent me three texts."

He sighs. "Did you do what Sodorov suspects you of? Did you find a way to pull money from his house account, you naughty girl?"

"No." I wish I could slap him across the face through the phone. "*Absolutely* not." *How the hell does he even know about this?*

"Seems hard to believe this is all just a coincidence," he says threateningly. "And hey, more power to you if you figured out how to pull it and squirrel it away. I didn't think you were that smart, to be honest."

"Wow. How nice of you, Peter." I feel both sick to my stomach and the surge of rage boiling.

"I'm just saying. You owe them money, so it makes total sense that you'd try to get out from that debt faster than planned. But to attempt to do that *with their own money*? Kinda genius, also crazy risky." He chuckles into the phone and the sound resonates like a rattlesnake at my ear.

I grit my teeth so hard I feel like I might crack one. "I did not do it. I'm making my payments. If I were some crime genius, I'd be long gone, not still here working at my crappy job—*in the same building where this crime took place*—getting roughed up every few days while still making my payments each and every month. Think about it, Pete."

He makes a noise that tells me he is not convinced of my innocence. Then he asks, "Who's the guy, Reggy? Is that where you were all night?"

The hairs on my arms stand on end. How does he know I wasn't home all night?

"I don't know what you're talking about, Peter."

"Don't lie." He exhales from his cigarette. "Tall, tatted up, and handsome? Good head of hair? Who is he?"

"None of your business."

"Aww, come on now, Reggy. Guy comes out of nowhere and beats the living shit out of one of Sodorov's best guys? And now he's hanging around, getting in the way of his business? Maybe they need to have a conversation with him? Maybe I'll suggest it to them as a way to get you to come clean."

"Fuck you, Peter." I hate this. I hate him. *How does he know what Mikhail did? How?*

I know his reaction before it even happens. The stupid, grating laugh. I can imagine the smirk on his face. And the words. "Well, we did plenty of that, now, didn't we? Wasn't anything to write home about, from my perspective. Maybe things are better with this new guy. Who is he, Reagan?"

"None. Of. Your. Fucking. Business."

Peter sighs dramatically. "Well, it probably doesn't matter anyway. You're a slut. I'm sure he'll be replaced soon enough since you have a whole revolving door of men stupid enough to crawl into your bed."

"I don't sleep around. Since you seem to be stalking me, you must know that."

"Come on," he says, his tone getting nastier, more aggressive. "You whored your sweet, little body around and crawled for every dollar. This one will figure you out in no time and he'll be gone. And you'll be begging for my help. Again."

"Your help?" I ask, half laughing, half crying. *He's a bastard. Such a bastard.* I hate my history. Hate it. But I hate this excuse for a human more. "You think you helped me? Maybe you're just jealous that I left you. That I realized what a loser you were, and I just walked away."

"Careful what you say to me, Reggy."

"Why? Are they listening, Peter? Did they make you call and check in on me? See if I'd tell you something different than what I've told them a thousand times? I did not take their money. I wouldn't."

"Ding, ding, ding, ding," he singsongs. "Just give it all back, little one. Give it back, and all will be forgiven."

I hang up on him.

A shiver rocks its way through my body as I sit on my couch and stare at the wall. The minutes tick by, but I can't move from my spot. I just keep staring at the wall where a photo hangs of me and my mom together in happier times.

I curse the day I let Peter Pellton into my life.

The anxiety is so overwhelming that I end up in a ball on the couch. My ears ringing, my stomach hurting, my heart pounding. I'm going to die. These guys are going to kill me.

It's all I can imagine happening.

The tragic ending to the story of the sad, short life of Reagan Marlowe.

Two hours later.

I COME AWAKE IN A RUSH, realizing I've moved from the couch to the floor at some point in my misery. A truly miserable wretch of a human, with my arms locked around my knees, my head buried between them, doing nothing more than simply existing.

I try to focus on my breathing. Just breathing in and out, deeply and slowly. In and out. In and out. My head is a roar, my heart is a caged animal, and my stomach is a volcano ready to erupt. At moments like these, I question every life decision I've ever made. I question life in general.

And then, there's a knock at my door.

Oh fuck.

16
number nineteen

Mikhail

Reagan opens the door slowly after, I'm sure, checking the peephole first. *As she definitely fucking should.* But she looks so different from the woman I was with last night.

Her eyes are swollen, dark circles blooming beneath, a strong contrast against her pale skin. Her hair is a mess, and she's still in her dress from the night before.

Without saying a word, she leaves the door wide open as she heads to her couch, flops down, and buries her head under a throw pillow. I take this as an invitation to come in, shutting the door quietly and finding a spot to sit at the end of the couch, pulling her feet into my lap.

For the longest time, I don't know what to say. There's so much to this story of Reagan that I don't know. And I want to ask why she left. Why does she keep leaving? What else is going on? Did she do something for real? Do those guys have a reason to be after her?

So many questions, but not a one of them comes out of my mouth.

"I've always lived in my father's shadow," I say, surprising myself at where my brain is taking me. "He was a god of a hockey player. You don't get to live among the Greats unless you're really something special, you know? And I was the only son. I have two sisters—I think I already told you that?—and hockey was a boy's sport as I was growing up. Not many girls played, you know? So, I was it. I was the only one who could hold up the legacy my father had built."

I fiddle with a loose string on the Crush hoodie I hastily pulled on when I woke up and found Reagan had disappeared. *Again.*

"I've played hockey since I was old enough to get into skates. I was, like, three maybe? I don't remember those early days much, so it often feels like I've been on skates my entire life, you know? My dad just expected me to play and nothing much else really mattered. And I just pushed myself. I kept pushing myself, but nothing I did was ever really good enough for him. I'd make one milestone and he'd set another. He never praised me or even said, 'good job, son.' He just kept telling me how inadequate I was, how much work I needed to do to be good enough."

Reagan extricates herself from underneath her pillow, turning to her back, her eyes tired as she watches me with interest.

"I was kind of a loner in school. I played hockey all year long, and we were always traveling for games and tournaments plus stuff my dad was doing, so I couldn't have friends over or anything. Because of that, I started reading comic books. Got really into superheroes." I let out a light laugh, feeling like the dork I totally am. "When I graduated high school, I went straight to the pros. I was just three months shy of twenty when I took the ice for the first time as a starter with the Crush. And I was a grade A asshole. I used to pretend I didn't speak English and spoke Czech instead, just to have an excuse not to have to talk very much. I did it every time a new teammate joined the Crush just to make it harder for them to get to know me. Such a dick move on my part, I am aware. I never tried to make friends on the team because, you know, why bother?"

"You probably didn't know how," she says, letting out a big yawn.

I nod. "Yeah, deep friendships weren't a part of my life equation. I just focused on the game, got the starting position, and left it all out on the ice. Nineteen-year-old starter on a top NHL team. When they asked me what number I'd like to wear, I didn't hesitate to pick number nineteen out of what was available even though my father's number eight was available as well. You'd think my dad would've been gushing with pride, right? Nope. Still not impressed."

"Why are you telling me all of this?" Reagan asks softly, her pretty brown eyes glittering with what could be leftover tears from before I got here and began this epic crygasm of a tale.

"Good question," I say with a chuckle. "I don't talk about this stuff with many people. My teammate

Aiden knows there's some tension between my dad and me, but he doesn't know half of what I just told you. But I don't know. I guess it seems like maybe you've got some stuff going on in your life—a lot more than you've shared—and I want you to know I'm here. You can talk to me about any of it because I'm a good listener. I thought it might help if you heard about my baggage first, I guess."

Reagan is quiet for a long time before she says, "Everyone has parent issues. I have them, too, among the many other ways my life is in chaos."

"Do you want to talk about it?"

She laughs and shakes her head. "We'd be here all day. I doubt you've got that kind of time."

I check the calendar app on my phone, and I really do need to get to a morning training session at the practice arena.

"I do have to go to training, but I'll be back this afternoon. Do you have to work tonight?"

"No, actually. I'm off tonight."

"Good. Look, Reagan, I'd like to give you someone to talk to. A friend to talk to. Someone you can trust."

"I'll admit I don't have many of those."

"Do you want to grab dinner? I could take you out somewhere fun? We could eat a ridiculously expensive meal and talk about our issues? It'll be like a caloric counseling session."

This makes her smile. "That sounds perfect."

"Awesome." I pat her ankles as I stand up. "I'll figure out the details and come grab you around six?"

She nods and I debate bending down to give her a kiss. She bites her inner lip, looking tentative, so I bail on the idea. Maybe I should just take a step back from the physical and be a good friend to her. *Fuck if I want to do that though.* I've enjoyed good sex in the past. Last night was a step above anything else I've ever done. But the woman in front of me seems so... heartbroken, and I want to be the man she can at least lean on. Maybe even heal some of the hurt.

I run my hand through my hair and stand there awkwardly, not sure what to do or say next.

"Mikhail, I'll be fine," she says, bringing her hand up to cup my cheek. "Thanks for checking on me. And for telling me some of your story."

I turn my lips into the palm of her hand and give it a kiss. "Okay, I'll see you tonight."

17
my friend. with benefits.

Reagan

Somehow, Mikhail's appearance really did make me feel better. Not totally better, but somewhat better. It was sweet that he tried to calm me by telling me about his relationship with his dad. Mikhail is a quiet guy, so I'm guessing he isn't chatty with others about his feelings. For him to admit he feels like he can't live up to his dad's expectations is probably significant. I hate that for him.

I'll admit, I don't know if I'm worthy of his trust or his friendship. Sex I can handle. It's basic and instinctual, and it doesn't have to mean anything apart from mutual pleasure. Sex is the easy part. And the sex with him was spectacularly easy *and* outstanding.

But I left for a reason. Mikhail doesn't need Sodorov in his business. He's a good man with a good heart, and he has nothing to do with the mess I'm in. Somehow, though, I don't think Mikhail will be all that easy to shake. I think he's developed some sense of responsibility for me, and while I'm thrilled to know someone cares enough to look out for me, I also don't want him getting hurt because of me.

Still, the fact that he showed up, that he didn't just let me disappear, energizes me enough that I push myself up and into the kitchen to make some coffee. Caffeine in hand, I survey my apartment, which I still haven't really re-organized after the break-in, and I decide it's time to focus on my living space. I have to start somewhere, and this will take my mind away from the litany of fears plaguing me for a little while.

I spend the day organizing papers, cleaning cabinets, and dusting floorboards. I organize my closet and panic a bit—I have no idea what to wear to dinner tonight. Like, are we going somewhere fancy? Do I need a dress? Am I paying for my own meal, and if so, how do I afford it? I mean, this isn't a date, right? He said he just wanted to be a friend to me.

Ugh. Anxiety sucks.

Adding to the despair, my phone rings, and it's my mom. She's already texted once, and since I didn't respond, here is the resulting call. I almost don't answer. It's likely to be some new crisis or drama with her, and I simply can't take any more right now.

I love my mom. I'd do anything for her, but sometimes she can be a lot. I weigh the risk versus the reward and decide that, in my current state, I would like to hear my mom's voice.

"Hey, Mamma." I try to sound as light and unbothered as possible.

"Hey, Bug." She sounds good. I breathe a small sigh of relief. "Just checking in. I haven't heard from you in a few weeks."

"Oh, yeah, sorry, Mamma, I've been working a lot lately."

"Well, I miss you when you don't call," she says in a mild scolding. "Any luck on the job hunt?"

"No, not yet." I sigh. "It's been pretty frustrating, actually. I could get a job in event planning, but those entry-level jobs pay less than my job running casino games. I can't see taking a pay cut right now, so I feel kinda stuck."

"Those are hard decisions to make, I agree. On some levels, it might be worth it to start fresh in the area you want to be in. Take the step back just so you can get your foot in the door."

She doesn't understand my debt load—she doesn't understand a lot of things—so I just grunt an agreement in order to get off the subject. "How are you?"

"I'm doing fine. I've been working part time at a used bookshop," she says cheerfully. "It's been fun. I'm learning how to repair old books. Something different. I sure wish you'd come home for a visit. Or...more? Maybe you could find an event planning job here in Columbus?"

There are a thousand reasons I don't want to go back to Columbus, and the first is that I cannot live with my mother again. I just can't. I love her so much, but we cannot be roommates. It just won't work.

"Maybe someday," is all I say. "I'm not ready to move yet."

I can't move yet. Not with this Sodorov stuff hanging over my head. If I left, it would be like an admission of guilt. And since I'm not guilty, I can't leave. An unending circle of hell.

"Is there a reason you're not ready to move? Maybe you're seeing someone new these days?"

I can't help grinning at her tone. It's so mom-like, nosy, interested in my love life. Or whatever she's feeling about me. "I actually do have a friend-date tonight. With a hockey player. He plays here in Vegas for the Crush."

"Oooh," she says. "Tell me about him. What's his name?"

"Mikhail."

"What position does he play?"

"Uh, I don't know the title of his position; I'd have to look it up. I know next to nothing about hockey, but I know he wears number nineteen."

She tsks at me. "Reagan. Seriously?"

"I don't know, I'm just not that into sports stuff. He's a big deal, though, and I'm taking an interest now. I'm trying to watch his games and learning about the rules. He said he went pro right out of high school, and that he's been starting on the Crush for five seasons. He's a few years older than me. Women always want to take their picture with him, and men, too. They'll talk to him about his play in the most recent game and such, so he's recognizable."

My mom laughs. "Well, I'd say you better do some homework, then. Up your game, so to speak. He must be really handsome, then?"

"Yeah," I say, a breathless laugh escaping. "Very. He is a certifiable hottie."

"Well, that's exciting. I hope it all works out."

I get a little teary, my throat constricting as I try to shove back the waterworks. This is such a normal conversation, more normal than I usually get with my mom. Discussing my future. Asking about my love life. She seems so happy for me. She misses me.

So normal.

But it's not…not really.

AT TEN MINUTES TO SIX, I finally decide on a pair of skinny jeans and a flowy blouse in a bright floral print paired with some nude peep-toe heels I bought for job interviews. It seems casual and chic, and since I've never seen Mikhail in anything other than sports gear or jeans, I feel safe in assuming he won't be too dressed up tonight.

He's knocking on my door at six on the dot. I open the door, ready to make a joke about being stupidly punctual, but he looks so good that my mouth goes dry, and I think I forget how to make words for a few seconds. He just looks ultra-sexy, in a turquoise plaid flannel, dark jeans, and unlaced combat boots. He wears a leather bracelet on one wrist and his hair is *on point*, all coiffed into a messy pompadour.

Lord, help me.

I've seen this man really, really naked and that is a sight to behold, but he looks just as mouthwatering with his clothes on.

"You look really beautiful tonight," he says, his eyes roaming from head to toe in a way that makes wetness pool between my legs. Which are about to fail me. I feel like I need to sit. Mikhail Zelenka is going to be my undoing; I can feel it down to the tips of my red-painted toes.

I fan myself with my hand. "You probably make all kinds of panties drop with that look, sir."

He chuckles, a dimple appearing in one cheek. "It isn't like that, but I'm glad I'm making you feel some kind of way."

"Oh, I'm feeling some kind of way, all right," I say lightly. "I might need to sit down to recover."

"Well, if you sit, then I'll be on my knees, and we'll never get out of here," he half-growls. It turns my insides gooey. Holy hell, I guess he's feeling some kind of way, too.

"We should go," I say quickly.

"Agreed." But he's still smirking.

We head out into the early evening, Mikhail holding my hand as we walk. It feels so natural I almost forget that we're not together. We're not a couple. He is my friend. With benefits.

Truly.

And that will have to be enough because I am not good for a man like this. Not for any reason related to vanity. I think I'm pretty enough, and I have a brain in my head—but I'm *not good for him*. I have too much baggage. There's too much drama, too much noise. He doesn't need that in his life, nor should he entangle himself out of some misplaced feelings he's having "to save me."

I'll just enjoy whatever this is while it lasts. I'll cut him loose before things go too far, and I'll make sure he knows it's only because I want to protect him from the shitshow that is my life. He'll understand. I know he will.

He takes me into a little hole-in-the-wall, Amadio's Italiano Eatery, I've never been to before. It's only got maybe ten tables, all placed far enough away from one another to feel private. There are lit candles dancing on each table.

"This place is so cute," I comment as we're led to our table.

"I asked the guys for recommendations," he says, blushing a little in the dim light.

We order some wine and an appetizer, focusing on the menu. Once he closes his and sets it aside, I say, "Thanks a lot for this morning. It's been a while since I've really had someone to talk to."

"Well, you didn't do much of the talking," he says, busying himself with rolling and unrolling the straw wrapper that came with the glass of water.

"True," I admit. "But I appreciated that you talked to *me*. It really helped. When you came over, I...well, I wasn't in the best mental space."

"Do you want to talk now?"

The waitress comes to take our order just as I'm about to tell my story. The way she looks at Mikhail makes me want to jump across the table and throttle her, but he doesn't seem to notice.

After she leaves, I venture to ask, "Does that happen everywhere you go?"

"Does what happen?" he asks, eyebrows furrowed.

"Women ogling you, looking at you like you're the meal?"

He rolls his eyes. "I don't know. I don't think so? And I didn't notice her doing any of that."

"Humpf."

He grins. "Come on. Have I given any indication that I'm the type of guy who goes around looking for that kind of attention?"

"No," I say begrudgingly.

"So, back to your story. You came to UNLV for school from Columbus, Ohio. I know that much. What's next?"

"Well, I think I've told you I meant to be a wedding and event planner, right?"

"Right. What made you interested in that?"

I take a big inhale. "Well, I used to plan events for my dolls all the time. They got married, and I planned out the whole venue and decorating scheme and I made all their clothes for them—it was a whole industry in my bedroom."

Mikhail chuckles at this, twisting his wineglass by the stem.

"I was always the kid in class who wanted to help the teacher get the room ready for class parties, too. I ended up getting an internship in high school with a local wedding planner. She paid me a few dollars an hour under the table, but I loved it. And I love weddings, frankly. I love the aesthetic of them, the flowers and the dresses. They make me so happy."

Mikhail looks up and meets my gaze, his face frozen and looking kind of horrified.

"Relax," I tease, "I'm not looking to get married myself or anything."

He laughs. "The only marriage I have for a frame

of reference is my parents'. They're still together, but my dad's such a disagreeable asshole all the time, I can't imagine my mom would describe it as marital bliss. Frankly, I don't know what she sees in him, and the dysfunction of it sure as hell doesn't make me want to race to the altar."

"Yeah, I get it." I take a sip of my wine. "My dad left when I was young, and I haven't had contact with him in nearly a decade. He's not even in the states anymore. Costa Rica was the last place I knew of. My mom pretty much raised me alone and always told me I didn't need a man to be whole. Which was good advice, you know? It made me independent. But at heart—not gonna lie—I've always been a bit of a romantic. Sorry." I shrug a shoulder and give him a rueful look.

He lifts a shoulder in response. "Nothing wrong with hoping we can do better with our own choices."

I lift my wineglass. "I'll toast to that."

He tips his glass to mine. "To making better romantic decisions than our parents did."

"Here, here."

"So you lived with your mom?"

I nod. "I lived with my mom, who has...bipolar disorder. She's been dealing with some serious mental health challenges throughout my whole life. Persistent and pervasive, her doctor always says. There can be calm times when she's fairly normal"—I make finger quotes—"but there can also be times where she's... fairly difficult." *Difficult. That word is an understatement.* When was the last time I told *anyone* about my mom? I feel both ashamed and sad.

Mikhail reaches over and takes my hand when he see me blinking back the fucking annoying tears starting to pool in my eyes. "You love your mom."

"I do." I nod emphatically. "She's caring and loving and creative. But she has struggled for most of her adult life. She can't really hold down a job. It's just—it's been...so difficult for a really long time. And it always felt like a dirty little secret. It wasn't something I wanted to talk to friends about, and I couldn't have friends over for fear something crazy would happen. So, I just, you know, stuck to myself."

And I think he does know, based on what he told me this morning about his own childhood.

Loners.

Both of us.

18
lasagna confessions

Mikhail

"You know,"—I reach for a piece of warm bread in the basket—"mental health issues aren't so stigmatizing now. Things are different around those conversations. Athletes come out every day and talk about their struggles with anxiety, depression, and whatnot."

"I'm sure that's true," Reagan answers carefully, "but those athletes have teams of doctors and counselors and trainers who can help them. And they're not, like, wreaking havoc all over the place."

I can't help chuckling. When Reagan's mouth turns down in a subtle frown, I squeeze her hand. "Hey, I'm only laughing at the phrase *wreaking havoc*, like she's a comic book baddie or something. Also, that's the name of my first professional team, Henderson Havoc."

"Well, she's certainly not that, but her mental health struggles have caused a ton of upheaval over the years. For instance, one of her signature moves during a manic episode is to go out and spend a bunch of money. She racks up enormous credit card debt and doesn't have the income to pay it back. It's a whole thing she does. When I was in, like, middle school, she took a whole bottle of sleeping pills because she got sued for like eighteen thousand dollars that she'd put on a credit card and couldn't pay back. A credit counseling program helped her reorganize the debt, and she got a bunch of it written off because of the suicide attempt."

She sighs and pulls her hand from mine, grabbing her wineglass, and taking a sip. I get the sense that she's not done talking, so I just sit back and give her the space to get her thoughts together.

"Toward the end of high school," she says after a long, brooding pause, "she seemed relatively stable. She'd landed a good job as an executive secretary. They paid her well, treated her well, and she got in a good place with her regular bills. I'd planned to stay close to home for school, but I'd also applied at UNLV thinking it wouldn't be likely I could go so far away, but she seemed genuinely good, so I decided to go for it when they accepted me. One thing I can say for my dad, he set up a fund for my college when I was a baby, so I had that at least by the time I was ready to go."

"But she wasn't good?" I ask, interested in hearing everything she will tell me. I feel like I'm on borrowed time here. Like at any moment Reagan will shut down and stop talking. And I don't want that.

She shakes her head sadly. "No. She was not good. At the beginning of my junior year here, she called me crying. Said her car had gotten repossessed and the house was about to go into foreclosure. She'd lost her job. And I was like, *Mom, what the hell did you do?* Apparently, she felt she was in a good enough space to go off her meds."

"Oh, shit." I can't help cringing, but I catch it quickly.

"Yeah. That about sums it up. So, I came home over a long weekend and tried to sort it all out, called all her creditors, talked to a bankruptcy attorney, got an emergency psychiatric evaluation, and got her back on her meds."

Our food arrives but it feels weird to dig into my meal while she's telling such a serious story. Still, she waves a hand and says, "Let's eat. I'm starving. I think I forgot to eat today." She takes her first bite of Amadio's signature lasagna and closes her eyes, letting out a moan of approval.

"Good?" I ask, my cock reacting to the sound of her enjoyment. *I want her underneath me again making that sound at me while we're fucking.*

She blushes prettily. "Best meal I've had in a long time. This place is top shelf." She kisses two fingers and her thumb together, smacking her lips and fanning out her hand. "Sorry, I got a little dramatic there."

"Not dramatic. I'd call it sexy from where I'm sitting."

She bites her bottom lip and looks up at me from beneath her long lashes. "Well, that's good, then."

I clear my throat and shift in my seat. "You were, uh, talking about your mom. Junior year, got her figured out…"

She holds out her hand and does the "so-so" gesture. "Kind of. There was just so much debt and no income because no job, and there were things we needed cash for right then. I just wasn't sure where it was going to come from, you know?"

"I don't know," I admit. "I grew up in a high-income household. My father was a millionaire before I was born. I'm embarrassed, I guess, that I don't have any of that perspective."

Her lips flatten. "Well, it's not a fun place to be so good for you."

I can tell that this bothers her. The haves and the have-nots thing. We come from different backgrounds and very different life experiences. "But that doesn't mean I don't understand struggle at all."

"Sure. I guess." She has a distant look in her eye that I don't like to see. "The one-percenters have struggles, too. Mental health and abuse and addiction and illness and whatever. Those are human things, and they have nothing to do with your socioeconomic strata, but surely you can see that the approach to dealing with those issues is drastically different depending on how much money you have. If you have money, or power, or access, then the path to recovery is much more easily managed."

"Yeah, I can see that. So, what did you do? You said there were some serious issues that weren't easily fixed financially. What happened after that?"

She stares at me for a moment before taking a bite of her meal. Following her lead, I focus on my food. Am I supposed to apologize for being born into a household with money?

When she speaks again, she says, "I'm sorry. None of this has anything to do with you, and I'm projecting my frustrations. It's not right."

"There's no need to apologize. You have a lot going on. And, frankly, you're right. I come from a different place, and I don't have the frame of reference to truly understand what you went through."

"It's also..." She takes a big breath in and then lets it out in a long sigh. "People who were in a position to help found ways to exploit the situation. It's like, no one does something just out of the goodness of their heart, or because it's the right or kind thing to do, you know? They find a way to gain something from it. You scratch my back and I'll scratch yours."

"That's why I turned you away that first night." I wait until she looks up at me. "Reagan, I never want you to feel that way with me. Like you have to give me something to have my friendship or help or whatever."

"I don't feel that way with you, Mikhail. I know you're the exception, but here's my frame of reference. When I got back from that weekend with my mom, I was freaking out, right? I needed to make some quick cash to help her out. I mentioned it to one of my roommates and she suggested I go work at one of the strip clubs. She thought I could maybe make some good tips serving drinks or whatever. So, I went." She gets that distant tone in her voice again as she plays with the stem of her wineglass. "They asked me to dance after a week of working there, which was mortifying at first, but when they told me what I could make in a night, I decided to go for it. The place seemed clean and safe, and I figured it was far enough from campus that no one from school would see me there."

"So, you were a stripper?" All kinds of images start forming in my head of Reagan stripping up on a stage that are impossible to suppress. Biology and all that.

"I was. And it's not a proud moment for me." She's looking ashamed now, and it kind of breaks my heart.

"Well, I'm not judging," I tell her honestly. "It's a way to make a living."

"Yeah, and it helped somewhat. I made some immediate cash each night and used most of it to pay some of my mom's bills. I also met this guy. He was a regular, a little older, but he seemed really nice. His name is Peter. We flirted a little at the club and eventually he asked me out. He was...a distraction. An ego boost. But eventually, I grew to trust him, and I opened up to him about my situation. I told him I was hardly making a dent in my mom's debt. She wasn't working, still, and had even gone off her meds again. It felt like I'd never get free. And he offered to help. Asked how much I needed, said he could front me the whole amount, no questions asked. I could pay it back monthly."

"Seems too good to be true," I say, frowning.

She tips her forefinger to her nose. "Bingo. You know, I thought it was a personal loan from someone I cared about. Who cared about me."

"But it wasn't."

"It was not. It was Sodorov money."

My jaw nearly hits the table. "What?" I have to take a drink to give myself a moment to process. "So, you do owe money to the guys who've been roughing you up." It's not a question.

"Yes, but I had no idea. I just thought Peter was trying to help me out. I hated the stripping, and it'd be so much better for me to just pay him back than to keep doing something I hated so much. So, I took the money and was able to help my mom keep the house and get her financials sorted." She twirls her glass back and forth on the tablecloth. "I went out and got my job at Tangiers so I could slowly pay Peter back. I have never missed a payment since, and I increased the amount I pay him once I graduated and got more hours. There is no reason for them to think I stole from them. None."

I sit back in my chair, letting out a low whistle. "Whoa. That is...crazy. And stressful."

"Uh, yeah."

"And does your mom know about all this? Is she better now?"

"She doesn't know. I just told her I was working extra hours to help her out. She has no concept of money. It's like, sometimes I feel like I'm the parent and she's the child." Reagan's eyes fill with tears, which she dabs away with her napkin. "And I don't want to tell her, you know? Because I'm worried it will set her off. She's been stable lately, but honestly, it can all change from one call to another. So, every time the phone rings, I worry some new crisis is about to unfold. I get anxious talking to her. She can be good and med-compliant for a year and then, *boom*, she's off her meds and everything is spiraling out of control."

"I'm so sorry." It's all I can think to say to her after hearing her story. I knew there was more than she was letting on, but now all the pieces fit together. Now, I understand. All this trouble she's in—it's all for her mom.

"It's not your problem to worry about," she says sadly.

"I know, but I just...well, that's a lot. For anyone. And you still made it through college. You finished and graduated, even while you were doing this thing for your mom. You figured out a way." She's tiny, but Reagan Marlowe is tough as nails.

She smiles, tears still flowing. "It doesn't feel like it sometimes. It feels like I'm in this endless tunnel and I'll never see the sun again."

"But you *will*," I tell her with a firm nod. "You will. I believe it because you're smart and capable and brave."

"And alone," she says. "I lost touch with all my friends here because I was so stressed and busy. I couldn't go out, couldn't spend money. I was always worried. And I couldn't confide in anyone because I was so ashamed of the whole situation. So, I was alone."

Not anymore.

"Well, you don't have to be alone. If you want a friend, I'm here."

aka mr. hockey

Reagan

"Why are you so kind to me?" I ask, still sniffling pathetically. "You could have left me in that alley. You could have told me to go away at any point. You don't need this drama in your life. You're a professional hockey player. You don't need some nobody causing you grief or putting you at risk."

"That's the second time, at least, that you've called yourself a nobody," Mikhail says with a deep frown. "I'm not a fan of it, for the record."

"Well, it's how I feel."

"You shouldn't." Mikhail tilts his head and folds his arms over his chest. "Look, I know what it feels like to do your best, but never feel like you can quite reach the top. And before you tell me you can't even get on the mountain, let alone make it to the top, I think you're wrong. Because you've fought really hard to get to where you are right now. You're fierce. You fought for someone you loved. You sacrificed. You finished school and you're still standing."

"I guess..." I can feel my cheeks burn at his intensity.

"You're *not* nobody, Reagan Marlowe. You're a person who persevered despite some real shitty circumstances. You're a person who gave everything to help another person. And you know what? This doesn't have to be your life forever. You're still so young. You have so much time."

We stare at each other, and I can't decide if I want to burst into a full-on ugly cry or crawl across the table and kiss him. A little of both, I suppose, but it's all rooted in the feeling that, for the first time, I feel like I have someone in my corner.

"Can't you just go? Start over somewhere?" he asks after a minute.

I shake my head. "The debt load is still pretty high, and I can't leave Vegas until it's paid. Once I broke things off with Peter, that's when it got ugly. He fessed up about the money he loaned me—that it wasn't his. He told me it was Sodorov money, and I had to pay it off or work it off."

"Work it off?" Mikhail's voice is flat.

"Yeah, as in on my back." I hang my head and continue, because I need to finish telling this, and I can't bear to see the reaction on his face right now. "Among Henri Sodorov's many organized crime endeavors here in town, running drugs and prostitutes are top of the list. Using trafficked sex workers from Eastern Europe, most likely. So, I chose to pay it off, obviously. But I was told that I shouldn't leave the area, or they'd find me and everyone I care about."

"Fucking assholes."

I laugh. "That's putting it mildly."

"Would you go home if you could? To Columbus?"

"No," I say. It comes out more sharply than I intend. "I love my mom, but being away from her allows me space to breathe, you know? I don't worry constantly about her mental state the way I am when I'm around her in person."

"Makes sense," Mikhail says.

The conversation tapers off from there. I'm not sure what else to say about my shitshow of a life. It means a lot that Mikhail is here to listen, that he's not judging me, but the depressing vibe is still heavy in the air.

So, I change the subject and ask, "How did you like your dinner?"

"The chicken parm was excellent." He's as grateful for the topic change as I am. "Not quite as good as my mom's but close."

"I'll have to try it sometime." I can't think of anything else to say to him because my mind is busy picturing Mikhail's nice and normal mom, who is obviously a great cook, bringing out a big platter of chicken parm to serve to her family at the dinner table. It's a nice vision in my head, at least, something good to remember about him when he's not around anymore. I also feel bad that I was so into my lasagna I never paid attention to what he even ordered tonight.

He insists on paying, which is no surprise, but when I offer to split the check, he shuts that suggestion down immediately—or more like ignores it altogether—while distracting me with something else entirely. "It's a nice night tonight. Want to take a walk with me?"

"Um, yeah, I'd like that."

Outside, it's warm and arid. Mikhail takes his flannel off and wraps it around his waist, leaving his muscular arms with their ribbons of ink mostly exposed in a dark gray, super-soft T-shirt. He might be the sexiest guy I have ever seen, let alone known personally.

We hold hands as we walk, companionable in our silence for a few blocks. I feel lighter for having been able to tell him my story, for having someone to talk to about this stuff. But still, it's all the *unsaid* stuff nagging at me.

"Mikhail, I want you to know I'm in no way expecting you to fix this for me."

He looks at me sideways. "Okay."

"I'm serious. You've been awesome and I'm sorry I dragged you into this, you know?"

"You didn't drag me into it. I saw a person being assaulted, and I stepped in to help. That was my choice."

"But then I came to your apartment that night. I should've left you out of it. Now they know we're...acquainted."

"Reagan, I am *not* worried about it."

"Why? *Why* aren't you worried about it? I'm worried about it, about someone coming after you just to get to me."

He shrugs. "I'm just not. Sodorov didn't get to

where he is by being stupid. He won't risk exposure voluntarily attaching himself to the National Hockey League, even by the loosest association. He's already on the radar of Las Vegas PD, and certainly the FBI, who eagerly await the first opportunity to arrest him. If Sodorov comes after someone like me, all signs point to him. He does not want that."

I slip into my own thoughts again. Must be nice to be strong and famous and rich. It's a position from which a person can face the reality of a crime syndicate and shrug off the risk.

Mikhail seems to recognize where my thoughts have gone. He squeezes my hand to get me out of my own head. "Hey," he says softly, nudging my shoulder, "I'm just saying, I think I've proven I can handle myself. And also, I like knowing I can help to protect you. I *want* to help."

"Well, I'm learning how to box, so maybe I can protect myself."

Mikhail grins. "Yes, I'm sure you're a real madwoman in the ring, all hundred pounds of ya."

I pout, but it doesn't last when I end up breaking into a grin. He stops walking and turns to me. "I love it when you smile. I know life hasn't given you a lot of reasons to do it lately. You're really beautiful, Reagan. You're a strong person, a smart person. And I've got your back, okay?"

All of those words, I can barely keep from throwing myself at him. Kissing him, wrapping my legs around him. I want to attack him right here, right now, on this busy street. But because I'm me, though, I sort of scowl at him and say, "Must be nice to be so perfectly confident in yourself."

He gives me a look that says, *Really?*

We're still holding hands though, but instead of dropping mine, he just turns and pulls me along the sidewalk, walking us toward the ice hockey arena where he plays his games for the Crush. For my part, I'm embarrassed by what a jerk I'm being to him. He's been nothing but kind and supportive. He's a serious guy, so he can handle serious conversations without getting twitchy. He's also a good person and I think he means it when he says he's got my back. I should have said thank you. I should have told him how much his friendship means to—

"Here you go."

Holy hell. I look up and there is a larger-than-life banner sporting Mikhail's image hanging down the side of the arena. It's in full color. He looks like he's mid-game, in helmet and uniform. Fierce is how I would describe it. And hot, let's not forget *hottt.*

"Wow, no wonder the ladies go crazy for you," I say, letting out an awkward-sounding laugh. "I feel really inadequate right now."

Mikhail points at a picture of a long-haired guy and says, "That's Georg Kolochev. He was an alcoholic, playing a moderately okay game on a moderately okay contract. He was a major prick, but he met the love of his life and got sober in the same year, then scored a goal in the championships from a defensive position. Was awarded the Norris Trophy that season—the highest honor in the league for a defenseman. He turned his life around. Now he's got a wife, two kids, and a fat contract. He's only a minor prick these days."

We walk a little farther and he points out a banner featuring a guy with a blond undercut and a tattoo peeking up through the collar of his jersey. "Tyler Lockhardt. This asshole's got the biggest mouth on the team. Dude literally cannot shut up. It drives me crazy, but you know what? He grew up with a drug-addicted mom and nobody knew it. Nobody. We only found out because she showed up at a game in Boston and got herself arrested in front of his two little siblings. He brought the kids back here and got things sorted out for them, gave them a chance at a stable, new, life."

"Why are you telling me about these guys?" My heart is beating like crazy inside my chest.

"I guess because I feel like you have this image of me as this guy who doesn't understand the depths of life's problems. And it's true, I'm from a different background and the stuff that I struggle with is very different from the stuff going on in your life. But it doesn't mean I can't empathize or care or help or whatever." He runs his hands through his hair and looks back up at the giant banners. "These guys look like gods when they're positioned like this. People treat them like gods, but they're just human beings who have problems of their own, you know? Problems they've overcome, for the most part. And you can overcome your problems, too."

"Who knew there was a life coach hiding under that big buff body?"

"You're deflecting, Reagan. Again."

I scan the arena courtyard. There are a bunch of

people milling around, looking at the banners, taking pictures. A sigh involuntarily escapes. "I know." It's all I can think of at first. "I've been alone at this for a long time, with no one to trust, no one to talk to. This whole having someone to talk to is new for me. I'm sorry."

He holds out his hand and I take it as we start the walk back toward the apartment building.

"What would your teammates say about you, Mikhail Zelenka?"

"They'd probably call me an asshole and a prick, too," he says with a chuckle.

"Would you agree?"

"If I'm being honest, yes. I didn't come to the NHL to make friends. I came to play and to be the best."

"How's that working out for you?"

This makes him laugh again, but he doesn't answer. In fact, he doesn't say anything for the last bit of the walk home. Nothing at all.

He hits the button for my floor first, walking me to the door of my apartment. I want him to kiss me, to come inside, to undress me. I want those things so badly because I know how he feels inside of me, and I want to feel it again. Because I like him. And I think I trust him.

He leans in and my belly does a nervous flop as he kisses me lightly on the cheek, then backs away, turning my nervousness to anxiety. I feel my brows knit together, my face obviously twisting into some expression of confusion.

"Did I do something?" I ask.

He puts a hand on my cheek and shakes his head.

"I won't be some asshole trying to get you to fuck me all the time, Reagan."

"But what if I want you to?"

This elicits a chuckle, but he shoves his hands in his pockets. "I want you to feel safe, and I want you to trust me. And I want to be your friend first because I think you need that. And frankly, so do I."

"You, sir, are a tease."

"I am a gentleman."

"That, too. Thanks for a very nice night. And for being a good guy. There aren't that many of you out there, I don't think."

As he heads back toward the elevators looking broodingly hot AF with a salute of his tattooed hand, it comes to me in a flash.

His superhero name.

Mikhail Zelenka, rescuer of my hot mess self, will otherwise be known as Mr. Hockey.

20

sometimes a win just isn't enough

Mikhail

We're suiting up for a home game. Aiden is jabbering on and on about a woman he took home a few nights ago and how crazy she's been since.

"I mean, Defcon ten-level crazy," he says with wide eyes. "Showing up with coffee and donuts one morning, unannounced. Leaving me cards at my apartment door. It's fuckin' ridiculous."

"Well, you're the one who took a random chick to your apartment," Nathan Cross chirps from his other side. "You never take the randoms to your inner sanctum."

Aiden looks at me, and I just shrug, hands up.

"How's your relationship going with crazy casino lady?" he asks, trying to shift the conversation.

"She's just a friend," I tell him. "She needs one."

Aiden grins. "I can't remember the last time I put my dick into one of my friends."

"I never said I put my dick into her." Even though I've not told him anything about Reagan and me, he's probably figured it out all on his own. He did graduate Yale, as unlikely as that seems sometimes. He's not as dumb as he pretends to be.

From the other side of the locker room, Kolochev chimes in. "Don't worry, Aiden, Zelly's always this cranky. It's nothing personal."

"Eh, the cranky ones make the best of friends sometimes," Tyler says. "Look at me and the big dummy."

Viktor rolls his eyes and says, "As long as you don't try to put your dick in me."

"Oh, for fuck's sake," I mutter.

Coach Brown and the GM come in for a pre-game pep talk. Coach talks about how we're playing fine, but he doesn't see the old spark out there, and we need to find it. He wants to see sparks tonight.

Grant says, "I know we've asked you guys to try something different. Well...different for this team. I give you all props for getting with the program, and more than that, for getting serious about your conditioning and nutrition. It shows, at all levels. Coaching and management are all happy with the progress of the second and third string players. The whole point of giving every player more minutes was to build a dynamic that isn't totally dependent on six or seven guys. The superstars are superstars for a reason. They kick ass and take names. But what if one goes out injured? What if one decides to hang up the skates and head to the front office? Then what? We're building a team that can lift itself up, no matter who's out there, no matter the lineup."

A quiet moment follows, the guys reflecting, once more, on the message we've been hearing all year. It's not like this style of play is different from any other organization. It's just that our organization's difference seemed to make the magic happen.

Of course, it's the loudmouth that speaks up. Tyler says, "Sir, it's all well and good what you're saying. I get it. We all get it. Subs are part of life on the ice. But the chemistry here is between the starters and that can't be ignored."

We all wait, wondering if the new GM cares to hear players voices or not. He's a big man, Grant Gerard. He used to play, so he knows the modern game a lot better than our last GM. He says, "Thanks for speaking up, Tyler. I understand what you're saying. And I know I'm just one voice among many. The coaching staff and players all matter. Everyone has to buy in and trust each other for this to work, and for trust to happen, we have to speak up."

"Well, I'm speakin' up," Tyler says. "And what I'm sayin' is that you have a wicked good starting lineup that you're sacrificing for whatever this is that you're tryin' to build."

"Just give it time," Coach Brown says. "Trust the process."

Tyler rolls his eyes, folds his arms over his chest, and leans back against his locker, unimpressed with the process. I don't blame him.

Grant says some more about how he wants every

line to be championship strong. The guys are restless, but no one is about to speak up after seeing Tyler get shut down. Players' voices matter, my ass. And it's not that I don't understand what they're saying, what they're doing. I do. It's just that the team's magic has crapped out since these changes.

After the weird "pep talk," the vibe is off. We head out and the play is clunky. A lot of missed passes and chasing down offensive runs by the LA team. They're firing off shots left and right, and we can barely get our sticks on the puck. Our goalie, Cal, is a beast, knocking back shots left and right, holding us to 0-0 in the first period. No one else seems to get their rhythm.

We break, and Coach tells us to get out of our own heads, to chuck our egos and our opinions and just get out there and earn our paychecks. "We're here to play hockey," he growls. "Stop dicking around and fuckin' get out there and play some motherfuckin' hockey."

At the buzzer, we head back out, but the nonsense continues. LA scores twice, and a sharp check against the glass causes a fight between Tyler and one of the LA forwards. At the end of the third, down 0-2, I'm fairly certain this is the worst game we've ever played.

In the final period, our full starting lineup is out on the ice. The crowd cheers for us and the energy of it is like the sun to Superman. I tap my stick on the ice and rock side to side as we wait for the start of the period. Play is fast and furious, our defenders in the same head space I'm in, seemingly. We get our passing under control. Our pace is better. And when Evan wings me the puck, I get up on the goal, only to sneak it around the backside, slipping it into the net with a confused goalie, wondering where the hell I just came from.

The crowd goes nuts, my big mug showing up on the jumbotron, along with a replay. I hop over the sideboard as one of the second stringers come in for me. Coach gives me a fist bump as I pull off my gloves to grab a drink.

Things look so much stronger, starting with the fact that Evan gets about three good shots on goal. They all go wide, but it's a far cry better to have their goalie on guard than ours. Finally, with about three minutes to go, Boris hit a shot so hard that the goalie literally ducks to save himself from a certain death in between the posts. It goes straight into the net as the horn sounds. Coach says, "Christ, Boris nearly took that kid's head off."

Tied up, the lines mix up again, and LA uses it to their advantage, putting us on the defensive. Kolochev is a one-man band out there, holding off a hell of an effort by LA's left wing forward. He takes off, looking for Evan, but finding our French-Canadian wunderkind Giroux there instead. He slows down and I can see the frown on his face when he realizes his best friend isn't there, where he expects him. Still, he gets the puck to the kid, who skates right past the LA defender, slipping in a tight shot that sets off the horn again. A minute later, the buzzer goes off, and we've managed to win, but barely. The crowd is happy, cheering, and loud. We should be celebrating, but honestly, I think we're all in some mixed space of relief and anger. I pull off my helmet and head down the tunnel without sparing a look back.

Chatter fills the locker room post-game. Some guys are like, *Hey, it's a win, but I'm not happy with it. It took us two full periods to get our shit together. We easily could've lost.* I don't participate in the talk. I just shower, dress, and take off, walking toward home.

I get a text from Reagan as I'm walking.

Reagan: Saw part of the game. It was on the bar tv

Mikhail: It was a stupid game

Reagan: Why? You won, right?

Mikhail: Sometimes a win just isn't enough

Reagan: Well, at least ur not working a roulette table w/ a guy whose laugh is so sharp it can break glass & breath smelling like 6 types of cheap beer.

Mikhail: How can you text from the table?

Reagan: On a quick break. I get off at midnight.

Mikhail: I'll pick you up

Reagan: K. Thx

AFTER SHOVELING some grilled chicken and a salad into my face, drinking a metric ton of water, and changing out of my dress clothes into regular ones, I feel moderately less pissed about the team situation. Around eleven thirty, I walk over to the casino, hanging at the bar, William telling me he liked my "sneaky goal" tonight. To which I just thank him and leave it at that.

A little after midnight, Reagan joins me, having changed into ripped jeans and a tight green T-shirt that I'd love to peel off her body. With my teeth.

I'm genuinely glad to see her, and not just because she's my flavor of female and I'm attracted to her. I've thought about her a lot since she told me about her situation with Sodorov. And yes, most definitely appreciating the incredible night we shared together in my bed, but it's more than that, too. She's become someone I look forward to seeing, and more unexpectedly, someone I worry about. *All the fucking time.*

"So, you scored tonight. I saw the replay, and it was both weird and cool that I was seeing my friend on TV's all throughout the casino."

Her friend. That's how I've labeled it, right? So why then, do I feel slightly annoyed hearing her say the word? But now is not the time to analyze it, so I deflect instead. "I did score tonight. But that's my job."

"So humble, for a guy with a huge poster on the side of a building not five blocks from here."

"Meh," I grunt. "The team's kind of a mess right now. It took us way too long to get our footing. We could've easily lost that game. It's a miracle we didn't."

We walk along in silence; the warmth of her small, delicate hand clasped in my much bigger one feels right, like it's the most natural thing in the world for us to be holding hands while we just walk along the boulevard together toward home.

"I have to admit, I know next to nothing about hockey, Mikhail. Or any sports, to be honest. So, even though I enjoyed watching *you*, I was clueless about a lot of it." She sounds apologetic telling me this, but she doesn't need to feel that way from my perspective.

"It's okay. I appreciate being able to not think hockey sometimes."

"Still, I feel like I should be watching your games or something. I want to learn and understand the rules better."

The thought of Reagan *wanting* to watch me play thrills me in a way I haven't felt before with anyone that I can recall. "Any time. I can get you in if you're off when we have a home game. I'll set you up at Will Call with standing home game tickets for Reagan Marlowe. Just give them your name at the window and you're good to go."

She smiles up at me and mouths the words, *"thank you, friend."*

My gorgeous friend, *you're so fucking welcome.*

She *is* freaking gorgeous right now, smiling a true smile for once, looking happy and relaxed. If this is something I can help make happen for her, then I'm going to do it every chance I get and be damn proud of myself for it.

When we get to the building and step into the

elevator, Reagan asks, "Wanna watch a movie or something?"

Fuck. Yes.

Although the "or something" probably more than the movie.

My answer to her question is the same for both.

"Your place or mine?"

21
superhero 101

Reagan

ikhail has decided on superhero movies. He said he couldn't care less if I knew the game of hockey, but superhero culture was non-negotiable.

Starting with *Iron Man*, which he claims, "launched the Marvel movie enterprise." I have no clue what this means, but I nod and go along with it. I guess, in addition to upping my knowledge of hockey, I'm also going to have to learn what the heck Marvel is.

It's adorable, actually, him so into this whole superhero culture. I know it means something to Mikhail, more than just regular entertainment, because he got jazzed when I told him he was my own personal superhero that one time.

"Do you ever wish you had superpowers?" I blurt out the question.

I figure he'll laugh or something, but he seems to have put some serious thought into this. "Well, I think the average person has the capacity to be a hero. I don't mean that they'll have some adrenaline rush and lift a car or some cliché like that. I just mean they can step in and do the right thing when the right thing is needed, you know what I mean?"

"I do." I nod, thinking back on how he stepped in to help me in that alleyway.

"You're thinking of me right now, but I'm thinking of you. I'm thinking of how you stepped in and took charge for your mom. You put yourself in harm's way for her. You're the hero in that story."

"I don't think of it that way. And besides, that's not what I asked. I asked if you'd ever want to have actual superpowers. Like super speed or super strength or whatever."

"Sure," he answers, sitting back on the couch, hands clasped behind his head. It shows off his carved, inked biceps, otherwise known as *thirst traps of hotness.* "I've wished I could have all kinds of powers throughout my life. One seems cooler than the next. But I also like the idea of normal people being heroes. I mean, look at Tony Stark. He's a genius, sure, and he's uber rich, but he doesn't have any actual superhuman traits."

"Who's Tony Stark?"

Mikhail sucks in a horrified breath. "What? Seriously?"

"What?"

He looks genuinely offended. "Tony Stark is Iron Man, Reagan."

"Oh."

"Have you lived under a rock your whole life? How

on earth did—I just can't even with you—what you just said to me—" He stammers, making me laugh out loud at his frustration with my Tony Stark ignorant self.

"Sorry." I hold my hands up in surrender. "Okay. I'll pay attention. We can add Superhero 101 to my list of things to do. Tony Stark is Iron Man."

Mikhail reaches over and tickles my side, telling me I'd better get up on my superhero game, or we simply cannot be friends. I giggle and kick at him, but he's overpowering and ends up hovering over me, between my legs. Everything stops. Time stops. The space between us feels magnetized as we consume each other with our eyes.

Tony who?

My mind's on one, and only one, superhero right now. His name is not Tony Stark *or* Iron Man.

But Mikhail doesn't give me the chance to tell him any of that. The part about how I'm only interested in one superhero on the list—the one I put up top of mine.

Mere mortal, Mikhail Zelenka, living a double life by showing up at just the right moment for people in desperate need of a savior. And don't forget to add that he's also super-hot, uber-ripped, excessively tatted, and the famous professional athlete I named Mr. Hock—

Because his lips come crashing down on mine.

His tongue. His teeth. His cock feels dangerously hard behind his jeans as he pushes between my legs. Too much denim between us. Too much.

My hands work at his fly, undoing the button, unzipping the zipper. I push my hand beneath the fabric of his boxers to press down on his cock as he moans and kisses me with such force I forget to breathe, let alone tell him about the cool superhero name I created for him.

I push on him, and he backs away, kind of dazed, as I tell him to get on his back. He pulls his shirt over his head and lies down, his jeans undone, his hair a wild mess, his cock out and hard for me. "God, you're hot." I pull my shirt over my head, my jeans down over my hips. I'm in plain cotton underwear, both thong and bra. Not the sexiest of lingerie by a long shot, but it doesn't matter. When I crawl on top and straddle him, the only thing between us is the thin cotton of my thong, and we aren't caring about underwear choices even a little bit.

"Did you score tonight?" I ask, leaning in, my lips hovering so close to his but just out of reach.

"I already told you I did." He laughs, but then he sees the expression on my face. His changes to a half-smile and a raised eyebrow as he says, "Nope. Not yet."

I move my hips, the friction of my panties and my clit and his cock giving me all the feels between the legs. Mikhail's fingertips play at my nipples through my bra as we kiss and kiss, sloppy and sensual and deep. "I fucking love your tits...in my mouth," he growls, his big hands roughly pushing my bra aside to get to them. The sight of him devouring my breast might just be the hottest thing I've ever seen. Watching him kiss and bite and suck at my nipple sends me over the edge when the whole sensory experience culminates into a sudden and blinding orgasm. I howl at the unexpected release, throwing my head back and going somewhere not of this world, grateful for his strong arms holding me from falling back onto the floor.

When I open my eyes, Mikhail's dark blues are looking up at mine with his lips still grazing my nipple. Still just as hot of an image after my orgasm as before, but I can tell he is looking for reassurance from me when he asks, "Fuuuck...what just happened there?"

"You. You happened and rocked me out of this world."

"Well, I guess I rock, then." He grins and pulls up to kiss me, his tongue spearing in deep to tangle with mine while his hands snake down to my ass. His busy fingers pushing aside my thong and dipping down to bury between my folds. His fingers press inside me where I'm wet and ready. The sensation of rubbing myself against his cock from the front, while having him finger me from behind, is nearly enough to set me off again. His mouth returns to my nipple, but this time, it's the other breast. I'm making all kinds of noises, like an animal unleashed as I feel the buildup begin again, another orgasm is coming for me.

"So responsive...it's fucking hot," he growls, moving his mouth back up to find mine once more. "Now come here and sit on my face."

Turned on by the direct order, I peel away my panties and scoot up, hovering over his mouth. He puts his hands on my hips and pulls me down, tongue probing. My hips move as I ride his face, my hands braced on the arm of the couch. I really do feel like a wild animal, totally free and uninhibited. I feel dirty and sexy and primal. He doesn't stop until I've forgotten my name, until I come so hard, I stop breathing. Until I fall onto him, my legs wobbly and my breath uneven.

I lie along the length of him as I float back to earth, his fingertips tracing along the bare skin of my back. "Can I just stay here forever?" I ask, feeling dreamy and far, far away from my problems.

Mikhail doesn't answer, and when I look up at him, his eyes are dark. I move my hand to his cock, gripping it, sliding against it. He moans as his hips push up to meet my touch. It's only minutes before he flips us over, pulling my legs up on his shoulders as he leans in for a fierce kiss that makes my toes curl. When he pushes his cock inside me, I cry out at the fullness. He moves slowly at first, but then goes deeper and deeper, the friction building as his pelvis rubs against my throbbing clit. I scratch my fingernails down his back, frenzied as he fucks his cock harder and harder into me, as deep as he can go.

He pulls out just before his release, and I take over from there. His big cock in my small hand, but I get the job done. I watch him as I stroke up and down his shuddering length, feeling powerful when he begins to come on my stomach. His face is fierce and beautiful. His eyes never leave mine the whole time he's coming.

Good God, this man is sexy.

Sex with Mikhail is the most erotic thing I've ever witnessed, ever done, ever experienced.

After an intense few moments of just looking at each other, he reaches back to find his T-shirt from wherever it landed when he took it off, his inked bicep flexing as he stretches for it. He uses it to wipe away the cum from my stomach before falling to my side, pulling my back to his front, his strong arms wrapped around me, holding me close.

We lie together like that, spooning, for a long time. I think I nod off a few times, until Mikhail's voice wakes me back up. "Don't ghost me again, okay?"

I open my mouth to respond several times. Eventually, I settle on "I won't, but I just don't want to pull you into all of my nonsense."

"But I'm a big boy," he says, kissing my shoulder. My whole body erupts in goose flesh. I shiver, so he pulls a blanket free from the back of the couch, throwing it over our naked bodies. "I can handle myself."

"Yes, you are a big boy," I say, innuendo thick in my tone. He pumps his hips toward my backside in response. "Still, these are criminals. You caught that guy off guard in the alleyway that night. We can't guarantee you'll catch them off guard a second time."

"I'm not afraid, Reagan. What kind of man would I be if I left a friend without someone at her side?"

You wouldn't be my superhero. My lovely Mr. Hockey protector. But I don't say that to him out loud. Instead, I turn to face him and cup his cheek in my hand. "You dear, sweet man, I'm so thankful for you. In so many ways. But I cannot deal if they come after you too, Mikhail. I could never forgive myself if they hurt you because of me."

"Hush," he says with a hard squeeze of his arms around me. "It's not even something you need to be afraid of, okay? I'm good. And you're good." He starts kissing me again, probably to shut me up about a topic he clearly doesn't believe bears his concern, but it's still lovely to be kissed to sleep, held safely in his superhero arms on this night.

So lovely, yes.

And I will never forget this wonderful night with Mikhail, making me feel sexy and desired and safe and protected. He's making it very hard for me to think of him as just a friend. He's so much more than that already.

Even so, other nights will come and go. We both know he can't be in two places at once. He might be my Mr. Hockey, superhero extraordinaire, but he's no immortal. I won't fuss anymore about it tonight and ruin the moment. He's made his feelings clear, and he's not worried for himself.

Even though I am. And I will be until this Sodorov business is behind me.

22
this ain't a democracy

Mikhail

I've only just put my bag down in my bedroom after a quick trip to Austin for a game when I get the text to come back to the arena for a team meeting.

I'd planned to go to the gym to box and meet Reagan but there goes that plan. I send her a text.

> **Mikhail:** Back in town but I've got a team meeting right now

> **Reagan:** ☹ I was looking forward to watching you punch people in the ring

> **Mikhail:** Sorry. I'll make it up to you somehow. Meet up later?

> **Reagan:** Yes please. To both. ☺

Oh, I plan on it, gorgeous.

THIRTY MINUTES LATER, I'm listening to Coach Brown express his frustrations about our inconsistent play lately.

"We're mostly winning, but it's not the kind of winning we've done during championship seasons," he's saying. "We need to talk this out or this sloppy bullshit is going to catch up on us and we'll find ourselves out of the running. Other teams are looking good. We can't rest on our laurels, here."

The guys all mutter amongst themselves. Grant says, "Look, guys, we talked about this before. Tyler spoke up and we appreciate that. We need to hear more voices. We need to know what's going on in your heads when you head out on the ice."

In true Team Captain fashion, Evan speaks up first. He clears his throat and looks around the room. "With all due respect, sir, the first string is like a well-oiled machine. There's history and chemistry and a bond that's been built game after game after game. We know where to send the puck, sometimes without even looking, because we know how each other thinks. And we trust each other. That kind of trust doesn't just show up because you wish it into reality. It takes trials and tribulations to build it up and once it's there, you just don't do anything that will knock it down."

You could hear a pin drop in this place. Coach nods a few times before saying, "But what happens if you go out for a season on injury? Or worse yet, if an injury takes you or one of your guys out permanently? What happens then?"

"It's happened," Evan says. "We've had a few bad injuries and guys have had to sub in as needed.

They've done a good job. Nothing wrong with their play. But there's a difference between subbing for injury and subbing whole lines in and out the whole damn game. You get comfortable on a line and then, next second, there's a bloody new player out there."

Grant pinches his nose between his fingers like he's got a headache. He says, "You know, I was a player before I was a suit. I know exactly what you're talking about, here. And what we're trying to build is a scenario where all these guys feel exactly the way the starters feel about each other. Where it doesn't matter who's out there with you, you feel supported and trusted and connected as players."

"Great, sounds like utopia," Tyler says. "Look, all these guys are on contract for a reason. There's no one sayin' that they can't play or whatever. But when our line is out there, magic happens. Why mess with magic?"

Next to me, Aiden grunts loudly enough that the room turns to look at him. He grimaces, like he didn't mean to attract attention, but then says, "I didn't expect to get much playing time my rookie year unless there was a retirement, or I had some kind of crazy pre-season. I knew what the front line could do. I wouldn't expect anyone to mess with it."

There are a few other comments. A few guys wonder why the starters get treated like they shit gold. Every other team subs in and out. We've all learned to play that way since we were little kids, and it helps with the whole team dynamic. Other guys agree that the chemistry on the front line is so crazy good that it's obvious it needs to stay intact. It's about fifty-fifty, honestly.

Coach is stiff-backed with his hands in his pockets. He jumps back in and says, "Look, boys, this ain't a democracy. Every one of you sits on a fat contract that says you play the game we tell you to play. This is a team, and we need bench strength. I need guys who get what we're trying to build who can also gel out on the ice. So, get your heads straight and outta your asses real fuckin' soon. Figure it out or find yourselves traded. You all are professionals. Act like it."

He storms out, which shocks us all. Coach Brown is always honest and blunt, but I've never seen him pissed like this. Grant hangs back, though. He bites at his bottom lip as he thinks about everything that's been said. "I know change is hard and you like things the way you like them. That's human nature. But we want this team to be strong to the foundation and I know you want that, too, in your bones. This is something to be proud of, what you all have built, and we can honor those who stood at the front while still building up the rest of our players."

He turns to head out but stops at the door. Turning back, he adds, "Good win in Austin." But it's quiet after he goes because we all know it wasn't a good win. It was an okay win that should have been a blowout. LA was a messy win. New Jersey was a messy win. There's a pattern emerging, and if I'm reading things right, it won't get better unless we stop trying to replay the past.

We all head out, and as I'm walking home, I get a call from my father. I let it ring for a bit before I finally sigh and answer. My reward is my father not even saying hello. He just launches into me. "What the hell was going on out there in Austin?"

"Yeah, it was kinda brutal," I say, with nothing better to add.

"The team doesn't seem like they can get their shit together. And you, where were you? You let two passes slide by you and spent two periods trying to wake up before you seemed to get your head in the game."

"I'm just not sure what you expect me to say, Pop. I agree, the team's not playing its best right now."

"I just think you can do better. I can't say anything to those other yahoos, but I can coach you. And what I'm seeing is a player who is not worthy of the starting spot he's secured. Your play is halted and weak. You need to put more power into what you're doing out there."

He rages on and on, telling me what I did wrong at every turn of the game. By the end, I feel like I've been doused in cold water, I'm so numb. I should be used to it, I suppose. It's no different than any youth, junior, high school, or AHL game I've ever played in my life.

I've learned over the course of my life that arguing with Jozem Zelenka is pointless on all levels. You just don't do it. He thinks he knows the game better than anyone else, and he's not interested in excuses.

So, I don't say anything.

I just grunt to acknowledge each statement as I walk, turning toward the boxing gym instead of the apartment building.

By the time he hangs up, I really need to punch something. I head in, go straight for the locker room, change, and proceed to the stationary bags. One of the trainers comes over and asks if I want a guided workout, but honestly, I just want to punch and kick shit, so I tell him I'll freestyle until the ring comes open for sparring.

"Your game is weak right now. You don't deserve to be a starter with the play I saw in Austin. Remember the name on your back and play like it or you'll find yourself traded to a shitty team."

Every comment, every dig, it all comes out as I punch and kick that bag. Someone says, "Take it easy" from behind me, but I don't want to take it easy. I want to let out every one of my frustrations on this inanimate object so that I don't let them out on anyone else.

I don't stop until I see a short, dark-haired figure out of the corner of my eye. I stop and turn, and Reagan gives a little wave as she jogs over to me.

"Hey, sweaty. I thought you had a team meeting?" She's smiling at me and it's the best thing to happen to me so far today.

"I did, and it did not go well. And then my father called to pick apart my game in Austin. So, I came straight here. Sorry, I should've texted you."

"No biggie." She gives me one cute shake of her head. "I get it. You okay?"

I push my lips together and make a noncommittal noise.

"Okay, so then, that would be a no." Reagan laughs. "Well, do you want to spar with me?"

"I was hoping to hit someone I didn't care about hurting," I say carefully. I don't want to offend her, but there's no way I'm gonna blast anything at Reagan.

"Well, I can use the sparring time, so suck it up." She's so damn sexy when she's feisty. *It's not sparring I want to do with her right now. I want to rip her clothes off her sexy-as-fuck body, have her tits in my mouth, and have her riding me hard and fast. Then I'd take her from behind, fucking her even harder so she can barely walk in the morning with my name on her kissable lips.*

But that's not going to happen in the middle of the gym, so I will myself to think about hockey stats.

Once we get the go-ahead and she's wrapped her hands, we climb up into the ring. The trainers put on our headgear, slip us our mouth guards, and help us put on our gloves.

Not gonna lie—Reagan looks very small and fairly helpless to me in this venue. I know she's been training, and I know she's strong for her size, but she *is* tiny. And I am large. So, we mostly work on footwork and combos. The trainers give her pointers throughout, so it's not really a true sparring match, but it's fun, and she seems to really enjoy it.

We get a five-minute warning and the trainers back off. I take it easy on her, landing a few kicks and punches that barely graze her. She gets extra feisty, though, and picks up her speed and footwork. I can see her expression turn competitive, and, honestly, I have to work at it to keep my cock from going hard. Seeing her go fierce like that is a serious turn-on. And because I'm thinking about milk and cookies or the colors of the Peruvian flag to avoid major embarrassment, she lands a square, hard punch straight to my jaw.

I back up with an "*oof*" sound, my eyes going wide as she dances around, super proud of herself for landing a bona fide haymaker to my dumb face.

The bell sounds and we touch gloves before crawling out of the ring.

"I'm so sorry I hit you that hard," Reagan says, pulling off her gloves and touching the spot where she landed her punch.

"No, you're not." I'm laughing. "You were dancing around like Muhammed Ali. You were totally pumped and proud of yourself."

"Okay." She's grinning up at me. "I was. But I didn't mean to hurt you."

"It's fine," I say, waving it off. "I feel good about your ability to clock someone. It's a good thing."

We wander back toward the locker rooms and stop in front of the door to the all-gender changing room. I lean in and kiss her. "I have to admit, I was turned on out there."

Her grin gets wilder, wickeder, as she pushes me through the door to the single occupancy room. She locks the door and pulls off her workout shorts, baring her pussy to me. I pounce, of course, shoving her against the door, fingers probing inside. She moans and nearly crawls up my body as we kiss—hard—her hand freeing my cock from my shorts as she shoves the waistband down and aside.

I'm inside her in a heartbeat, holding her up, hands on her ass as I pound into her. She begs for it, harder, faster, and I oblige, filling her to the breaking point until she comes with a loud cry that I smother with another searing kiss, swallowing her cries of pleasure.

My orgasm follows and I pull out, spilling my release on the inside of my bunched-up shorts, my forehead against hers as I ride the wave, her hand pumping me dry the way she's perfected. I fucking love having her delicate hand wrapped around my cock while I get off.

She wiggles down to stand on her own. "Wow," she says, giggling at me. "Welcome baaack, Mr. Hockey!"

"That was—wait, what did you just call me?"

"Yep," she says, pulling on the other leg of her shorts while I grab a paper towel to clean up my mess so I can walk out of here and into the shower. "Mr. Hockey is your superhero name. I told you I needed to think of one for you and that's it. And yeah, whatever you're thinking about what *that just was*—it was the best part of my day so far."

"I'm so glad, and I'd like to try improving on the 'so far' if you'll let Mr. Hockey take you to dinner." The nerd in me is stoked she thought about and came up with a superhero name for me. How fucking cool is that? It's a good one, too. I dig it. This girl. I think...*I think she might be the most special person I've ever met.*

"Can't," she says with a pout. "I have a shift tonight."

"Bummer." I mean it. "I missed you while I was gone."

She smiles and it nearly brings me to my knees. "I missed you too."

"Well, I guess I'll just stay home and feel sorry for

myself. Mr. Hockey all alone waiting for some superhero job to do."

"You'll be fine. And hey, guess what?"

"What?"

"I got a call from a real wedding planning company. I applied for a job there and I have an interview on Thursday."

"Hey, that's cause for celebration!"

"Don't jinx it," she says. "But I'm excited."

"Well, I'll make a dinner reservation for the night after. We'll either drink to our sorrows or celebrate our successes. Sound good?"

She pushes up on her tiptoes to kiss me. "Okay. Sounds good. Now give me a thirty-second lead so people don't see us sneaking out of here together. I don't want anyone razzing us for being naughty."

I'm grinning like an idiot as she peeks out the door and makes a run for it. I definitely don't wait thirty seconds, but I do give her the lead, and then stroll out and down to the men's locker room for a quick shower.

Outside the gym, I'm waiting for her so I can walk her home. She looks surprised to see me. "I wasn't expecting you to wait for me."

"Eh, I assume we're going to the same place." We walk while I mull over what I really want to say. "You know, I went to the gym to blow off steam. But seeing you? It had the same kind of effect."

"Well, orgasms will put anyone on cloud nine. Great orgasms, especially." I feel my cheeks heat, and she giggles at the sight of me blushing. "I like seeing you happy, though. Smiling. You do it so rarely. You're so serious all the time."

"I could say the same about you, Reagan."

"You could, but I wasn't always like this. I was silly and lighthearted. Hard to believe, huh? Since I'm such a drama magnet now?"

"No, I can see it, still. You're in self-protection mode. It's hard to shine when you're just worried about survival. But I can see it. It's the thing that makes it hard for me to stop thinking about you."

Reagan blushes a deep shade of pink at my comment. She covers by joking, "Is it hot out here?"

"You're hot," I say, winking.

"No, *you're* hot," she says. "Especially when you do that one thing…"

"With my tongue?"

She laughs, but it slips from her face after a moment. "I'm sorry I brought all this drama into your life, though. Seriously."

"We've already talked about this, Reagan."

"I know. I just…I guess I wish we'd met before all of this. I wish you could have known me when I was more carefree."

"I like you just the way you are, though. I mean, I've never been carefree, so it's not something I look for on a résumé."

She snorts. "Yeah, you probably came out of the womb brooding."

I pull a face but don't deny it. "I do understand you, Reagan. I like where your heart is at. I like that you protect the people you love. And I'm glad we can make each other smile, despite life's bullshit."

Holding hands, we walk the remaining block, content in each other's company.

She smacks me on the butt as I step off the elevator at my floor. "I'll see you in a couple of days, okay?" she sings at me with a tilt of her head.

I turn and watch as the elevator doors start to close and shove my hand in to keep it open. "For sure, but if you need me to bring you home tonight, just throw me a text and I'll come. I should be awake."

She clutches her hand to her heart and looks up at me, all gorgeous and smiley. "'Texting Mr. Hockey at Midnight' sounds like a movie. Okay, I will." She blows me a kiss as the elevator doors are closing, the sassy smile on her face giving me all kinds of ideas for later, when I have her in my bed. Where I can make her come until she can't keep her eyes open. Then I can watch her sleeping and know she's safe beside me and nobody is going to hurt her.

Why do I suddenly feeling like this "friendship" needs to be something defined as a lot more than just friends with benefits?

You know why, *Mr. Hockey*.

You're falling in love with this girl, and you need to tell her.

23
big guy with the ink can't protect you 24/7

Reagan

Henri Sodorov is here. I feel sick.

He's alluring as a snake, with his dark hair slicked back and his pointed nose. His suit is custom, fitting his wide shoulders like it grew right out of him. Women, and some men, are magnetized by him as he wanders around the casino as if he owns the place. He oozes money and power, a heady combination for likely everyone but me. For me, he looks like the Grim Reaper, ready to harvest my soul.

He smiles and laughs and raises his drink glass, the life of the party, as he welcomes himself back to his favorite casino. People scurry to meet his demands. When he takes his seat at the blackjack table, he's smiling, but when he slides his attention to my roulette station, the smile melts away, and his eyes go hard. He's not here to have fun. He's here to show me he knows where I am, that he still doesn't believe I don't have his money.

It sends a shiver straight down my spine and into my shoes.

Thankfully, it's busy tonight, and I get a lot of action at my table. It doesn't take away the skin-crawly feeling I have, knowing how closely I'm being watched, but it does help me focus on other things. Still, the moment someone comes to give me a fifteen-minute break, I go straight to Raul.

"Sodorov won't stop staring at me. Can I go work at the restaurant tonight? Or somewhere away from the blackjack section?"

"Reagan," he says, not even looking up from his ever-present clipboard, "It's too busy tonight and I'm already understaffed. We have a tour bus that just unloaded. Please, just work your station and ignore him."

"How can I ignore a man who has clearly positioned himself to intimidate me?"

He sighs loudly, throwing his head back. "Just go take a breather. Get a drink of water. Get back out there and finish your shift. Nothing is going to happen to you here."

"Sure, but the minute I walk out the door—"

"Reagan," he snaps, "stop being a conspiracy theorist. Just get to work."

My teeth hurt, I'm gritting them so hard. Raul has not, for one second, taken my safety seriously throughout this ordeal. "I have given statements; they've done a sweep for fingerprints on and around the financial computers. There is nothing tying me to this crime, and yet I've been abused and intimidated ever since. And he's still allowed to walk in here and get treated like a king while he continues to abuse and intimidate me."

Raul meets my eye. "Money talks, Reagan, and he has a lot of it. He was the one whose money got stolen. He was the one who was robbed."

I stare at my boss for a long moment, long enough to make it uncomfortable, before stomping off. I do as he told me. I get a drink of water. I do a breathing exercise. I go back out to my station.

Late in the shift, one of Sodorov's goons comes to the table and places a bet. He's the scarred one from the alley. I act professionally, as if I don't recognize him. As if he's just another customer. He stares me straight in the eye and smirks.

He loses his bet but places another. And another. Every time, he smirks. He stares. And every time, my anxiety ratchets up a notch, my stomach flipping wildly, the noise of the casino blending into an incomprehensible roar in my ears. My throat tightens.

By some miracle, I stave off the panic attack that threatens to leave me in the fetal position on the floor. I breathe and smile and act like nothing is wrong until my next break. It's a long shift today. I'm tired, and I'm emotional, and I run straight to the bathroom to throw up. I work to get my breathing back under control. I cry for a moment just to get it all out. When I finally feel calm enough, I wash up and head back out, only to run straight into Peter. *Oh fuck. Could this night get any worse?*

"Hey, Reggy," he says with all the warmth of a snake. *He is a snake.*

I can't believe I ever thought he was handsome. Or good. Now, all I see is a skinny dude in a cheap suit.

My face hurts, I scowl so hard. "Don't call me that."

"Henri tells me he might have proof it was you who took his money. Last chance to come clean on your own."

"Fuck off, Peter," I snarl. "The FBI has questioned me. I am not a suspect."

"Maybe not to the FBI," he says, examining his fingernails, blasé to the max.

"There is no reason for them to consider me a suspect when I'm paying on my loan. On time. Every month. I'm not running. Any evidence they claim to have is a lie. Why would I still be working here if I had any money?" *Asshole.*

He makes a noise that tells me he doesn't think they care. As I move to shove past him, telling him I need to get back on shift, he grabs my arm roughly. "There are ways to work it off, as you well know, Reagan."

"And you well know, Peter, I'm not doing that, ever." They can't force me into sex work, even though he's tried suggesting it before.

Peter smirks at me and says, "The big guy with all the ink can't protect you twenty-four seven."

I ignore his comment and pull my arm loose, feeling the sting of an emerging bruise as I head back to my station. Looking around, I realize Sodorov has left the blackjack table. He's surely elsewhere in the casino. I'm relieved he's not there to stare at me, but I'm also nervous about what corner he might be lurking behind.

At the end of my shift, I debate calling Mikhail to come walk me home. I know he will, but I also don't want him thinking he has to come rescue me every time. He's my friend, not my bodyguard. As I clock out and change into sweatpants and a hoodie, I think about how lonely the past couple of years have been. I plodded through classes and work, trying to dig myself out of this dreadful hole I've been living in. But I miss the friends I made when I came to school. I miss having friends, period. I miss meeting people for coffee and going out to a club dancing. There was a time when I was relatively carefree. As I said to Mikhail, I once felt positive and felt like I had my whole life and all kinds of opportunity in front of me. *This is definitely an "old and new me."*

Mikhail has given me reason to hope I can have it all back. His friendship has been everything to me lately. And here I thought he was one of the bad guys when I first saw him.

Also, I know I more than like him. Maybe a lot more. As in I might love him.

Should I tell him? I'm just not sure. He's tried so hard to set boundaries between us, to show that he cares for me as a person, as a friend, not just as a sexual partner. But the chemistry between us is just as real, and we both know it. I've tried pushing him away, but I can't deny that I feel something for him I haven't felt…well, ever, for anyone who came before Mikhail Zelenka, my superhero, my gorgeous Mr. Hockey.

I nearly float to the front of the casino as I think about all of this. I think about going and surprising him from here. Showing up at his door and telling him tonight just how much I care about him and that I want to explore this *more than friendship thing* happening with us. I even think about telling him I'm falling in love with him.

My romantic thoughts are curtailed straight back into harsh reality as I step outside of the Tangier's doors.

I don't feel safe walking, what with Sodorov lurking about tonight, so I hail a cab, eager to make the short commute back to my apartment building. I'm about to text Mikhail to see if he's up as I slide into the seat. What I don't expect is the big Russian who slides in next to me, shutting the door and giving an address that is most definitely not mine.

As the cab moves, I feel a gun pressed against my side. The goon leans over and whispers, "Keep your mouth shut or I will shoot you."

So, I keep my mouth shut, my hands on my phone, hidden in the pocket of my sweatshirt.

And we ride away into the dark night.

It takes forever until we finally pull into a long drive far outside of town. As soon as I see the mansion, I know it must belong to Henri Sodorov himself.

No!

How can this be the end?

Just when I've found something worth living for.

24
i think you're it

Mikhail

We're running offensive drills at practice, each of us analyzing each other's movements and instincts, trying to get a sense of which players will work well with each other. It's been going okay, and we've been at it long enough that we start chattering on the ice as we run the drills.

One of the younger players, Ethan Smith, asks what it was like to grow up hockey royalty.

I just grunt in response. My least favorite subject.

"Yeah," Smith says. "The Great Zelenka. What was it like growing up with that guy? I mean, obviously, it worked out for you, since you played starter from the beginning."

I'm sure I look thoroughly unimpressed. "Yeah, he made training my number one priority."

"But was it cool?" he prods. "You know, being the son of a hockey Great?"

"It depended on the day, I suppose."

Thankfully, Evan jumps in, aware of my ambivalence when it comes to talking about my dad. He says, "Most guys have some kind of pedigree in hockey when they get here. Their dads played or coached. Or they've been on skates since they were three. Or they played in the Olympics. Pro players don't usually come from nowhere."

This moves the conversation away from The Great Zelenka and toward everyone's individual accomplishments. Actually, a smart strategy by our team captain. It helps level the playing field, so to speak, and gives some of the players who get less playing time the chance to see that there is no one on this team who doesn't deserve to be here.

After practice, Evan asks if I want to get a bite to eat. I look at my phone to see if Reagan has checked in. I was hoping we could hit the gym or something, but she never texted me last night, and today, she's been MIA, as well. With no word from her, I agree to grab a bite with the captain.

Down in the pub, we order our food, and Evan asks if I'm okay lately. "You haven't been the cocky rookie I'm used to these days."

I can't help but laugh. "Well, I haven't been a rookie in, what, five years now. Six maybe?"

Evan nods but looks surprised. "Damn," he says, kind of shocked. Then, "*Damn.* Time sure as hell flies, doesn't it? I mean, I'm going to have a kid in kindergarten next year. How's that for crazy?"

"Crazy, yeah," I say, wondering why the hell I'm sitting here. Evan and I are cool, but we're not best buds or anything. We ran into each other a few times at a cooking class taught by the team nutritionist back in the summer. But classes have been paused since Devon went on maternity leave. So, I don't see Evan outside of a hockey arena. We don't grab drinks and eat burgers at the pub together. We don't share our feelings with each other. I like the guy, but we don't do this.

"I'm thinking of retiring," Evan says without missing a beat.

This sure as hell gets my attention. My eyes snap up to his face to see if he's joking, but his expression is serious. "Why?"

He lifts a shoulder and stirs his glass of lemonade with a straw. "There's been speculation for the past year or so—which isn't at all why I'm thinking about it, to be clear. But I'm rolling further along into my thirties. I've got a wife and three kids. My contract is up for renegotiation after next season."

"None of those seem like reasons to me," I argue. "You're still playing like fire. And next season is next season. You're in top shape. Play it through."

"I'm not the only one."

"Vik?" I ask.

Evan nods. "Viktor and Scarlett have been talking about going to Russia. His mom is there, her dad is there, and they want a big family of their own. Vik said he's not going to be the dad who's never home for his kids. He wants to coach their sports and enjoy the life he's earned for himself over a long and remarkable career. I get that because I want the same for my family, too."

I sit back in the booth, whistling. "Well, the focus on bench strength makes so much more sense now."

"Kind of," Evan says. "Neither Vik nor I have given them a timeline, so they've just asked us to be up front about how we're feeling. And we have. Both of us still want to play, but if hockey becomes second or third on the priority list, then it'll probably be a pretty good sign it's time to go to the front office or go coach or whatever."

"Yeah, I guess I get that."

"And honestly, they're not wrong, even if we weren't thinking about what's next. There are seven of us out there, with Cal, who makes shit happen. Game after game and, yes, it's magic when it works the way it's supposed to, but as Coach and Grant have asked, what if one of us goes down with a catastrophic injury? What happens then if no one else is conditioned enough to jump in full-time? They get paid good money; they need to do good work."

Our food comes and we take a few bites before I ask, "Why are you telling me this, man?"

"Because I need you out there as a leader."

"I'm no cheerleader, Evan."

"I need you to be." He nails me with a hard look. "I do the best I can, but someone will need to take my place when I decide I'm done. And I think you're it. You're serious about the game. You're not out at the bars partying it up."

"I'm also the son of The Great Zelenka." I can't help rolling my eyes at him.

"No," Evan says sharply. "No, Mikhail. You're your own man. Your style of play is your own. Your countenance is your own. You do not have to live, or lead, in your father's shadow. You can grow into whatever kind of player you want to be—whatever kind of man you aim to be."

"You're too weak to lead a team. Too soft when a captain needs to be tough. Indestructible. That's not you."

I can't help but hear my father's words and attempt to weigh them against what Evan is saying.

"You do not have to live, or lead, in your father's shadow. You can grow into whatever kind of player you want to be—whatever kind of man you aim to be."

Whose words do I listen to? My captain's? My father's? Evan doesn't shoot the shit aimlessly. He also speaks his truth. This proposition seems so surreal.

Me? Captain of the Vegas Crush?

Evan's message is not lost on me. He wants me to be more than just a steady scorer, a quiet force on the left wing. He wants me to step up and be more. I'm speechless, my throat tight at his encouragement, at his belief in what I can be. My father has never talked to me this way, has never given me any sense that he believes in my ability to lead or grow. His comments are always negative, always focused on what he would've done that would've been better.

As we finish our lunch, he asks what I've got going on outside of the team. I'm not going to go into any detail on Reagan's situation, but I do mention that I'm seeing someone.

"Oh yeah? Is it serious?"

"Um, I'm not sure, actually?" I laugh. "She had some stuff going on and really needed a friend. But it's, you know, more than that now. We haven't put a label on it even though I'm ready."

"Well, I chased my wife around like a panting dog, so I knew just exactly what I wanted there." He grins. "I guess you'll know when you know."

He insists on buying my lunch, and as we head out, he says, "Have a think on what I've said."

I do. All the way home, I think about what he's said, what he's shared. It's more than a little insane to think about the Vegas Crush without Evan Kazmeirowicz. The guy is an institution here, and—as hard as it is for me to admit—he's grown into a damn good leader for the team. I sure gave him grief when I first started here as an untested rookie. We've come a looong way since that first season of butting heads at every opportunity. If and when he decides to retire, I'm sure the Crush Foundation will grab him, or the coaching staff. Or broadcasting will lure him over. Or he'll go on to train future NHL players. Who knows? The point is—he's a machine, and if he moves on from playing, it will most definitely leave a void on our team.

I need to step up my game if he thinks I'm the one to fill it.

25
find a way

Reagan

As I blink to consciousness, I'm confused. I'm in an unfamiliar, but lavish, bedroom in a strange house.

My mind races. How did I get here? Where am I? I sit up, realizing I'm sprawled out on a bed in the sweatpants and hoodie I remember putting on at the end of my shift. I remember getting a cab and having one of Sodorov's men slide in beside me, a gun to my ribs. I remember the long ride out of town and the anxiety rippling up through my rib cage. I vomited as soon as I got out of the car. And as the taxi drove away, I tried to run. Then everything went black.

As I look around the room, a man's figure goes from blurry to clear. Peter. He's smoking a cigarette.

"What the hell..." I trail off as I wince at the sharp pain in my head. Reaching up, I find my hair matted with blood, tender to the touch.

"Pistols do some damage, don't they?" he says evilly. "Even when they're not being fired."

"Why?" It's all I can manage to get out.

"*Why?*" he repeats, like I'm an idiot for asking the question. "Why bring you here? Why pistol-whip your lying ass? What?"

I just grit my teeth, putting my energy into staring daggers at this man I once trusted.

"Look, Henri's given you plenty of time to fess up. To return what you stole."

I laugh kind of hysterically. "And I didn't steal *anything.*"

"Hmm."

"I have a job interview. How long have I been here? I need to be back by Thursday for my interview."

Peter sighs. "It seems unlikely you'll make that appointment, Reggy. Or any appointment, for that matter."

My stomach drops. "What day is it?"

"Wednesday."

I nod, swallowing back the bile that threatens to rise in my throat. I haven't missed the interview. That's my thought. Not, *I'm going to die.* Or *I need to figure out how to get out of this.* No, I'm still worried about missing my job interview.

And I'm worried about Mikhail. I didn't get to contact him after work. I've been missing for a day. Surely, he would know to tell the cops about Sodorov. Surely, someone is out there looking for me.

It's too much to hope for, to be rescued again. He's rescued me too many times already.

Peter stands and walks toward the bed. I stiffen as he touches my arm with his fingertips. "I miss watching you dance, Reggy. Will you dance for me like you did when we first met?"

"I was getting paid to do a job," I say, not daring to move. I think I'm barely breathing. "It wasn't for your benefit."

"But it was for a while, though, wasn't it? When we started fucking? When you accepted my money to solve your mom's problems?"

"You make me sound like a prostitute, Peter. I thought you cared for me. I thought you were being kind. I didn't know it was money from Henri Sodorov until you told me later. Which I would never have accepted if I'd known it wasn't your money to loan." *Motherfucker.*

"So naïve," he says, clucking his tongue. "Come on, do a little dance for me? I'll talk to the boss. Maybe he'll let you stay here. Work off your debt."

I shake my head furiously, and he grabs my throat, leaving me clawing at him, gasping for breath.

"Listen," he snarls, "you got yourself into this. You'll pay off your debts either way."

There is nothing good in him as he bares his teeth at me like a rabid animal. My vision gets spotty before he finally shoves me back. I fall in a heap on the bed, willing myself not to cry, throw up, or to show any sign of weakness.

"Just remember, I offered you an option," he says as he walks toward the door. "If you're a God-fearing person, you might want to say your prayers. I don't think Sodorov will keep you as a pet. Not for long anyway. You're too small and delicate to survive him. He's a brutal fucker when he takes a girl to use."

He locks the door from the outside. The outside. Which means I'm not the only person who's been stored here, awaiting his or her fate. There's no reason to create a cell if you rarely have people to imprison.

My thoughts are a jumble, my head's throbbing, and my throat's on fire, as I lie there where he left me. Terrorized and numb and alone. Eventually, though, my eyes do close, and the darkness mercifully takes me once again.

WHEN I WAKE for the second time, I know exactly where I am.

I force my legs over the edge of the bed, my feet onto the carpeted floor. I will my body forward toward the luxe bathroom attached to my room. I throw up in the toilet, then drink water straight from the tap in the sink. I start the shower and strip off my clothes. There is soap and shampoo and conditioner, and I can't help wondering why a prisoner's cell would be stocked with good-smelling personal hygiene items. I wash my hair carefully, my temple tender and bruised, nearly passing out from the pain and the sight of blood as it stains the suds and disappears down the drain.

After showering, I pull my clothing back on and return to bed. I'm so tired and emotionally drained, I struggle to stay awake. They must have drugged me before. I lie in the strange bed, staring at the ceiling, thinking about Mikhail and how much I wish I could have his arms around me right now. How I wish we'd had more time...

Somehow, sleep comes to me once more.

IT'S COMPLETELY dark when I awaken. I still don't know what day it is, but I'm more alert than I was the last two times I've come to consciousness. My stomach rumbles, and I can't believe no one has brought any food or water. They must really mean to kill me.

The race of my heart and the whoosh in my ears tell me a panic attack is imminent. I crawl to the floor and curl up in a ball, attempting to breathe through it. I can't just sit here and wait for these guys to kill me. I need to get it together. I must find a way out of here.

I crawl on my hands and knees to the window and look out. There are bars, which doesn't surprise me. I think I could shimmy through them, but I'm on the second floor. *There's nothing to grab, even if I got out. Nothing to catch my fall. Come on, Reagan. You're no superhero, but you have to find a way out of here.* I look around the room, trying to stay calm when I feel anything but calm.

"I don't think Sodorov will keep you as a pet. Not for long anyway. You're too small and delicate to survive him. He's a brutal fucker when he takes a girl to use."

No. Do not think about that. You're still alive, you're rested, so—

What's that behind the bed? There's a large HVAC vent hidden in the wall beneath where the bed is. I crawl to it, using my fingernails to unscrew it. They're bloody by the time I finish, but I don't care. I pull the cover from the wall and push myself inside. I fit, but just barely.

Now what?

Now, you're going to figure out a way to get yourself out of here.

26
so much more than like

Mikhail

It's a home game against Toronto, and we're up one goal after playing the whole first period with the starters, apart from a few short sub-ins. It felt good being back out there with the players I know.

The buzzer goes off for the period and we head to the locker room. "I've missed this chemistry, boys," Coach barks at us in his familiar tough-love style. The crowd noise indicates that the home fans have missed it, too. "See what I mean? They've also missed seeing your ugly mugs up on the big screen."

I get his sentiment, but I've been thinking about what Evan and I talked about ever since I left the pub the other day, so I speak up.

"You know, I miss that chemistry, too, but I think I've come around to this new idea. We need to move forward and get the team fully engaged. We need chemistry for the future, not just the now."

Everyone stares at me for a heartbeat long enough to show their surprise that I'm speaking up. And more that I'm in agreement with management. Evan gives me a subtle nod, and I know I did the right thing. Coach says, "It's good to hear from you, Zelly," and then he lays out a plan for the second period.

He mixes things up in the second and third periods, and, somehow, things go smoothly. Maybe what I said helped—though I think it's more likely due to the excessive drills and team building bullshit we've done lately. Still, we win decisively—something that should've been happening all season.

Back in the locker room, it's loud and celebratory. The vibe is so different than it's been, and I can't help but wonder what helped us all turn the corner. I guess just time. New things are uncomfortable until they're not new anymore, right?

Aiden slaps me on the back and congratulates me on my goal in the third period. "You want to go out for a few beers and celebrate? It's been a hot minute since you've had to carry me home."

"Yeah, and I'm still not interested in carrying your fat ass back to the building." I grin at him though.

"It's muscle," he whines, fake pouting. "Seriously, though. Your crazy lady is probably working. Just come out for a while."

I check my phone. No texts from Reagan. I've called a few times and texted a few times. Not enough to be stalkerish, but enough to let her know I'm worried about her. I haven't heard from her since Tuesday afternoon. It's now Thursday night. I've either been ghosted, which seems par for the course with Reagan, unfortunately, or she's busy with her job interview, which she said was today.

"All right." I sigh. "I'll come out for a couple."

Aiden whoops happily, and thirty minutes later, we're at some bar I've never been to.

"Why are we here?" I ask, looking around.

"Cal's fiancée's band is playing tonight," Aiden explains. "They're a big deal now and this is where they got their start."

We all sit at a high-top table just off the dance floor. Right now, someone's playing deejay—badly. A few women come over, congratulating us on our win. Aiden basks in it, the rookie soaking up every speck of attention he can get. A few want pictures with me. One asks if she can sit by me. I mostly ignore them.

The three who have been hovering around us head to the bar, and Aiden lays into me. "What the fuck, dude? Crazy casino lady got you pussy whipped?"

"Maybe," I say, sitting back in my chair, arms folded over my chest. "And she has a name."

"Regina?"

"Reagan," I correct him.

"Whatever. Is she better than Gia?"

"Gia who?" I laugh. "I'd almost forgotten about her."

"So, I'll take that as a yes. I wouldn't peg you for liking the crazy ones, but okay."

"She's not crazy. She's actually smart and compassionate. She's funny. I like her."

As I say it, I realize it's so much more than like. At least, for me, it is. I wanted to provide friendship and security for her, free from attachments. I didn't want her to think I was using her, that I wanted anything from her. But we've gone past that now, haven't we?

The thought of my fingers inside of her, my tongue between her legs—

I have to sit up and breathe to keep my dick from going hard. I want her. And more than that, I care for her. A lot.

Why am I here? I should go to the casino and tell her how I really feel. I shouldn't let her push me away. As much as I wish I could leave now, I don't. And I won't. Before Evan found his girl, he went out with the team...*and maybe that's what I'll need to do more of as well.*

Maybe two beers into the night, the band finally comes out to play, and people go kind of crazy for them. Billie Hirsch, the purple-haired drummer of Love Scrum, and also our goalie's fiancée, is on a meteoric rise to fame in the music world at the moment. We can see Cal up front doing roadie duty or something, totally focused on his girl, as he should be. Dude is kind of strange and abrupt, but he loves playing hockey, and he loves Billie. He can stop a puck like a fucking robot predicting the future, too. Aiden is rambling in my ear about Billie's brother being some A-list Hollywood actor, to which I tell him I couldn't care less unless he tells me her brother was one of the Avengers.

"Nerd." He smirks at me, one of the puck bunnies sitting on his lap now.

The band is good, I have to admit. They play a couple of songs before a lot of the people hit the dance floor, Aiden among them. One of the girls tries to grab my hand and drag me out, but I wave her off. "No, no, not tonight."

As soon as no one is looking, I settle my tab and head out, eager to check on Reagan. When I get to the casino, she's not on the floor. I try the restaurant, but she's not working there either. Finally, I stop by the bar, asking if anyone has seen her.

"Nah," William informs me. "She hasn't been about for at least two days. Raul is cursing her name."

I thank him, tap the bar, and head out, dumbfounded. Where could she be? Maybe she took a few days off to prep for her interview? But it was supposed to be today, right? But still, if she did that, I feel like she would have told me.

Something doesn't feel right. I book it to my apartment building and run the five flights of stairs up to her apartment, pounding on the door. I jiggle the handle, finding it locked. I bang again, pulling my phone out and dialing her number.

It goes straight to voice mail. The texts I sent earlier are marked "undelivered." In fact, as I'm looking, none of my texts since Tuesday night have gone through.

Okay, now I'm starting to fucking panic. We don't see each other every day, but we had been texting or calling nearly every day. And I thought we were past the ghosting thing. We talked about it. I know she can get skittish—maybe her interview didn't go well? Maybe her mom had an emergency, and she went home?

Christ. My heart is beating so hard right now.

I do the only thing I can, which is head back down to my apartment. I make myself some food that I can't taste. I sit on the couch and stare mindlessly at the television until I drift off.

When I wake up on the couch, the TV is still on from the night before with the morning news chattering away. My blood turns to ice when I see the headline scrolling across the bottom of the screen...

Police attempting to identify the body of young woman near Tangiers casino.

I sit up and watch the reporting in disbelief and horror, wishing like hell I was still asleep, and this was just a very bad fucking dream.

The unidentified body of a petite woman with short, dark hair in her early twenties was discovered behind Tangiers casino late last night. The Las Vegas Police Department encourages anyone who might have information about her identity to call the number on the screen.

Fuck. No. No. No...

It can't be...

I'm shaking with fear as I start dialing.

27
not like the movies

Reagan

I don't know how long I've been crawling through the vents. I just know I've been moving slowly so that I don't make noise and attract attention. I also know that it's much easier to do this kind of thing in the movies. The vents in the movies are bigger and cleaner, and these are small and full of dust and don't seem to go to any obvious exit point.

I'm hungry, my stomach a constant drum of the reminder it's been days since I've eaten. I'm so thirsty I want to cry. I curse myself for not drinking from the tap before I crawled into this rat's maze. I think I've fallen asleep once or twice. I'll probably die in here. Which is worse? Dying and rotting in the vents of the criminal's mansion or being sexually abused to the point of death by the same criminal?

I think I've lost it.

This seemed like a good idea at the time, but I have no idea how to get out of here. I just crawl and crawl until, somehow, I've gotten myself back to my own room. I shove myself through the hole to the floor under the bed, lying there for a long time.

When I finally persuade myself to move, I crawl out from under the bed and stumble to the bathroom, slurping water from the sink and washing dust from my hands and face. I trudge back to the bedroom, only to find the door wide open.

Wide. Open.

Someone must have come for me and found me gone. Did they think I'd pulled a Houdini? Did they see the vent cover on the floor beneath the bed? Did they think someone else had come to grab me? I laugh and it's an insane sound, void of any real humor. *Oh God. Now I'm delirious.*

I tiptoe to the door and peek out into the hallway. Finding no one, hearing no one, I make a run for it, down the hallway, past a row of identical, closed doors. I find a door marked Staff Only and push through it, finding a set of stairs. I go as fast as I can on weak legs, holding on to the rail, holding my breath, clinging to any shred of hope I can make it out.

At the bottom, there are two doors, and one of them literally goes outside. I hesitate. What if it sets off an alarm? But I can hear people in the kitchen. So I push and, hearing no alarm, make a break into the back yard.

The lawn is soft sod, well-maintained. It's an odd thought to be enjoying the feel of grass between my toes as I'm running for my life, past the pool, into the vast yard. I stop short at a tall fence. It's tall, built more like a prison wall than a fence for someone's home. It's not meant to be climbed.

I look around desperately, spotting not one but at least two or three cameras.

I'm going to die. This is it. There is no way out. They will spot me on the cameras and come to get me. They'll probably make it extra painful because I tried to escape.

I slink along the perimeter, which is likely futile, since they've surely got me on camera at every angle. When I hear a commotion back at the house, I run toward the pool house, slipping inside. I find a towel bin and open it up, folding myself to fit inside, a dirty towel over top of me.

Outside, I can hear the men yelling. "She went this way!"

They open the door. From inside the bin, I see the flash of lights and hear heavy boot steps. "Where the fuck did she go?" someone asks.

I just focus on not breathing, not moving, not making a sound. The boot steps retreat, the guy yelling "Fuck!" as he trips over something. I hear something fall to the ground as another muffled voice from outside tells him to go back inside and look.

It's not until it goes quiet that I poke my head out of the basket. I'm alone in the small space, taking huge gulps of air, silent tears streaming down my face. And then I see it.

The guy dropped his cell phone. It's face-up on the ground beneath a towel rack. I scramble for it. *Oh, thank God.* It's unlocked.

I dial 9-1-1.

"Nine-one-one, what's your emergency?"

"This is Reagan Marlowe. I'm at Henri Sodorov's

mansion, against my will. I've been kidnapped and beaten. They're going to kill me. Please. Come quickly. I'm hiding in the pool house, but they will find me soon."

"Keep the line open and go back to your hiding place in the pool house, Reagan," the dispatcher says in a steady, calm voice. It helps.

"Okay. I—I'm g-going to be in the t-towel bin."

"Reagan, you can do this. You're brave, and you just hold on now. We're coming to you."

I stay on the line, again trying not to breathe, not to move. I hear footsteps again, but beyond that, nothing else.

Then I hear...sirens.

Alarms go off all around the property. People start shouting and running. I hear cars start as tires squeal. I hear women screaming and shots fired.

When the pool house door opens, I hear a man's voice. "Police. You're safe." But I stay put, not moving until the basket opens, an older police officer peering in, offering his hand. "Reagan Marlowe?"

"Yes, that's me. Thank you," I breathe. It takes everything I have to stand, to take his hand, to step free. My earlier adrenaline rush crashes, and I collapse against him, no longer able to stand on my own.

He wraps me in a blanket and carries me across the property, somewhere, to a waiting ambulance. To precious freedom and safety. *I hope.*

How I hope this nightmare is finally over. That I'm finally free.

28
you like saving people
Mikhail

It's Friday, and I was supposed to have dinner with Reagan tonight. We were going to celebrate success or drink away failure after her job interview. That was the plan.

The plan was not for me to be sitting in a Las Vegas morgue, waiting to identify her dead body.

"Mr. Zelenka?" an older man in a lab coat says from a secure doorway.

I snap to. "Yeah, that's me."

"Come this way, please."

I follow him down a long, sterile hallway, walking in silence. When we enter the morgue, I guess it's about like anything I've ever seen on television. It's cold enough to make the hairs on my arms raise. Smells weird. Several metal tables are scattered throughout the middle of the room. A wall of small, square doors make gridlines from floor to ceiling. Behind each one, the space to hold a corpse.

Please don't let Reagan be one of them.

He opens one and slides out a long drawer. There's a body on it, under a sheet. *Please don't let that be her.*

"Are you ready?" he asks, his hand taking hold of the edge of the sheet.

I frown deeply but nod at him. Fuck you, sir, but no, I'm *not* ready. The fuck is anybody ever ready for this? *Please don't let it be Reagan.*

I have something like an out-of-body experience when he pulls back the sheet to reveal a young woman with a single bullet hole to the middle of her forehead.

I lose my shit. Tears fall from my eyes when I see someone I don't know.

"That's not her." I breathe shakily, bent over with my hands braced above my knees to keep from collapsing to the floor. "Thank fuck, it's not her."

"This is not Reagan Marlowe?" he asks to confirm.

"No. No. No." My head goes back and forth. "Not Reagan."

"Do you recognize this woman?"

I shake my head, wiping away my stupid tears with the sleeve of my flannel. "No, I'm sorry. I don't."

He writes something down inside the shiny metal chart holder, draws the sheet over the dead woman who is definitely not Reagan, pushes the drawer back into the wall, and closes the metal door latch with a clink. He walks me back down the hall, thanks me for coming in, and sends me on my way.

I sit on a bench outside for a long time, trying to pull myself together. That was rough. Could've been a lot worse though. I am relieved, to say the least, but my worry remains. Where the fuck is she?

Back at my apartment, I pace. I can't help it—I just

walk back and forth, probably scuffing the crap out of the flooring with my boots. I try sitting, watching television, but I can't concentrate. I get back up and pace some more. The local news starts breaking with a story of a raid on Henri Sodorov's remote Las Vegas mansion complex. Details are sketchy at first as it's just developing, but some information comes through, along with images of very young women being led out of there among cop cars and emergency vehicles surrounding a ritzy looking walled compound. A sex trafficking bust at the Russian crime lord's crib, perhaps?

Looks a lot like it.

Could Reagan be mixed up in that fresh hell?

Why won't she answer her phone?

Probably because she doesn't have her phone.

I must finally succumb to emotional exhaustion because when I hear a knock at the door, I'm lifting my head from the kitchen table. I jump up and run to the door, flinging it wide open.

There's a police officer. But there is also Reagan.

Reagan, wrapped in a blanket, hair a mess of dust and debris. Reagan, with a blooming bruise on her temple and angry, red marks on her neck. Reagan, who cries as soon as she sees me, stepping into my arms, sobbing into my chest as I pull her close.

"She wanted to come here first instead of her place," Officer McNabb explains. "You her boyfriend?"

I look down at her. We haven't had this discussion yet. I don't want to do this without her consent, but I still answer, "Yes," because that's what I want to be.

"We're going to have more questions for her," he

says, handing me a business card. "Whenever she's ready, just have her come down to the precinct and ask for Detective Stone. There are still a lot of pieces to put together, but there were other women at the compound. All locked in rooms. And we think Sodorov is connected to the recent casino murder."

I feel sick at the memory. Thinking that was Reagan. I just nod and thank him. He tells me to have a good night and heads off.

I hold her there, just inside the doorway, for a long time. Finally, though, I detach from her, set the business card he gave me on the entry table, and lead her into the bathroom. "Let's get you in the shower."

Reagan is running on empty, barely able to hold herself up. I pull off her sweatshirt and sweatpants, her underwear and bra. When the water is warm, I take off my own clothes and help her into the shower. She immediately slides to the floor, sobbing. The only thing I can think of is to wash her. So, I lather her hair, carefully inspecting the tender injury on the side of her head. With the soap, I lightly wash her body, scrub her dirt-caked and bloody fingernails, and take note of the bruises on her arms. Her feet are covered in scratches that the paramedics obviously didn't deem a problem, although given the bandages, there are more that were. *Fuck. What happened to her?* I massage her shoulders, and she relaxes enough to lean back against me, her head against my chest, her eyes closed.

After a long time, she lets out a strange little laugh and says, "I guess I didn't get the job with the wedding planner. You know, on account of not showing up to the interview."

"There will be other interviews. Other opportunities." I kiss the top of her head.

She doesn't answer. I know she must be in terrible shock, but she needs to go to bed and rest.

I stand and help her to her feet, turning off the water. Wrapping her in an oversized towel, I pick her up and carry her to my bedroom. We crawl under the covers together, still a little damp, and I pull her to me, wrapping my arms around her tightly.

"I was so worried about you," I whisper against her neck. "I went to the morgue." A long, tense pause feels very loud in the strange silence between us. "Cried like a baby when I saw it wasn't you."

"I'm so sorry you had to experience that, but it could've been me," she says after a long moment, sounding very detached and weirdly calm. "I haven't eaten since they took me. They never brought me any food, and I had to get water from the bathroom sink. I think they might have meant to kill me."

"Let me get you something. I'll be right back and then you can tell me what happened to you."

One vanilla protein bar, Vitamin Water, and a few Advil later, she starts talking. Her voice is clear, but the weight of the world weighs heavy on her, I can tell.

It nearly breaks *my* heart to hear her talk about her ordeal, but I sense that she has to tell me as much as I have to hear every horrible word of her story.

"Henri was at the casino, eyeballing me all Tuesday night. His minions were there including the one you beat up. Peter was there. I asked Raul to move me, to protect me, and he refused. I changed in the locker room, thinking I could sneak out after my shift without being recognized. I took the front way, grabbed a cab, but one of them slid in with me, put a gun to my ribs. I was just starting to text you when he hopped into the cab with me."

I growl at this image. Literally, growl like an animal. *I wish you would've called me when they first showed up.* I don't say this to her out loud, of course, she's a wreck right now, but I sure as fuck think it. Why didn't she call me from inside the casino?

"We rolled up to this mansion out of town. I tried to run, but they pistol-whipped me. Knocked me out. When I came to, I was in a bedroom and Peter was there. It wasn't…good. He was threatening and mean and even choked me to scare me into breaking, but he wasn't s-successful," she says with a shaky voice, like she's remembering more than what she's telling me about her encounter with *Peter.*

That shit-stain motherfucker is so done bothering you. Again, I keep it to myself and just press my lips to the side of her hair to keep her talking.

"When he left, I tried escaping through the vents, but I couldn't find a way out of the maze. It brought me right back to the room where I was being held, but the door was left open like they'd been in there and found me gone. So, I just ran. I ended up hiding in a laundry basket in the pool house and by some dumb luck, one of the guards dropped his cell phone. I used it to call nine-one-one. The operator told me to leave the line open and stay hidden in the pool house laundry basket, so that's what I did."

"You're a hero." I kiss her head again. "You got out of there. And saved other women, as well. I saw it on the news. They were bringing so many women out of that house tonight."

"I don't feel like a hero, but I'm glad they have something on Sodorov now."

"What happens next?" I ask carefully.

She sighs. "They arrested Sodorov and some of his guys, but I doubt they'll stay behind bars for long. He'll post bail or some overpaid attorney will get him off. He'll get out someday and I'll always have a target on my back because I was the one who put him there. And quite frankly, I still owe him money. On top of what he thinks I stole from him."

"I don't think that's true anymore. They know you didn't steal from them. And they know that because a petite young woman with short dark hair was murdered in the alley behind your casino last night. I went to the morgue to ID her. She stole the money. And they figured out it was her and then they killed her. You told me she looked like you."

And she did look like Reagan, from a basic perspective of age, body type, and hair style, but thank fuck she wasn't. I will never forget the look on her face, a bullet hole clean through her forehead without any other mark on her body. Her dead eyes sightless and dull, her head jostling slightly as her drawer was slid back into its refrigerated compartment. *God help me.* That woman from the morgue will be in my nightmares forever now.

"Well, that's both horrible for her, and only a little bit better for me, but not by much. I still owe like twenty-thousand dollars from what I borrowed through Peter."

"You know I have a multi-million dollar a year contract with the Crush, right? I have investments. I'll take care of your debt with that douchebag ex of yours. Fuck him. Peter Pellton won't be bothering you ever again. And Sodorov most likely has a one-way ticket back to Mother Russia, because they're gonna either indict him or deport his ass, so you really don't have to worry about him, either. And you can stay here with me where you're safe. We can go get your stuff from your apartment and move you in here tonight if you want. You aren't going back to your casino job, are you? I don't think you should work there anym—"

Reagan maneuvers her body to face me and kisses me firmly on the lips. She lays her hand on my cheek and taps my lips with her pinky in a silent gesture to please stop talking. I was laying it on thick with the demands, so I'm sure she'd love for me to shut my mouth. I never talk this much, but this is fucking important, and she needs to know all of it.

Also, I know I'm not going to like whatever's coming out of her mouth next.

"You're the most wonderful man I've ever known, Mikhail Zelenka, but you can't always be my personal savior."

"I'm not trying to be your savior. I care about you, and I want to help you."

"I know," she answers softly. "And you do, by being my friend. By being one of maybe two people in this world who care what happens to me."

"Rea-gan—" Everything I want to say to her gets caught in my throat. "But isn't it obvious to you that I want to be more than just your friend? What we have is more than just friendship, right? For me, it *is* more."

She kisses me again, which turns into her hand dragging slowly over my chest, making its way down a path to my cock. She grips me, strokes me, as I kiss her neck and work my thumb against her clit.

She moans and it brings me back to my senses. I can't fuck her when she's injured and traumatized. Sex is not what she needs right now. So, I pull away and roll to my back before slipping off the bed and turning on the bedside lamp.

"I want you, always, but you need time to heal. And we need to talk about this."

"About what?"

"About all of it." I pull on a pair of boxers from my dresser drawer. I toss her a T-shirt and she pulls it over her head. "About what needs to happen to make you feel safe again. About the fact I just said I want to be more than friends and you didn't respond."

Her eyes well with tears. "Mikhail, I am not your problem to solve."

"You know that's not what I'm saying at all."

"You have a career," she says with a sad shake of her head. "A good one. And you've earned that money. Why would you throw it away like that?"

"I don't see it that way. I see it as freeing you from all this bad shit that's holding you back. I see it as giving us a chance to be together without all this ugliness getting in our way."

"And you like saving people."

I open my mouth and then shut it again. "I can help you. *I want to help you.*"

Reagan slips to the floor, holding out her hand to steady herself. She manages to square her shoulders and stand upright, her chin sharp as she raises it almost defiantly. "I need to figure this out for myself, Mikhail. I have to help myself for once."

"You have been," I argue. "You work so hard."

She puts up a hand to stop me. "I won't let you do this. This is my problem. I need to be the one to solve it."

She shuffles to the bathroom and grabs her pile of clothing, pulling on the sweatpants and balling up everything else before heading out of my room toward the door.

"Why are you pushing me away again?" I ask desperately, my feet holding me like lead weights to the floor.

"I'm not pushing you away. I'm protecting you."

"Protecting me? From what? Why are you really doing this, Reagan?"

"Because I care about you, Mikhail, and this is what I need to do. I'll text you—oh shit—I lost my phone. I'll get a new one or something, but I'll figure it out and be in touch, okay?"

I don't respond, and I don't look at her, the floor becoming my point of visual attention.

After a moment or two of silent tension, I hear the front door open and then close.

Sounds I don't want to hear.

She's gone again. I only just got her back, and now?

"I'm not pushing you away. I'm protecting you."

It's bullshit, that's what it is.

And I feel my heart breaking into pieces.

29
silver & golden events

Reagan

I realize I have no keys. I think I may have left them in my locker when I was trying to make a fast getaway from the casino, so that gives me some level of relief, but I still have to trudge down to the office to ask the building manager to let me into my own apartment.

I know I need to eat something more, but I'm so, so exhausted. It's all I can do to grab a box of crackers from the counter before I collapse onto my couch. And I can't eat anyway. The threat of a desperate cry is lodged in my throat, my chest gone tight, because I am a big jerk. I'm a big jerk who just hurt a man I care deeply about.

In time, the ugly cry does come, and it gives me a spurt of angry, frustrated energy. I rage around my apartment, crying and screaming and talking to myself. I was on my way to tell him my feelings. I was going to tell him I wanted more. And here he is, telling me he wants it too, and I'm pushing him away. He's not wrong. No matter how I frame it, this is on me. I'm the one giving up something good.

But I can't go back. I can't grovel and tell him I was wrong and that I very much *do* need his help. I'm going to figure this out for myself. I will think this through and come up with a plan. I should go back to Mikhail only when I'm clear and free to be normal, to live a normal life.

He deserves better. I want to be better than this for him. And for myself. Because I can't live like this anymore. Living in fear has fucked me up and made life into a daily trauma. But most of all, I hate that I'm leaving Mikhail hanging when he's done so much for me. Again.

There's no other choice though.

I start throwing things into a duffel bag. I pull on some halfway-decent clothing, make sure I'm presentable enough for public viewing, and head out, locking up with my spare key. I book it to Tangiers, slipping in through the back door unnoticed, finding my wallet and keys in my locker as expected. I definitely can't face Raul right now. *What if he'd listened to me? Made sure I was protected?* No, I can't think about it anymore. My time at Tangiers is done. That much *I know.* My cell phone was lost somewhere in the kidnapping, but whatever. I hail a cab out in front and instruct the driver to take me to the airport.

Ninety minutes later, I'm boarding a flight to Columbus, Ohio. I fall into a deep sleep as soon as the plane lifts off the ground.

I do not dream.

My mind is silent.

Like it just needs dark and quiet for a time to reset me back to a level of basic functioning.

WHEN I GET TO COLUMBUS, I'm ravenous, so I stop for my favorite pizza on the concourse before walking out to catch a cab to my mom's, shoving hot pizza in my face as I walk. I eat it all, still feeling hungry as we pull up to her house. I wait outside for the longest time, wondering if I made a mistake in coming here. What if she's not doing well and her problems compound mine?

I take a deep breath in and let it out slowly before climbing the front stairs, knocking lightly on her door, artfully adorned with a wreath of eucalyptus leaves.

When she opens, her dark eyes go wide with surprise. "Oh, my baby girl." Seeing I'm about to lose it, she pulls me into a fierce hug—the kind only moms can give. She pulls me inside and takes my bag, tossing it in a corner and leading me to the kitchen table. I sit as she fusses, making tea and warming up food. As I look around, I finally allow myself to take a sigh of relief. The place is tidy. There's nothing lavish sitting around. There are no signs of mania.

As I pick at a bowl of broccoli casserole, Mom asks if I'm okay.

"I need a place to lie low for a while. Is it okay if I stay here, Mamma?"

"Of course. I miss having you here. You can stay as long as you like, but you didn't answer my question. Are you okay, Bug?"

I've been avoiding her eyes, trying not to lose it, but I look up and see the concern there, and the waterworks start up all over again. I shake my head. "No, I'm not okay. But I need to rest before I can talk about it."

She reaches out to take my hand across the table, and it takes me right back to that restaurant, with Mikhail holding my hand, not judging me as I told my story. My heart hurts so badly I want to claw it out of my chest. Why do I have to mess up good things?

I eat a little bit of the casserole, at her insistence, and then head back to my old bedroom to crash. And crash, I do.

When I wake up, it's the next morning, and I've slept for something like eighteen hours. The smell of coffee, bacon, and eggs fills the kitchen as I shuffle out, still in the same clothes I was wearing yesterday.

My mom hugs me, her familiar scent and the weight of her body against mine, a huge comfort in my wretched state. "Whoo, girlie, you are ripe," she says with a wave of her hand.

I'm sure. The last shower I had was at Mikhail's, and I don't even know how many hours or days ago that was because the calendar has escaped me at this point. "Sorry, I'll go hop in the shower."

She grabs my hand to hold me in place and gives me a squeeze. "I made some breakfast. Figured it would bring you out of your coma. Grab a bite and then you can get cleaned up."

I nod and take a seat as she loads up a plate for me —a plate I aim to completely ravish since my appetite has finally returned.

"So, my darling, I don't want to push, but I am curious what's going on with you," she says after I've eaten a good portion of my food.

I think for a moment. Where to start? Sometimes it's best to just unload all at once. And for better or worse, I feel Mom is in a place mentally where she can handle the truth now. It's time.

"Well, I was abducted on Tuesday. I was pistol-whipped and strangled, and pretty sure I was going to die."

Mom's mouth hangs open. Shuts with a tilt of her head. Opens again. Shuts again. I take this as a sign to keep talking. So, I tell her everything about Henri Sodorov, about the case of mistaken identity. I tell her about how I borrowed a crap-ton of money from a guy I was dating just so I could stop stripping, only to find out it was Sodorov money. I tell her how trapped I feel. I hated the casino, but I had to make these payments and still be able to live. I tell her Sodorov is behind bars for now, but who knows what will happen down the line.

"How did you get into so much debt? Why would you need to borrow so much money?" she asks in confusion.

"Mamma, how do you think you still have possession of this house?"

She still looks confused.

"My junior year, you had a particularly rough patch. Do you remember?"

She frowns. "Only vaguely."

"Yeah," I say with a bitter laugh. "Well, the car was repossessed, and the house was about to foreclose. You lost your job and had no way to pay for any of it, in addition to racking up a bunch of credit card debt. I came home and got you into short-term treatment, back on your meds. I consolidated things. I made deals with creditors. But there were some things that needed to be paid right away and neither of us had it. I took a job at a strip club to make some fast cash, but it wasn't fast enough. I met a guy and we started seeing each other. He offered to help, and I unwisely borrowed the money from him. Flash forward to now and here I am."

I can see the whole array of emotions my mother processes as she takes in the info dump I just dropped on her. She often doesn't remember things she does when she's in the throes of a manic episode. I don't expect her to remember, and I didn't want her to know what I did. Her mental health has been so volatile that this kind of thing could have really set her on a spiral at certain low points in her life. *But it's time I give her my truth. I'm allowed to do that.*

"All of this…is because of me?" she asks in a clipped voice.

"It's a choice I made, Mamma. To help you. It's not your fault."

"But it is, though," she says sadly. She makes a face like she's swallowed something rancid.

"No," I say firmly. "It's not. You were not well, and I did the best I could to help. Taking that loan was my own stupid fault."

My mom's name is Audrey. My grandma named her after Audrey Hepburn. She kind of looks like her namesake, I guess, with her pale skin and super short dark hair. She's always been slim and pretty, even when she's crying or raging or having a mental breakdown. And now, as she processes the reality of this thing I did for her, she loses it. I mean, loses it. She sobs uncontrollably, her face splotchy and red. I've never seen my mother look like this, like she's really feeling a real and true emotion that isn't tuned into paranoia or anxiety or some other mental health frequency.

I let her get it out. And then I go to her side, putting my arms around her, telling her that things are going to be okay. She keeps crying, saying she can't believe someone would hurt her baby, that she hates what her struggles have done to me.

After a long time, when she's back to calm, I tell her the most important part. "You know, I think that I'm a stronger person because of all of this."

"Well, I'm sorry that I did this to you."

"You didn't do anything to me, Mamma. You've been sick and I love you. I wanted to help."

"If I'd been med-compliant, maybe..."

We go back and forth like this for what seems like a very long time.

I let her process through all of it. The regrettable emotional salad that must be dealt with while just telling her again and again that it's not her fault. That I love her. That she means the world to me, and I wouldn't change my choices because it was the right thing to do—helping her.

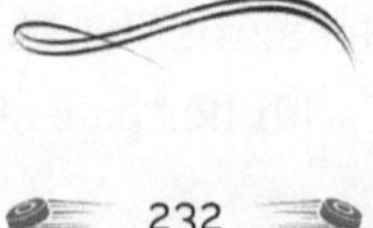

WHEN I'M in the shower, I think of Mikhail, of course, and how he washed me so lovingly after my ordeal. And it occurs to me that I am not so different from him in how I've helped my mom. That he would jump in to help someone he loved in the same way. He'd do whatever was necessary. He's told me this—so many times—that he doesn't see us as so disparate from one another. That he thinks I'm strong and compassionate. And worth saving. Worth protecting.

In my mom, I see the same thing. I see someone worth protecting, worth helping. She has a mental health disorder, but it's only a small sliver of the person she truly is. My mother has taken in friends and even the kids of friends who needed a place to stay. She's always volunteered at community events for charity. She has always supported me in what I wanted to do, even when it hurt her. She is kind and caring, and she loves me.

Later, once she's calm enough, she wants to know the details of what I did to take care of her finances during that manic period. I walk her through everything, meticulously recorded, and show her how everything gets paid and managed now that she is on disability benefits.

"I'm so sorry I disappeared," she says. "I can't believe you did all of this while you were still going to school. Where was I?"

"It's fine, Mamma."

"No wonder you didn't ever want to come home these past couple of years."

I shrug. I didn't want to come home. It worried me too much. What if I'd come home to another crisis?

Another financial wreck? I don't say any of that, but I know she understands.

"I've been stable for a long time now, Reagan. I have a good doctor and we've found a nice combination of medications. I have my moments, here and there, but therapy has made me more aware of the signs. There are people I trust who help me reach out for help as soon as they notice I start doing something that seems out of the ordinary."

"That's great, Mamma. Really great."

"I know this is the way of this disease," she says, looking over the paperwork I've put in front of her. "It cycles. It comes back. So I can't say I won't have another episode in this life. But I am committed to staying on my medication, to staying connected to my doctors."

I stare at her, my face caught between a cry and a smile. "I love you, so much."

"As I love you, my darling daughter. I bless the day you were born and chose me to be your mamma."

"I NEED to get a replacement for my cell phone," I tell the T-Mobile rep at a kiosk inside Columbus Towne Center. "I lost it in an accident."

Shea at T-Mobile gets me set up in no time and sends me on my way with a brand-new phone covered by my replacement plan. My first call is to one Detective Stone at LVPD using the card Officer McNabb gave to Mikhail when he took me home. I saw the card sitting there by his front door when I left.

Just remembering my emotional state as I was leaving, with Mikhail begging me not to go, takes my breath away as I wait for the call to connect.

As I'm sitting on a bench at the food court inside the mall, the gruff detective tells me they have my phone in evidence, but it seems to have been run over by a vehicle. It probably fell out of my pocket or hand when I got out of the cab. He asks why I didn't stay in Vegas for questioning, and I tell him I needed to see my mom. I get an earful about leaving, but I end up answering his questions over the phone and promising to check in at the police station as soon as I return to Las Vegas.

My second call is to the wedding planning company, Silver & Golden Events, in Henderson. The person who was supposed to interview me, Veronique, is dubious when I tell her why I didn't show up for my interview.

"I'm so sorry, Veronique. There was an emergency completely out of my control. My phone was lost in the chaos. It's taken me a few days to recover. I would really like the opportunity to interview if the position is still open. This is what I went to college to do, and I don't want to miss an opportunity. I'm a hard worker and I'm ready for the next chapter. I hope you'll consider giving me another chance."

"You know, I don't usually give second chances," Veronique says. "We're in the business of making dreams come true and we don't get second chances on wedding days. Our reputation is built on delivering what we have promised, and on exceeding those expectations."

"I know. And I would be so thrilled to be part of building that for your clients. Please, just a chance to come in and talk about the opportunity."

She's quiet for a long pause, but then she speaks. "Okay, Reagan. I feel like I can believe you, that you really did have an emergency. I'd still like to take a chance on you. Let's schedule another interview."

Oh, thank you, God. Maybe, just maybe, my life is turning around for good.

LATE AT NIGHT, alone in my room with my new phone in hand, I get brave enough to face all the texts and voice mails Mikhail left while I was missing. It's hard for me to acknowledge just how much I've hurt him by always pushing away after letting him in.

But face it, I must.

Once everything downloads from the Cloud, I read his texts first. The early ones are the usual short messages and emojis we use with each other, mentioning his game schedule or meetups at the gym. He sent one on Thursday morning, wishing me luck at my interview. And another that night asking how it went. He sent one on Friday morning, reminding me we were supposed to have dinner that night to celebrate success or drown our sorrows, whichever fit the situation.

The voice messages are worse, not because of the words, but because I can hear the worry and concern in his voice. He doesn't say a lot, because he's not a chatty guy in person or on the phone usually, but I can hear the worry loud and clear even through those few voice mails he left for me.

Then everything stops after Saturday when I left Las Vegas. After I pushed him away for the last time. But then I see he's left me a text with no message—just a song attachment, dated yesterday.

"Breath" by Breaking Benjamin.

I hit the link and listen as the song starts to play on my shiny new phone. I sit there frozen as it plays, my guilt for the hurt I've caused him only growing stronger as I listen to what the words say:

> *You take the breath right out of me*
> *Left a hole where my heart should be*
> *You got to fight just to make it through*
> *'Cause I will be the death of you*
> *This will be all over soon*
> *Pour the salt into the open wound*
> *Is it over yet?*
> *Let me in*
> *So sacrifice yourself and let me have*
>   *what's left*
> *I know that I can find the fire in your eyes*
> *I'm going all the way, get away, please*
> *I'm waiting*
> *I'm praying*
> *Realize, start hating*
> *You take the breath right out of me*
> *Left a hole where my heart should be...*

The tears come as I hit single repeat, so it'll just play over and over. I figure the punishment is what I deserve, listening to the angry words of a song that demonstrates to me very clearly just how much I've hurt him. Even more, made him mad at me, something I've never really felt from Mikhail before. I've pissed off Mr. Hockey good and truly, and that's a terrible thing to do to the best man I've ever known and probably will ever know.

I send him a single text.

> Mikhail, please believe me when I say I'm so terribly sorry for everything I've put you through. You didn't deserve any of it. I'm only safe because of you, and when I can, I'll be home soon. xo R

I try to suck it up when he doesn't reply.

THE WEIGHT on my shoulders feels lighter already, just being away from all the bad consuming me over the past two years.

Reconnecting with my mother is probably the best medicine of all. Doing simple things together. Just accepting the love and support from another person throughout the day and knowing they'll still be there for you (and you for them) tomorrow and the next day, has helped me tremendously.

Mom and I have been taking long walks around the old neighborhood, visiting with people and their dogs and families walking with babies in strollers. I've even introduced her to the basics of kickboxing, which is hilarious, but she's into it. We watched *Wonder Woman* one night, and all I could think about was Mikhail and his encyclopedic knowledge of the DC and Marvel universes. How he would explain Wonder Woman's backstory to me, wanting to help it all make sense for me.

One night, when I turn on ESPN to watch the Vegas Crush playing in New York, Mom turns to me.

"You haven't mentioned your hockey friend since you've been here. Something I'm missing, Bug?"

"Well, there's not much to say. He's a wonderful man, but we'll only ever be friends."

"Which one is he again? It's hard to tell with their gear on."

I point to the screen. "He's the left forward—winger, I think it's called—for the Crush. I'm such a crummy friend though. I've been so wrapped up in my own craziness that I've barely asked him about his stuff."

"*He's* your friend?" she asks, as Mikhail's image and stats pop up on screen. "That hot, professional hockey player is your friend?"

I laugh. "I know, it's *insane*."

"How did you meet him?"

"Well, first I accused him of being a creeper, when really, we just work out at the same boxing gym and live in the same building. Then, he saved me from a bad guy in the alleyway. We've been friends ever since."

I'm purposely picking at nonexistent lint on my shorts to avoid my mother's gaze. She is fully present these days and, therefore does not miss the slight blush that heats my cheeks.

"Friends," she repeats. "What kind of friends?"

"Um," I hum.

"Is it serious?"

"No, it hasn't been." Then I sigh. "Well, he'd like it to be. And I think I'd like it to be, but I keep telling myself he doesn't deserve to get stuck in this web I'm in. You know?"

"Well, he's a grown man, Bug. Shouldn't that be his choice?"

"I suppose." I think about her words. "He's a really good man. Kind of on the serious side. His dad was a pro player, too. A very famous one, from what I gather."

"Oh," my mom breathes. Then, "Ohhhh. The Great Zelenka. That's his dad?"

I pull a face. "You've heard of him?"

"When I was younger, I went to hockey games with my friends. He was quite the hockey poster boy back in the day."

"Well, I think he might be quite the asshole in the now. Mikhail seems to feel oppressed by him."

"I can imagine it's hard to live in the shadow of someone like that."

"I don't think he does, though. I think he's quite good on his own. Mikhail told me he started for the Crush in his rookie year."

"That's a rare feat. Well, maybe his father pushes him too hard? Makes him feel inadequate?"

"I think that's more like it," I say. "He's very serious

about the game. But he also has a thing for superheroes. Movies, comics."

"It sounds like he's worth getting to know."

"He's been a great friend." Even to my own ears, my voice sounds wistful. When I meet Mom's gaze again, she's wearing a knowing smile. "I think I'm in love with him."

"I can tell."

I blush again and focus on the game. I don't know much about hockey, so my mom, of all people, walks me through the rules as things happen. I ogle Mikhail through the television and wonder just how, amidst all this chaos in my life, I have managed to fall in love.

I just hope it's not too late for me to let him know.

30
weird clubs

Mikhail

The Crush are on fire tonight. I've scored twice in two periods, and we're playing full subs. Whatever hiccup there was between all of us on the team seems to have dissipated. Everyone is *playing like a team.*

Which is good because I really need something to keep my mind off Reagan.

Who I haven't heard from since she left, except for a single text apologizing for hurting me and letting me know she was safe and coming home soon.

I know she only sent the text because I was a dick and sent a song letting her know just how she was making me feel. It wasn't my best moment, and the lyrics are kinda mean, even though they're spot on with where my emotions have been.

For an entire fucking week.

I still worry about her. And look for her everywhere I go. She hasn't been back to the Tangiers for work, but William from the bar told me she cleaned out her locker. I'm not sorry she quit her job there though. It wasn't a good fit for her, and there are better jobs out there where I know she'd be a lot happier.

I did take care of a couple things on my own, whether she likes it or not. It's already done. And I won't apologize for helping someone I care about out of a serious problem when I have the means to do so.

With Boris and Viktor's help, who hooked me up with a fixer in Vegas who deals in such things as handling payoffs to the degenerate fuck who dared to put his hands on Reagan and threatened her with being sex trafficked or murdered (her choice).

DEBT PAID IN FULL—

The message Saul Heisenberg had delivered to Peter Pellton in his jail cell via a picture of Reagan with a second message written on the back and signed by me.

YOU DON'T KNOW REAGAN MARLOWE ANYMORE. FUCK WITH HER AGAIN AND FIND OUT. YOUR CHOICE.
—MIKHAIL "MR. HOCKEY" ZELENKA

So yeah, I did that. I know people now. And I *always* keep my promises.

But then, a few days after settling Reagan's debt through Saul Heisenberg, more news came out. Henri Sodorov was found unresponsive in his cell where he was being held before his arraignment. No video to show what really happened to him, either, because his guards were conveniently absent when it all went down in the early morning hours.

The fucker is dead.

Didn't even make it a week before someone unalived him in what's being called a suspected suicide/poisoning? That someone was not me, of course, but kudos to the mastermind who handled it, whoever they are.

The Vegas crime boss probably knew too many names and where all the "bodies" were buried so to speak. Probably had too many connections with high profile clients who didn't appreciate the very noisy federal raid on his compound. Doesn't matter why he was taken out, or by who. The important thing is Henri Sodorov got what was coming to him.

Saul Heisenberg assures me all the backroom books are wiped clean of Reagan's name, her debt, of her existence even, and that's all I care about. Whoever takes up the helm of the former Sodorov crime syndicate won't even know about Reagan Marlowe. She is free to move on with her life now.

Not very superheroish of me to be thrilled at the death of a person, I realize, but maybe it was on second thought, if I righted a wrong and protected someone I love from a literal bad guy.

Even though I'm still fucking pissed at her, I've accepted where I'm at with my feelings.

Which is flat out in love with her.

Even if she doesn't love me back. Or can't, or whatever.

I've learned you can't help who you fall in love

with, and that goes both ways. Even when they hurt you, it may not be on purpose and only because of the circumstances they're in. At least, that's what I tell myself to get through the days until she comes back—

"Let's go, muthafuckahs, and get Zelly his hatty in the third!" Evan busts through my deep thoughts in the locker room before delivering a few hearty slaps to my back with his big mitt.

Time to head out to the ice and finish off this game.

In the third period, we just keep dominating. Cal is not letting a damn thing through, and our defense isn't letting much get that far anyway. Boris is hungry, ready to prove exactly why he's called the Ice Dragon. He takes three rapid-succession shots on goal. One goes wide. He grabs it, jukes a Boston defenseman, and takes a second shot. It hits the goalie and bounces back, and he's right there again. *Boom.* Third time's a charm, and it's in. The horn is loud and obnoxious, but everyone in the arena is also loud and obnoxious. In short, it's awesome. Boris's face is huge on the jumbotron, and then the screen changes to his girlfriend, Talia, blonde and bespectacled, and the genius financial manager for a lot of guys on the team, including me. She blows a kiss to him from the stands, which he returns right back to her by way of the jumbotron in full garish Las Vegas style, complete with a cartoon dragon giving an air kiss with hearts floating around his head.

No hat trick for me tonight, but we finish four-zip, a shut-out at home, with a full tank of gas on the ice and on the bench. Coach comes in with our GM, and they tell us that this is what they've been waiting for. Tyler and Georg dump a bucket of ice water over Grant's head. And all over his expensive suit. I can't help but smirk about it.

"Hey, you're smiling!" Aiden says. He points and yells, "Hey, everyone, Zelly's smiling!"

I roll my eyes and shake my head, turning back to my locker, but the grin just gets wider. Sometimes, I forget how fun this game can be.

"You up for a celebratory drinkie-drink?" Aiden asks.

"Nah." I tap him on his pec with my fist. "I'm good. But you have fun."

"Lame, Mik, so very lame," he scolds with a slow shake of his head.

Evan claps me on the back, his British coming through as he tells me, "Fine work out there, my lad." There's a new understanding, I think, between us. I still don't speak up a lot to the team, but I do speak. Not just with words but with my play.

I walk home, as usual, ready to find some chow and try to relax with a movie. But as I step off the elevator, I see a small familiar figure sitting cross-legged in front of my door.

I think it's the most beautiful fucking sight I've ever seen in my life.

She stands as I approach, dusting off the front of her jeans. "I expected to find an eviction notice when I got back, but management tells me an anonymous person paid up my lease for the next three months."

I shrug. "Nice person."

"*Very* nice." She grins. "I've missed you."

I've missed you, too. So much. But I'm wary about the hope spreading through me. Cautious she's only here to say a final goodbye.

I unlock the door and invite her in. "Where were you?"

"I went home to see my mom for a while. I'm sorry I didn't check in."

"I tried calling for the first couple of days, but it just went straight to voicemail."

"I know." She sighs and pushes her lips together.

"Reagan, I don't think I can keep doing this, you know? You keep bailing on me." It's all I can do to not pull her to me. To kiss her, and more. I still want her. I still care for her deeply. And knowing she's here and safe? It's everything. I think I might be able to actually sleep tonight. But I'm also still raw from believing she was dead in that morgue, from the constant back and forth. And what I've said is true. I can't keep doing this. Getting close and then pushed away will fuck me up worse than I already am.

"I know I hurt you when I left. It was wrong of me not to keep in touch with you. I should have told you where I was, but I had some things to figure out. With my mom. With my life. And I didn't want to hurt you or your career."

"My career has *nothing* to do with this."

"If there had been word that you were involved, even peripherally, with Henri Sodorov? A criminal? You don't think that would tarnish your reputation in hockey?"

"*No*," I snap. "I'm not a criminal. And neither are

you. What's there to be afraid of? Especially now the fucker's dead."

"I guess that's really the difference between us. You live in this bubble. You have money and people know who you are. They care if something happens to you. You go missing for two days? The FBI will be out looking for you. I go missing for two days?" Her arms flap out helplessly.

"You go missing for two days and there's this hockey player who goes to the morgue, hoping and praying it's not your body he has to identify. He stays up for nearly two days straight, worrying and pacing." I shove my hands through my hair and groan. "You're killing me, here. We go back to the same arguments over and over again. Yes, I'm a pro athlete. Yes, I have money. Yes, I grew up with money. Stop using those things against me. I am who I am, and you are who you are. And you're worth knowing. I want to know you more, but you keep running away."

Reagan's shoulders slump. "I know. I know I do. But I'm done running away. Now, I'm running toward something."

I look up, still wary but hopeful.

"I had an interview today. This morning. The company I was supposed to interview with before everything happened with Sodorov. And guess what?"

"What?"

"I got the job!"

I force a smile, but I'm quite sure it doesn't register as authentic. Because I am happy for her, but I'm also disappointed. Disappointed that she hasn't yet realized that all these barriers she's putting up between us are a construct. They're excuses to avoid getting closer.

"That's great," I say flatly. "Congratulations. Now you can start to move on with your life. Use that college degree and do what you've always wanted to do."

There's an awkward moment between us. Me, checking my phone. Her, hunching her shoulders forward and a strange, shy look on her face. "I know it's late," she says with a dip of her head, her long dark lashes starkly contrasting against her cheekbones. Her beauty is perfection to me. I could look at her for hours and never be bored.

"Yeah. I'm whipped. We had a game tonight."

"I know. I watched it from my apartment. You scored twice. I watched your game at New York from Columbus, too. My mom, as it turns out, was a fan of your dad back in the day. Who knew? She totally schooled me with her knowledge of hockey."

I let out a huff of a laugh. "That's cool." And it is cool that she's having fun learning about hockey, but I do *not* want to talk about my dad right now.

Reagan opens her mouth, but nothing comes out at first. She licks her lips and looks around the room, then seems to focus again. "There's something else I learned when I was in Columbus."

"Okay."

"I...um...well, I think—I *know*...I love you."

I feel my face open up in surprise as my heart goes on a roller coaster ride. "But you just gave me seventeen reasons this can't work."

She laughs. "I did not give you seventeen reasons. I

just said I—Never mind. Look, I'm a dummy. I was a shell of myself the past couple of years, but you helped me fill in the lines again. When I'm with you, I feel like I can be a person again. A real person, with interests and goals. I've laughed again, smiled again. And you don't diminish me. You encourage me to be strong. You remind me that I'm strong."

"I sound kind of awesome when you put it like that." I can't help the grin I feel on my face.

"Cocky bastard." She does a sexy eye roll that slaps my little brain down below wide awake. "But yes, Mr. Hockey, you are a kinda awesome superhero dude. Who, despite my best efforts to resist, for your own good, mind you, I've fallen in love with. In case you missed it the first time around."

I step forward, pulling her to me, filling the space between us. My hands cup her cheeks as I lean in for the briefest of kisses. "I didn't miss it the first time around, but I really liked hearing it come out of your pretty mouth twice." Holding her face to mine, I whisper against her sweet cherry lips, "Mr. Hockey fell in love with you a while ago."

She bites back a smile. "I knew it."

"Now who's cocky?" I ask, but it's kind of cut off as she jumps me, wrapping her arms around my neck while my hands grip under her ass to hold her off the ground. She feels so fuckin' good against me again. She buries her head against my neck but then pulls away to look me in the eye.

"I'm so sorry for being stupid, but mostly for hurting you."

"I forgive you. And I'm sorry for trying to fix your problems all the time."

"That's not something to apologize for. I know you just want to help. And I know you think I'm capable and smart because you've told me so."

"I do think you're capable and smart. And really fucking gorgeous."

She blushes and I'm fully hard in an instant. I want to see if that blush spreads anywhere else on her gorgeous body. She wiggles against me and grins when she finds my erection saluting her right between her legs. "At least one part of you is completely happy to see me."

I set her down, reaching for her hand, ready to guide her to the bedroom. "All parts of me are happy to see you. But you know, we can still take this slow, if that's what you want. We can still love each other without a label or whatever."

She smacks me on the shoulder with her free hand. "No way, buddy. I read up on the Hockey WAGS website. There's a whole club and I want in."

Laughing, I lead my girlfriend to the bedroom.

"We have other business to attend to before there will be any joining of weird clubs, babe."

31
i'd like a gift

Reagan

One month later.

Well, this is awkward.

I'm in the stands at the ice arena, watching the Crush play their second game in a best of seven. It's playoff season, and the Crush are, according to Mikhail, in good position to win the Cup again. On my right are Jozem and Maria Zelenka, Mikhail's parents. On my left are his sisters, Iliana and Daniella, and his nephew, Roman. Me, smack dab in the middle of a family I only just met last night, over an uncomfortable dinner at an overpriced restaurant.

Maria is very sweet. She has an infectious smile, which is made even brighter next to her husband's stoic expression. Jozem Zelenka is as intimidating as I'd imagined. He has a hawk's eye on his son's every movement on the ice. I can tell he's making a mental tally of every perceived mistake, every missed opportunity. Even when Mikhail scores, which he has twice in this game, Jozem never smiles. Zero celebration of his son's accomplishments on the ice from the man.

Iliana and Daniella are both beautiful and dark-haired, like their brother, but their personalities are very different. Iliana is quiet, like her brother, serious. She's career-focused and will have to return to the East Coast for work on a red-eye that leaves tonight after the game. Daniella is a little wilder, it seems, a little less focused. She dotes over her son, who clearly looks up to his uncle. She tells me she's taking classes at a community college while she works at a coffee shop.

"You'll be joining us for dinner after the game, yes?" Maria asks as the third period begins.

"I'd be happy to join you. Thanks."

When the game ends with a Crush win, we all head out to a waiting town car. I offer to stay behind to wait for Mikhail, but they tell me to jump in and that he'll meet us at the restaurant. I guess he has to do a media thing. I'm still learning about the business of hockey.

At the restaurant, Daniella and Roman order appetizers, while Jozem literally sits at the head of the table, writing notes in a small notebook. I look at Maria for explanation, and she says, "My husband is a fierce competitor to this day. He likes to write down his notes so he can share them with Mikhail later."

Mikhail arrives about thirty minutes behind us, wearing a collared dress shirt and gray slacks, per the dress code for game days. He's ditched his jacket and tie, but he still looks yummy. I'm enjoying the dressier side of his wardrobe, as he's required to wear a suit and tie to the arena for games. It's a whole thing with the media filming the players arriving in their custom suits. He favors athletic gear or more trendy flannels and boots when it's not a game day, which is how I always saw him before we officially got together a month ago. He usually wears a leather bracelet on one wrist—a gift he tells me came from his sisters this past Christmas. I love everything about his style—from his hair to his many tattoos, to his clothes, to his stoic expressions. He's the perfect man wrapped in a perfect package, for me.

"Hey, sharp dresser," I say as he takes his seat beside me after kissing me on the top of the head.

"Ugh," he grunts. "I hate those stupid press events."

"Those stupid press events put your face out there to the world," Jozem says. "The fact that the press gives a shit about you is important. If they didn't care to speak to you, you'd know your relevance to the game."

Mikhail sighs next to me. I put my hand on his knee beneath the table just to show him some support and that I understand.

"Roman," Mikhail says, trying to change the subject without creating conflict, "did you have fun at the game?"

"It was a blast. Two goals for you, Uncle Mikky," Roman says with a couple cute fist pumps. "My hockey team sucks."

"Stinks," Maria corrects. "Don't say naughty words."

"Mama," Daniella interjects. "Sucks is not a naughty word."

Maria's pursed lips show that she feels otherwise. The ensuing silence at the table opens up another opportunity for Jozem, who tells Mikhail that he felt his reactions were slow tonight, his passes sloppy. He recaps about six different plays as we eat our dinner, telling his son, in precise detail, the ways in which he would've played differently, for a better result.

Mikhail just nods through it all. He just takes it, not taking the bait, not fighting back, barely looking up at his father, who clearly has no regard for his son's feelings. I feel so bad for Mikhail. *This is exactly what he meant when he told me about his dad.*

No matter what Maria or Daniella do to try to change the subject, Jozem stays laser-focused on Mikhail and on his game play. It actually makes me lose my appetite.

The waitress comes to take our plates and asks if we want dessert. Roman says yes, obviously, but Jozem firmly says, "No one needs those calories." He takes the check and slips his credit card into the sleeve, handing it back to the server.

Mikhail seizes the moment, standing abruptly. "You know, I'm pretty beat. I think we're going to head out."

I look at his parents and at his sister, not sure what to do. Mikhail holds out his hand to help me up from my chair. "Thank you for dinner," I say, smiling at Maria and Daniella and winking at Roman. I can't bear to really look at Mikhail's dad. He's oppressive even when silent.

Maria looks like she might cry. Mikhail stops to kiss his sister on the cheek and to give Roman a bear hug from behind with a buzz to the top of his messy little boy hair. Then he steps behind his mom's chair and puts his hands lovingly on her shoulders. He leans down to kiss her on the cheek and whispers something in her ear before turning back to me and leading me out of there.

He still stays quiet out on the sidewalk as he hails a cab. When one pulls up to us and we slide inside, he's finally able to let his feelings out. He puts his arm around me and tugs me close to his side, burying his head at my neck and breathing in. "I fucking hated you witnessing that. I'm sorry, babe."

"Why don't you stand up to him?" I ask honestly. Mikhail is a strong person with strong convictions. He does nothing on a whim, so it surprises me to see him overpowered by someone else like I witnessed tonight at dinner.

"The man lives for hockey. Everything else is secondary to the game. His wife. His kids. I'd be shocked if he even knew his grandson's birthday. Someone with that much focus, and who's had that much success? He doesn't give a shit what I have to say. No one is going to change him, so why bother wasting my breath or emotional energy on an argument I can't win?"

He has a point, I suppose. Still…"It's sad that he can't see you as your own man, your own player. Does he expect you to recreate his career or something?"

"He sees me as an extension of his reputation. Anything I do that's bad tarnishes how people see him."

"Does he treat your sisters the same way?"

"No. He does not. He's sexist that way. It was assumed I would play, but he's never pushed them, even though girls were definitely starting to play when we were growing up."

"But Roman plays hockey. Does your father push him, too?"

Mikhail laughs. "Ah, that'd be a big, fat no. Daniella would kill him if he pulled that bullshit with her kid."

"Family dynamics are weird," I comment. "I don't have siblings, so this was interesting."

"That's one way to describe it," he says, chuckling as we pull up in front of the building. He tosses way more cash than necessary up to the driver as we unload. "But welcome to my world."

Once we're inside his apartment, he says, "Thank you for being there tonight. I do hate that you had to sit through that crap with my dad, but I loved that you got to spend time with the rest of my family and they got to meet you." Mikhail pulls me in for a kiss. And another. And another. "So they could see for themselves how special you are."

My heart swells, having the support of this man. I wrap my arms around his neck, and he picks me up, carrying me into the bedroom. Off goes my dress. I take my time unbuttoning his dress shirt, running my hands over his chest and abs. I undo his belt and pants, savoring the unwrapping of this amazing specimen. "What a gift you are," I murmur, mostly to myself.

"Is that right?"

"Indeed, it is, Mr. Hockey." I stare at him, my beautiful man, admiring that exceptional part of him he'll have inside me soon.

"I'd like a gift from you." He tilts his head at me, his stance wide with his pants undone but still on his body, muscled arms folded across his bare tattooed chest, and his cock hard and gunning for me.

"Oh? What might that be?" I lick my lips at the thought of his cock in my mouth and how he feels when he's there.

"Probably not what you're thinking." He smirks wickedly.

"Well, put me out of my misery and tell me then." I lick my lips again and wait.

He groans under his breath, but then just says it in a rush, "Move in with me. That's the gift I want from you. Live here with me. Starting tonight."

Definitely not what I was expecting him to ask for.

I step closer to him and slowly look up his body until I reach his dark blue eyes, which are laser focused on me, and deadly serious. "Well, then, I say yes to that. I will happily give Mr. Hockey his gift because he deserves it, but mostly because I love him to infinity and beyond."

"Thank you, Reagan. And the Buzz Lightyear quote was a cute add."

"You're very welcome, Mr. Hockey. I try."

"Careful, now," he growls, but with a smile

underneath the growl. "You're going to give Mr. Hockey a big head."

I grip his cock and stroke it from base to tip with extra attention. "It's already pretty big as it is."

His response is to kiss me, hard, as he backs me against the bed. We end up on the mattress, Mikhail shaking off his shoes and pants, me nearly desperate to tear his boxer briefs away, to fully free him. He bites my nipples through my lace bra, rubs my clit through my satin panties. I'm moaning, my hips moving wildly, heat pulsing through my core as he works me to a frenzy.

When he pulls away my bra and underwear, I'm wet and ready. I open my legs wide for him, letting him see every bit of me. He buries his tongue in between the folds of my pussy, savoring, sucking, licking. When he adds his fingers, I nearly come on the spot. It's so good.

"Mmmm, Mikhail, I want you. Fuck me. Please."

He backs away, and I nearly cry at being left without his touch. He grabs a condom and holds it up in question. Always the gentleman, never assuming consent. "We don't need those anymore," I tell him. "I'm protected, and I need you to come over here and fuck me, *please.*"

His mouth quirks up in a very pleased with himself half-smile as he puts on a show of tossing the condom over his shoulder to fly across the room. When he positions himself between my legs, the vibe changes. This time, he kisses me softly. Tenderly. "I want to make love to you, Reagan. I don't want just a quick fuck. I want you to know how much you mean to me."

If that wasn't enough to make me self-implode, the slow burn of friction as he moves inside of me might. He holds my hands above my head as his powerful body moves slowly, leisurely, his hips pumping in and out at a pace that makes the buildup last forever. His eyes never leave mine, his lips dip to touch mine, his tongue tasting my bottom lip, his teeth nipping at my jawline.

I'm lost to him, to his love making. Good definition. It's exactly what he's doing—making love to me. When I come, it's long and luxurious—a trip to another place, another dimension. Endless. He rides the wave with me, his kisses deepening, whispering, "I love you, Reagan," in my ear.

I explode, a second orgasm that's nearly violent in the way it makes my hips rise. His cock dips deep inside of me, and he groans, picking up the pace.

"Fuuuck. What you do to me, woman."

"I love you, too. I love you, too."

It's like my mantra, a chant I can't stop repeating.

"I love you, too, Mikhail."

He pushes my legs back, nearly folding me in half to take him deeper.

His kisses are fierce and devouring, like he can't get far enough inside me to satisfy himself.

I love being loved like this by him.

And when he comes inside me for the very first time, it's with a very deep love and on a roar, my name falling from his lips over and over and over.

Reagan...
Reagan...
Reagan...

32
26 years is probably enough

Mikhail

Another month later.

This was not a championship year for the Las Vegas Crush. We lost the seventh game in a tied final series to Columbus, of all teams. Columbus, a team that hasn't won a Cup in, like, forever.

There was a silver lining though. I flew Reagan out to Columbus for games three and four and got to meet her mom, Audrey, and visit her childhood home. I can see where Reagan gets her feistiness from and have a pretty good idea how she might look in another thirty years or so. Still hot.

Two seconds after we were introduced, Audrey pulled me in for a bear hug and whispered in my ear, "Thank you for saving my baby. I can never repay you for that, but I'm going to try my best, son." She called me *son* and welcomed me as an honored member of the family. It was nice to be appreciated for something other than hockey or my namesake for once. But on my merits as a decent human. First time for everything, I guess. Either way, Audrey Marlowe and a guest will have standing tickets every time the Crush come to Columbus to play hockey.

Now we're all hanging by the pool at a private resort, the owner, Max Terry, blocked off for us to celebrate the end of the season. I'm stretched out on a lounge chair, Reagan between my legs looking sexy-as-fuck in a turquoise bikini. Aiden sits next to us, chattering about his plan to go teach kids how to play hockey in New England for the summer.

"I'm going to get a weird, Reagan-shaped tan line, babe."

"Too bad. Don't be vain," she replies.

"With hair like that? There's no other way to be," Aiden jokes.

"He does have very pretty hair," Reagan says.

I roll my eyes and flip Aiden the bird.

It's been fun introducing Reagan to my world. She was shy at first, but her personality has been coming out more and more as she gets comfortable meeting my teammates and their significant others. She's already been chatting with Tyler's fiancée, Zoya, about their wedding plans. She's on her way now, and I'm so proud of her.

Scarlett and Viktor wander over and I take the opportunity to introduce her because I know Scarlett has been on maternity leave with her second kid and wasn't traveling with the team during the playoffs. "Scarlett, this is Reagan, my girlfriend."

"Hiya, Reagan," Scarlett says. "Where did you come from?"

"She spotted me at the boxing gym and thought I was stalking her," I explain.

"I punched him in the jaw once," Reagan adds proudly.

Viktor grins. "He probably deserved it."

"What do you do for a living, Reagan?" Scarlett asks.

"I'm a wedding planner at Silver & Golden Events. But only for the past couple of months. I used to croupier at Tangiers."

"Oh yes, the Tangiers." Scarlett is nodding. "I worked there for a bit a few years back myself. Did double duty in the Crush PR department while I was busting my ass serving drinks at the casino before I met Viktor."

I can feel Reagan relax when she realizes there is someone else here who changed their career path. I know a little about Scarlett's story and I think she and Reagan would connect.

Max Terry gets up and taps a half-empty glass of some kind of fruity-looking drink. Coach Brown and the GM, Grant, join him. They all take a minute to talk, each of them saying how unique a season this was and how proud they are of our ability to work through discomfort. It's taken a couple of years to successfully build a full roster of players who all feel connected to the mission.

"And damn," Max Terry says, snapping his fingers. "We came so close again this year."

As Coach Brown is talking about the growth he's seen this year, my phone rings. I sigh and roll my eyes.

"Your dad?" Reagan whispers, missing nothing in my body language.

I nod and crawl out from behind her, walking off to take the call.

"Yeah," I answer once I'm out of range of the party.

"Congratulations on a nothing of a season," he says. "You all wasted so much time dicking around with line changes and new formations this year that you forgot who you were. You let it all slip away…"

I pinch the bridge of my nose between my fingertips, closing my eyes. *More insults. More ranting.*

Enough.

All I feel is fury.

"Stop. I'm so done with this."

"Done with what?" my father asks. "Hockey?"

I scoff. "No. I love hockey. You haven't beaten that out of me with your constant negativity, at least."

"My negativity?" Like he's unsure what I mean. "I believe I've only been providing feedback to make your play better. I just want you to be your best."

"You don't give two shits about me, Dad. You're worried about not having your legacy tarnished. I've never been good enough. Never been enough, period. And I never will be. I see that now."

"Son, you're letting your emotions cloud your judgment right now. Tread carefully. Think about what you're saying before you open your mouth again."

"Why? Because you don't like to hear the truth? Sorry, I'm done keeping my mouth shut just to preserve the peace. I've tried living in the shadow of The Great Zelenka, but now I'm done with that, too. I'm just going to live my own life. Make my own way. And I'm going to play my own game. If I want your advice, I'll ask for it. Otherwise, please just keep your opinions to yourself."

Then I hang up on him.

I have never done that. I've never told him off like that, either. *Never* have I ever gotten in the last word on one of his ranting calls.

Shaking, I head to the restroom and wash my face, staring in the mirror, seeing so much of my father's face there, sans the neck tats. I cock my fist, ready to smash the image but gather my wits before doing something very, very stupid.

"He does not control you," I tell myself in the mirror. I've spent years reminding myself of this. I was thrilled to move out West, just to get farther away from him. Today, though, it actually feels true as I say it.

I spend the rest of the party with a dull roar in my ears, halfway present and halfway still in the conversation as I process what I just did. You simply do not talk back to Jozem Zelenka. You just don't. If I were a kid, it would've meant extra drills on the ice, or heading to bed without dinner, even if I'd just burned off a day's worth of calories at practice. I learned not to argue because not arguing meant survival. It meant that there would be a tentative peace.

But have I done the right thing? It felt right.

Triumphant in the moment. *But what does it mean for my family?*

In the car on the way home, I stare out the window, holding Reagan's hand on the leather seat of the town car Max Terry ordered to shuttle us.

"What's wrong?" Reagan asks. "You seem agitated."

I lift a shoulder. "I don't want to talk about it."

"Was it the call from your dad?"

I pull my hand away. "I'm fine."

"You seem fine," she murmurs.

I don't know how much time passes, but she gets my attention when she puts the privacy glass up between us and the driver. She crawls on the floor in front of me, unzips my shorts, frees my cock.

She strokes and licks, watching for my reaction. I'm pretty sure I just scowl, but she's undeterred. "I'm trying to distract you, dummy. Let it go. Just focus on me."

I can do that.

I focus on her mouth around my cock, red lips parting to take me in. I watch as her cheeks turn pink under my scrutiny. I see her eyes go dark with lust as she finds her rhythm, feels me harden fully.

Reagan is just so gorgeous. Her skin is porcelain, her eyes dark as stone. Her hair is a slick bob to her sharp chin. She's small, with beautifully proportioned breasts and narrow hips. I worried, the first time we were together, that I might break her. But now I see her strength. I see how powerful she really is. Not just physically—though her workouts have certainly resulted in some lean muscle—but mentally, emotionally. She has complete control over me. Especially now, as she takes my cock deep into her throat, moaning as she fucks me expertly with her mouth.

I put a hand on the back of her head, guiding her to go faster, to take me deeper. One hand at the base of my dick, she digs the nails of her free hand into my thigh. My hips arch up and I come wickedly hard. She licks some more, swallows it down, takes her time finishing.

Laying my head back on the seat, I close my eyes as she zips me back up and crawls into my lap, her arms around my shoulders, her face buried at my neck. *What did I ever do to deserve this warrior princess?*

We stay like that the rest of the way home. We don't talk, and I don't feel any less angry, but I love her for making me feel good and forget for a little while. I plan on returning the favor at my first opportunity.

As soon as we get home and step inside the apartment, I have her sundress over her head and her bikini top on the floor. I tear the suit bottoms from her body. Moments later, I'm naked, and she's on the kitchen table. My cock is in her, no preamble. I fuck her, hard, and she begs me, "More. Deeper. Please, please, please."

When I feel close to coming again, I pull out, pulling her roughly to the edge of the table, shoving my tongue in her cunt, adding my fingers as she writhes, her hands digging into my hair. I don't let her come though, and she cries out in frustration at me when she's close and I pull away.

I pick her up and take her to the couch, pushing her over the arm so her ass is exposed. I finger her from behind as I kiss her neck and take her mouth with my tongue. She moans and cries out for me, begging me to fill her, to fuck her. It drives me wild, my cock so hard I think it might break.

My hands on her hips, I give her what she's asking for. I fill her. I fuck her. I own her beautiful body until she's coming around my cock, her pussy contracting, squeezing, begging me to come along with her for the ride.

And I do.

I come brutally hard, pumping myself through an intense orgasm that has me growling and gritting my teeth as I unload every last drop inside her.

There are no words as I pick her up and take her into the bathroom to clean up. No words as Reagan takes my hand and leads us to the bedroom. No words as we curl up together, skin against skin, our hearts still beating wildly.

"I love you," I finally say in the dark quiet.

"I know. And I love you, too."

But what happened?

She doesn't even have to ask the question out loud for me to know. It lingers between us, pressing into the dark quiet of the room.

I have to swallow a few times before I can form the words. For so many years, I've lived in my silence. I haven't had anyone to offload my frustrations with, so I'm used to internally processing with no outlet to articulate my anger. *Instead, I've been such an asshole to so many for so long.* But now, I'm no longer alone.

This woman loves me. She's selfless and kind. And it's okay for me to share my burdens with her. "I hung up on my dad today. I told him I was done with his criticism. I told The Great Zelenka I needed to make my own way as a player. As a man."

She doesn't speak for a long time, but when she does, it's exactly what I need to hear. "I'm proud of you. I know that can't have been easy."

"He called it a *nothing* of a season. Only negative things to say. I guess I finally had enough."

"Well, twenty-six years of it is probably more than enough," she says with a soothing caress of her fingers through my hair.

"Let's say twenty-three years." I try to lighten the mood. "I started playing when I was three."

She huffs angrily. "Who shits on a three-year-old for not being good enough at hockey?"

"My father had very specific expectations of me. You know what his new thing is? He thinks I'm worthless because I haven't played on an Olympic team. I mean, fuck. I can't fucking win with this guy."

"I'm so sorry, but I think you did the right thing today. I'm sure you just lost your cool, but this was a long time coming. He needed to hear you find your voice."

I don't say anything in response, but I think about her words. Eventually, Reagan's breathing evens, and I realize she's fallen asleep. I should sleep, too, but my mind won't shut down.

He needed to hear you find your voice.

That really sticks with me, but it mixes in with my worries about how my mother will react. Does she know I stood up to him? Will she take his side and ask me to apologize?

It's a long time, and a lot of anxiety, before I finally fall asleep. And the only thing that gets me there is the woman beside me in our bed.

Who loves me for no other reason than for *me*.

33
going for the knockout

Reagan

I adjust the straps on my dress and tap my fingers nervously on my thigh beneath the table. I picked a nice, but not too expensive, restaurant with outdoor seating. The sun is beating down in a way that makes me wonder if I'll regret choosing to sit out on the patio.

I see Mikhail's parents walking down the sidewalk and stand up to wave at them. They make their way through the gate and offer me polite hellos before taking their seats. I could throw up, I'm so nervous. I wanted to speak with them alone, without Mikhail, and here we are. But in no way did I ever expect them to fly to Vegas to meet me in person.

"How are you, dear?" Maria asks after we've ordered drinks and food.

"I'm okay. And you?"

She gives me a sad smile. "We're okay, too."

When I called to talk to them, Maria mentioned she knew Mikhail and Jozem had argued. She was the one who suggested a trip to Vegas, an in-person attempt to smooth things over. I can see that this rift causes her pain. Jozem, on the other hand, sits stoically, looking at his phone.

"So, Reagan," Maria says, "When we last met, it was a little chaotic. With the games and our daughters, we didn't get to learn much about you. I remember you went to UNLV. Are you from Las Vegas?"

I shake my head. "No, I'm from Columbus, Ohio."

"What made you decide to go so far west for school?"

"I wanted to do wedding and event planning. They have a good program here, and I figured there would be plenty of jobs in the Las Vegas area."

"And you do work in that field now, as I recall?"

"I do. I had a hard time finding something at first. I had some debt to pay down and the jobs in my field weren't paying as much as my job at the casino, so I just stayed put. But now I'm working for an awesome company. I'm learning a lot."

"That's lovely. It's always nice when you find your passion. Mikhail caught the hockey bug early. He's always been very focused. His sisters wanted nothing to do with the sport. Are you a fan?"

"I confess, I had never watched a single game before I met Mikhail."

"Sometimes it seems Mikhail has not watched a hockey game in his life, either," Jozem mutters.

I glare at him. This is the exact reason I decided to talk to them—this callous, demeaning dismissal of Mikhail's career and accomplishments. *Oh my God, what is his problem?*

"Let's let the young lady talk, shall we?" Maria says to her husband.

Jozem stares at me, an expression of distrust on his face. "So you did not know who he was when you met?" His expression is hard. He's handsome like Mikhail, but he lacks the warmth his son has in abundance.

"*Jozem*," Maria says, a touch of scolding in her tone.

He means, I realize, to ask if I am a gold digger who went after his son for his money and fame. I'm so shocked that I can hardly formulate a thought in response. However, this opens up the opportunity for me to say what I came here to say, so I steel myself and look him in the eye.

"I did not know who he was when I met him. I wasn't familiar with hockey any more than knowing it was a game played on the ice before we met. I mostly just worked and went home. I'd just started working out at the gym. Those were my three places. Work, home, gym."

"You don't have to explain yourself, dear," Maria says softly.

I shake my head. "No, I'm not. I mean, I'm explaining myself for a reason. When I met Mikhail, I was not in a good place. I had a lot of debt from trying to help my mother, who has a mental illness. I grew up without my father for most of my life, and with my mother's challenges, I had to make things happen for myself if I wanted them to happen at all. I worked to get scholarships for school. I worked several jobs to assure my mom's needs were taken care of. And I suffered for it. I made some unwise decisions and I paid for them, nearly with my life."

I am *not* going into that detail with them here, but I still have nightmares. Sometimes even feel Peter's hands squeezing around my neck. But Mikhail is there to hold me and remind me how blessed I am now, which helps the bad memories to fade. I'm reminded every day of my superhero and what he did to wipe away my debt to Sodorov to give me a fresh start. To get me disconnected from that world once and for all. Not because he loved me, but at first because he wanted to help a friend. I don't think it's possible to even express to his parents how much in awe of their son I truly am. How he not only saved my life, but he made it possible for me to *live*.

Maria looks over at me with sympathy and concern, while Jozem tilts his head at me, his harsh mask of politeness in sharp contrast to his wife. I take a sip of water first and then a deep breath to prepare myself for what I must say.

"But then I met Mikhail, and he was my friend when I really needed one. He helped me in so many ways. He helped me to believe I could see the sun again."

"What is your *point*?" Jozem asks, his voice making me jump.

"My point is, Mikhail grew up with a silver spoon in his mouth. He was born a crown prince of hockey, right? The Great Zelenka's only son. But he didn't have to take that path. He could have rebelled. He could have done anything with his life, but he chose to follow in your footsteps. The problem with following in someone's footsteps, though, is that you never get the chance to make your own path."

"My son has the makings to be better than I ever was." Jozem's voice is steady and his eyes cold. "He just needs to listen to me so that he can achieve higher."

"He needs to listen to himself." I'm surprised at how assertive I sound, but when I look over at Maria, her eyes are wet with tears. She dabs them with her napkin before reaching to take my hand. She doesn't say anything, but the way she looks at her husband tells me she doesn't have to say anything. It gives me more courage.

Jozem lifts his chin, defiant, arrogant, but I continue. "I've heard the things you've said to him. I can't imagine spending twenty or more years taking that kind of abuse from a person who is supposed to support and love me. And he never said anything, until just recently. He did every drill, went to every practice, listened to every rant. And he just took it."

Maria says, "Maybe that's enough for today." It comes out small. I know she just wants this conflict to end. My guess is it's because she thinks no one ever wins an argument with Jozem Zelenka. Well, I'm not giving up.

"You know," I say after taking another sip of water and another deep breath, "my mother couldn't hurt me the way you hurt him. Not even when she was at her most lost, her most manic. And you're his father, so I assume you only want the best for him. You've just said as much. So, I can't understand why you don't get that he's not a machine. He's not some robot that you can program to do what you want him to do. It's too much, and he's a human with other interests. He likes superheroes, he takes cooking classes and he boxes in the gym. And he takes the game seriously. He's not out partying and whatever. He's really focused on his fitness and his nutrition. He got a starting position at *nineteen*, his first year in the pros. And he's retained it all this time. He told me it was the reason he chose to wear the number nineteen in his first NHL game. I bet you didn't even know that. Mikhail is proud of his accomplishment. What, about any of it, doesn't make you proud as well?"

Jozem doesn't speak. Our food comes, and I can barely eat, my anxiety kicking in. What if I've done more harm than good? What if I've made his parents hate me?

Maria cries silently through the whole meal. We just sit there, eating. I can't taste my food. I've said my piece, and I've probably made a mess of things, but you know what? Mikhail would do this for me. He would stand up for me.

Once we've finished, Jozem pushes away his plate and looks around for the server. I intercept the bill, though. "I won't allow you to pay." I meet Jozem's gaze as steadily as I can. "I had hoped that we could talk, that you would see reason. And I've offended you, so I apologize, but I love your son and I was hopeful today that maybe you would hear me and understand the thing he needs most is a father who supports him, not a critical, merciless coach. He has a coach. He needs his dad. A dad who doesn't make him feel like he's nothing more than a projection of his father's great legacy. Mikhail will build his own legacy without the benefit of yours, if he must. It'll be on you if you're not there to be a part of his journey."

Something flickers across Jozem's face. It nearly looks like regret. "Thank you for the meal." He pushes his seat out and stands. "Maria."

Maria and I both stand. She pulls me in for a hug. As we part, I look at them both and say, "Thank you for listening."

I take a cab back home, but wish I'd been able to walk the miles instead, because I need to drain away all the tension inside me from facing off with The Great Zelenka by way of a long, hard workout. *Boy, do I need it badly.*

I hope Mikhail isn't home so I can change out of these clothes and get to the gym before telling him what I've done.

But it's not to be when I find him right in the doorway as I'm unlocking the door. He looks me up and down. "*You* look amazing," he says, holding the door open for me.

"Thanks." I step inside. "I was, um, out to brunch with your parents."

His mouth drops open. "I'm sorry, did you say you were out with my parents? As in, Maria and Jozem Zelenka are here in Vegas?"

Smiling ruefully, I give a nod. Mikhail's eyebrows draw high onto his forehead. "Why?"

"Well...um, I may have called them and asked them to talk."

"About..."

"I maybe, might've told your dad he's too hard on

you and that you're not a robot and that he needs to stop being a critical coach and just be a dad. Let you make your own legacy and not have to carry his." I wince, expecting him to be mad.

But again, and not for the first time, Mikhail surprises me and does something totally unexpected.

He barks out a laugh. Not mad at all, but looking rather...happy? "Holy shit, you are incredible. And brave. I can't believe you took him on like that. Alone."

"Your mom was there. I wasn't alone."

He makes a face. "She probably cried the whole time."

"She did. She held my hand, though. And she hugged me."

"My mother used to try to argue with him, but I think she gave up on that when she realized she'd never win."

"Well, what's done is done." I sigh heavily. "They probably hate me now."

Mikhail pulls me into a hug, resting his chin on top of my head. "Well, first of all, my mother doesn't hate anybody. But second of all, thank you. No one has ever done that for me before. Coaches, friends, other parents...they all saw him do what he does, and no one ever told him to back off or go easy on me. And here you are, a tiny prizefighter going in for the knockout to be my champion."

"I confess I never would have had that kind of courage before the thing with Sodorov. Before I met you."

He backs away only slightly, not letting go. I look up at him, and heat blooms low in my belly. What a beautiful man. I still can't believe he's mine sometimes. And the look in his eyes…I know I did the right thing. I'd do it again. For him, I'd do just about anything.

I stand on my tiptoes to kiss him, and it's sweet at first, soft. Quickly, though, I feel him stirring beneath his basketball shorts, and I reach down, rubbing up and down over his cock through the fabric.

He cups my ass and picks me up, pulling us together as my legs wrap around his hips. The hardness of him hitting me right where I need him to be, creating the most delicious friction against my clit. He bites at my jaw, and I moan, desire overtaking all other thoughts of past mistakes with crime bosses, tyrant fathers, crying mothers, or anything else at all except for my Mikhail.

But a terse knock at the door brings us crashing back to reality.

34
takes one to know one

Mikhail

I know it's them before I even open the door. And in spite of knowing, my heart still feels like it beats out of my chest as I brace myself for the onslaught. *My girlfriend is disrespectful. I'm a disappointment. He raised me to be a king and here I am, just a joker.*

Reagan smooths her hair and the front of her dress. Her cheeks are pink, her luscious nipples hard through the thin fabric.

"I'd rather ignore the door and fuck you until you can't remember your name," I growl, pulling her in for one more kiss.

She groans and points toward the door. "You can't say things like that to me when your parents are on the other side of that door."

Another knock, this time more impatient, and I know I have to abandon lust and deal with reality. I started this by telling him off in the first place. Now, I need to finish it.

I open the door and bow with a flourish to my father, a sweeping gesture to welcome them into my home. My mother grabs my hand and squeezes before walking right over to Reagan. They hug, and my mom puts her arm around Reagan's waist, pulling her in tightly, showing her allegiance.

I back away slightly, toward my kitchen. "Can I get you two anything?"

My father steps forward, shutting the door behind him. He doesn't answer my question. My mom doesn't answer my question. Instead, the two women who mean the most to me just stand there, watching my father and me engage in some sort of mental showdown.

My mom clears her throat and says, "Jozem," in a tone I rarely hear her use with him.

He looks at her, at Reagan, and then again at me, shoving his hands into his pockets. "Mikhail," he begins, his accent thicker than usual, "I know you feel I've been hard on you. I know you have not always liked hearing my feedback."

"Dad." I put my hand up to stop him. "If you've just come here to hand me some bullshit about how you pushed me so hard because you loved me, you can just head on back to Detroit. I'm not interested."

"No, I did not come to say anything like that, son."

"Right, yeah." I chuckle darkly. "Because I'm pretty sure I've never heard you tell anyone you loved them. Sorry, that was my bad."

"Stop, son, please." His voice is far less commanding than I'm used to, and I realize he's out of his comfort zone. "Yes, I wanted you to achieve at a high level. I wanted you to be better than I was, and anything less than that, for me, would have been a disappointment."

My hackles rise again, and I huff at him, ready to tell him to get the hell out of my home if he can't act like a decent human being.

He makes a face, and sensing my impatience with this conversation, he says, "Wait, please let me finish. I know I pushed you. Maybe further than I should have, and maybe at the expense of our relationship. But I saw so much potential in you. From the beginning, you understood the game. You took to skates as if you were born in them. I wanted to help coax out the brilliance I could see in you. I wanted to see your name beside mine on the list of Greats in our sport. I wanted glory for you—not for me, but with me. *Beside me.* I dreamt of it always."

"I've played hard. I've done well. I'm part of something really good with the Crush. And if I get traded, I'll work hard for that team, too."

"I know that. I see it. You have always had a good work ethic. You have always been serious about the game. And I'd like to believe that I helped develop that focus. So, I won't apologize for pushing you, for wanting you to be your best."

How do I respond to this? I hear him trying. Do I expect him to apologize? Do I expect him to suddenly become a man who says he's sorry or that he was wrong?

And yet, he surprises me.

"I will apologize for making my only son feel like he was nothing more than a projection of my own ego.

I will apologize for making you feel as if I did not care about you. Of course I love all my children. I spent so many hours there with you, more hours than I ever spent with your sisters. I thought you would know, somehow, that I just wanted the best for you, that I believed in your talent so much that I would give much of my time to assuring your success."

My mother is holding on hard to Reagan. Both of their eyes shine with tears. Reagan looks at me and nods.

"Dad—" I don't know what I expected to come out, but all that does is a sigh as I close my mouth again, the words evaporated.

"I hope you can forgive me," he says, looking me in the eye.

This is more than I could ever imagine from him. He has apologized. He has asked for forgiveness. I shove my hand out and he takes it, shaking on this new, tentative truce between us.

"I've never wanted to have conflict with you, Dad." He nods sharply. "And I do want to make you proud."

He looks from me to Reagan, who blushes under his gaze. "That one has balls," he says. "She will go somewhere in her life. You better keep her."

This makes me laugh. It's a new experience to laugh at a joke coming from my father's mouth, for sure. Mom and Reagan both move toward us, my mother pulling me into a hug, then turning to her husband and touching his cheek. She says something softly to him in Czech that I can't hear, and he gives her the slightest of smiles. Another rare thing: my father's smile. It means something, and this one is private—just between the two of them. It shows me that there is genuine love and real respect between them.

Slinging my arm over Reagan's shoulder, I whisper, "You are a miracle worker. My real-life warrior princess superhero."

"Takes one to know one," she whispers back.

My mother turns to me. "We love you so, so much, son, and we are so proud of the man you have become." Then, to Reagan. "Thank you for loving our son and for caring enough to talk to us. We are so grateful."

I offer to take them to dinner, but they have a flight to catch. My father has one of his usual charity events back home, but they felt that it was important to come out and hear what Reagan had to say in person. It goes unsaid that my last words to my father during our phone call left him unsettled. Left me unsettled, too. Despite the endless coaching and criticism, my father has been a constant figure, looming larger than life, since I was very small. The idea of not having him there at all left me feeling more than a little bereft.

There are many more words we should probably say to each other, but this is enough for now.

After they leave, I lock the door and turn to the woman I love. "Where were we, my superhero princess?"

She literally runs at me, leaping onto me, her legs locking around my waist, her arms around my neck, her lips on mine. I stumble back a bit, but get us steadied, my mouth not leaving hers as I navigate us to the bedroom.

She finds her feet and pushes me to the bed. "Take off your clothes," she orders.

I bow my head, grinning. "Yes, princess."

As I strip, so does she, pulling her dress over her head, revealing her beautiful breasts and a tiny, white thong. I could come just looking at her, her full round breasts tipped with their dark pink nipples calling to my mouth. She gives me a sly smile and touches them, pinching the tips, then sliding her hand down beneath the fabric of her panties. She touches herself, and it drives me nuts, not knowing if she's rubbing up and down her pussy or touching her clit.

"Take those off and let me see."

That little slip of fabric is on the floor in zero-point-four seconds.

Reagan stands in front of me, totally bare. Her two fingers are spreading her pussy to expose that sweet button, touching herself, her hips pushing forward as she closes her eyes, moaning in a way that has me stroking my cock like a teenager watching porn.

"Do you like this?" she breathes, her eyelids heavy as she rubs herself, slipping her middle finger into her slick sex.

I can barely breathe; I like it so much. I certainly can't formulate a sentence. My resulting groan is one of affirmation and need.

"Do you want me on top of you?" she asks.

"I do," I answer, huskily, reaching out a hand to beckon her to me. "Come."

She grins and crawls atop my lap, spreading her slim hips wide as she slides down on top of me with a gasp as my cock fills her deeply all the way to my balls. "Ohhh…I will," she says on a breathy sigh.

She moves slowly, at first, my fingers playing at her clit as she cups her breasts, pinches her nipples, her hips moving in a slow, steady rhythm. I could watch this all day, the way her body moves against mine, the way her creamy skin flushes as she grows closer to orgasm.

"You're so fucking beautiful," I murmur, sitting up slightly, taking one of her gorgeous tits into my mouth.

She moans, liking the closer connection, riding me harder, faster, her hands moving to my hair. I keep one thumb working at her clit, the other steadying my balance as she takes total control. I bite and suck and lick those tight, budded nipples. Reagan throws her head back, a gasp escaping as her orgasm crests, her pussy tightening around my cock, squeezing me tight as she rides the wave.

As it subsides, she blinks, slightly disoriented, then grins as she realizes she totally left the planet for a moment.

"Good one?" I ask.

Something nonsensical comes out of her mouth, making me chuckle as I flip us over without losing connection. I spread her wide for me and start to move —slow at first, but then faster as her nails dig into my ass, pushing me forward.

I kiss her long and deep as I sink into her, following her lead. She throws her legs up over my shoulders, giving me deeper access, her arms reaching back to grab the headboard.

"Fuck me, Mikhail. Please, please."

Well, when you put it like that...

I slam into her. She cries, "Yes, yes," chanting at me. "Yes, yes, Mikhail, fuck me. Yessss."

It's all I can do to hold myself back, but as I feel her tensing for another orgasm, I can't help myself from going over the edge. She's coming, and the sight of my cock spearing into her cunt as she makes sounds that can't be described with words sets me off. I follow her, an explosive culmination of pleasure and love washing over me as we both cry out each other's names like ancient prayers.

Collapsing, breathing heavily, I tell her how amazing she is. I tell her I love her so much. I tell her she's the best thing that's ever happened to me.

She rolls over on top of me and lays her head on my chest. "Your heart is beating so fast," she says between heavy breathing.

My hands travel up and down her naked body, dewy with the sweat of exertion. My hands find her ass, cupping each cheek, pushing her hips toward my still-twitching cock.

"I always want you. It never stops for me."

"I feel the same," she says with a press of her lips over the place where my heart beats just below them.

"I can't believe my dumb luck you came into my life, Reagan Marlowe. I mean it. So fuckin' lucky."

She lifts her head from my chest to look at me. "But I was the lucky one. I might not be here, if not for you...my superhero, Mr. Hockey, the love of my life."

A pang slices across my heart but I try hard to push it down. I don't think I will ever forget the terror of believing I'd lost her before I could ever have the chance to tell her I love her. I'll have to learn to use that painful moment for something good, but I don't know what that is yet. I'll figure it out. My alter ego will find a way to make that happen.

Kissing the top of her head, I sit up and carry her into the shower. I hold her and kiss her as the water warms, and when we step inside, she slips her feet to the ground, tossing her head back into the spray as I soap up my hands and gently clean the sensitive space between her legs. She gasps and widens for me, and suddenly, I'm not cleaning her up anymore, but instead pushing my fingers deep inside of her, watching her eyes roll back in her head as she comes again.

"Not done, huh?"

She sighs and moans as I continue pushing my fingers in and out of her, my free hand at her back, holding her up as she goes boneless, her hips flexing as her pussy clenches tightly around my fingers.

I'm hard again as she rides another wave of ecstasy, so I pick her up and pull her to me, impaling her on my cock, holding her against the shower wall. Burying myself as deep as I can go inside her, again and again, my mouth at her neck as she comes apart in my arms, my name falling from her lips. *Mik-hail...*

Which sends me over the edge to my own release the instant I hear her saying it. This time, when I pull out of her to come, she finds me quickly with her delicate hand and strokes me through to the end of the orgasm as she likes to do. This beautiful and brave woman who owns me...from yesterday to today to tomorrow to forever.

It takes us both several minutes to recover enough to finish getting clean; time we spend just holding each other, my chin on the top of her head as I like to do. She lets me dry her from head to toe with a towel and then carry her back to bed, where I can hold her some more. I have a lot of holding Reagan in my arms to make up for. For all those days and nights when I never imagined I could ever find this kind of deep connection of peace and love and acceptance with another person.

But I did.

Because once, there was this beautiful but lonely princess in terrible trouble who needed a hero. And by some random luck or accidental miracle across space and time, she picked me to be that hero at the exact moment she needed one.

It all happened just like that for us.

She chose *me*.

And when she did, she gave her heart to me in exchange for mine.

That deal is *done*.

Because Mr. Hockey will be keeping it forever.

epilogue

Reagan

Comic-Con
Los Angeles

"Are you sure anyone will know what I am?" I ask, running my hands down the green leather jumpsuit I'm wearing, then reaching up to touch the custom headpiece Mikhail had made, which he says makes my Mantis costume as realistic as possible.

"Yes, babe, for the tenth time, I promise people will get it."

He's dressed as Iron Man in an authentic metal-looking robot suit. My guy went all out on these costumes in a big way. And here we are, at Comic Con in Los Angeles, dressed as superheroes. I have now watched every Marvel and DC movie made at least once. Some more than once.

"I haven't dressed up like this since middle school," Mikhail comments as we wander into the large convention center space. It's filled with others who are, for the most part, dressed in costumes or character T-shirts. There are people of all ages, from babies to the elderly. Some costumes I recognize, most I don't. "I feel kind of stupid," Mikhail says under his breath.

"*You* feel stupid? But everyone here is dressed up. And no one will know it's you anyway. You're wearing a mask."

"Humph," he grunts at me in response.

We head over to a green screen where we wait in line to get our pictures taken. The photographer grins as we approach, commenting on our "sick" costumes. He has us choose a background and then takes a few photos. Just as we head to look at them on the screen, Mikhail taking off his helmet so he can see, we hear our names. "Mikhail? Reagan?"

We both look up, startled to be recognized, only to see Mikhail's teammate Boris and his girlfriend, Talia. Talia is in full Hogwarts robes, gold and magenta accents for Gryffindor, her hair in frizzy curls, a time-tuner hanging around her neck. Boris, I *think*, is dressed as a Fortnite character. He looks totally bizarre, and I can't help laughing as they run up and hug us, telling us how great our costumes are.

Mikhail looks slightly horrified to be running into one of his teammates here, when we're in full-on superhero nerd mode.

"What are you guys doing here?" Talia asks excitedly. "Who's the geek?"

I hitch my thumb at Mikhail. "He's been schooling me on all things superheroes. But it was my idea to come here."

"We've come the past couple of years," Talia says. "We love it."

We end up walking around together, checking out all the amazing booths and sitting in on a few exclusive, star-studded, movie sneak-peek events. As it nears the dinner hour, Talia asks if we want to change and get dinner with them.

A couple of hours later, we're at a swanky LA restaurant, finishing maybe the best meal I have ever eaten in my life. I've spoken to Talia a few times now, but we end up really hitting it off. Mikhail relaxes a bit, chatting with Boris about all things sports, comics, and video games.

As the server comes out with dessert, a champagne bottle also arrives. I look quizzically at Mikhail, who lifts his shoulders and shakes his head. But then, our attention is shifted to Boris, who drops to one knee in front of Talia.

"Natalia,"–he pulls a small jewelry box from his jacket pocket— "we have gone through some wonderful times together, and some hard times too. You have taught me so much and I am such a better man for having you in my life. I really want to be your husband and for you to be my wife. I want this to be forever with you, my love, my Natalia. Will you marry me, *krasotka*?"

Talia literally jumps out of her seat, squealing, and tackles Boris to the floor. She's kind of a klutz, to be honest, and Boris has to steady them both to avoid total disaster. He helps her back to her feet and, at this point, everyone in the restaurant is watching as he slips a massive ring on her finger, asking, "Is that a yes, *krasotka*?"

"Yes. Yes. Of course, it's a yes!"

There are claps from throughout the restaurant, and the server comes back to pop the champagne, pouring some into each of our glasses.

Boris is grinning ear to ear and Talia looks giddy enough to pass out as she holds out her hand, showing me the flawless diamond ring.

"Congratulations," Mikhail says, a genuine smile on his face.

We raise a toast, and Boris says, "I don't usually drink, so wish me luck."

It's obvious that the two newly engaged have important things to accomplish, because they pay their bill in a hurry, telling us how much fun they've had before nearly running out of the restaurant. Talia turns back to tell me she'll be in touch to talk wedding planning with me soon.

Wow. That's two high-profile clients from the Crush I've brought to Silver & Golden since I started working there. A proposal and a new client were not what I was expecting when we were invited to dinner tonight. I can't wait to share the news with Veronique, who has turned out to not only be a very gracious and warm boss but also my loudest cheerleader. I've learned so much and know with absolute certainty that it's the job for me. I feel as though all the hard, tough years have made me stronger and more confident at my job.

Mikhail and I catch a cab back to our hotel, holding hands across the seat, both still smiling at the sight of being there for such a romantic moment.

"I can't believe he didn't tell us to fuck off tonight." Mikhail shakes his head. "Like, he probably didn't plan on having company for that."

"Maybe not, but Boris seems like an easy-going guy to me, and I barely know him. If he minded, I certainly didn't sense it."

He hums an affirmative response, squeezing my hand as we pull up to the hotel.

In our spacious suite, we both undress and put on our comfortable sleepwear, snuggling on the bed while we search Netflix for something to watch.

"All that romance gave you some big ideas about marriage, huh?"

My head is on his chest, so I can't see his expression. "Um, no, not really. But since you brought it up, *Mr. Hockey*, would it be so bad, to marry me?"

"Not at *all*, babe," he says quickly. "I know it will be the opposite of bad, but we're both still young."

"Yeah, you're right about that." I let the topic drop since I was not the one to start us down the judgment road at his teammate's decision to welcome us to witness his proposal.

Some moments pass, Mikhail's fingertips running up and down my side, snaking my shirt up just a bit so he can touch my skin. "Besides, when I propose to you, it will be way more romantic than at a restaurant after attending some nerd convention."

"Who's the person with a thousand superhero books and movies and toys on his shelves? It's not a nerd convention, it's a Mikhail convention. And it seems like your teammate is totally in your corner about it."

He chuckles. "Fair enough. But still, Mr. Hockey will do better."

I look up, and his eyes are alight with amusement. I kiss him sloppily on the lips as he pulls me fully on top of him, an erection apparent as I settle onto him. "So, the vibe I'm getting here is *this*: Mr. Hockey sure likes talking about someday popping the question. *A lot*. He's the one who keeps bringing it up."

I wiggle my hips against him, and he smacks my ass playfully. "The future *Mrs*. Hockey has nothing to worry about. I'll bring it up for her, all right." He gives me a thrust of his hard cock, grinding it up against me for extra effect.

Aw. He's telling me without *telling me* he wants to marry me. Nothing is cuter than Mikhail in a teasing mood like this. Which is something I enjoy seeing more and more of since he and his dad have figured out the boundaries for their relationship. Wiggling some more, I plant another array of wet, loud kisses on his neck and chest.

"I'll bet he's really vanilla in lots of ways," Mikhail says, mischief in his voice.

"Oh yeah?" I stop kissing him and sit up.

"Yeah. Missionary all the way."

"Poor Boris is getting dragged here. And you think you're more creative?"

He just gives me a cocky, lopsided grin.

"Well then, Mr. Hockey, my love, you'll have to show me what you've got someday."

"Oh, I plan on it, future Mrs. Hockey."

I smile and then hum, knowing my Mr. Hockey is always a man of his word.

But then, with the speed and stealth of the superhero he is, he has our positions reversed in an instant and proceeds to pounce on me, holding me captive beneath his hard body.

"The future Mrs. Hockey is curious about this ultra creative plan of yours."

Still grinning and looking mighty proud of himself as he prepares to ravish me, he winks at me and says, "I don't think you'll have to wait all that long to find out, babe."

my thoughts about...

afterword

Extensive creative license was applied in portraying some elements of NHL games, fan events and awards, that would ***not happen in real life***. I did this intentionally to create a more enjoyable reading experience within the storyline. These stories have been carefully crafted for your reading pleasure and in no way meant to be a true and accurate representation of NHL best practices and/or official rules currently or in the past.

Hockey Romance F-I-C-T-I-O-N all the way!!!

vegas crush by trope

All books in the **VEGAS CRUSH** series are *STANDALONES* existing in a connected world centering around a Las Vegas ice-hockey team. You can read them out of order if you wish and everything will still make sense with only minor spoilers. I've made a list of tropes for you here.

CRUSHED

BOOK 1

Forbidden, Reformed "Player", Ukrainian/American Hero, Good Girl Heroine, Office Romance, Love in the Workplace, He Falls First, Sports Romance, Team Captain, Social Media Manager, Risking it All for Love, Band of Brothers

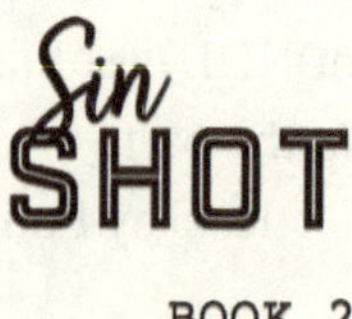

BOOK 2

Bad Boy Russian Hero, Virgin Heroine, Damaged Heroine, Forbidden, Office Romance, Hockey Defenseman, Team Physical Therapist, Love in the Workplace, Band of Brothers, Overcoming Self-Doubt and Addiction, Trust

Red ROCKET

BOOK 3

Grumpy/Sunshine, Russian Hero, Feisty Red-Haired Heroine, Forbidden, Office Romance, Hockey Defenseman, Public Relations Manager, Love in the Workplace, He Falls First, Brooding Alpha, Opposites Attract, Band of Brothers

Puck MONEY

BOOK 4

Opposites Attract, Forbidden Romance, Financial Advisor/Client Relationship, Russian/Romanian Hero, Nerdy Young Heroine, Fresh Start in Vegas, Dyslexic Hero, Gentleman Alpha, Good Guy Hero, He Falls First, Age Gap, Vegas Mafia Suspense, Savior Hero, Band of Brothers, Superstar Hockey Centerman

Smoke SHOW

BOOK 5

Friends to Lovers, Teammates Little Sister, Young Virgin Heroine, Russian Heroine, Boston Native, Bad Boy Hero, Forbidden Romance, First Love, Age Gap, Single "Dad" Vibes, Hardscrabble Upbringing, Band of Brothers, Hockey Defenseman, New Adulting, Found Family

The KEEPER

BOOK 6

Enemies to Lovers, Forced Proximity, Love in the Workplace, Neuro-Diverse Hero, French-Canadian Hero, Rock Chick Heroine, Socially Awkward w/ No Filter, Opposites Attract, Instant Attraction, Fish Out of Water, Band of Brothers, Superstar Hockey Goalie, Rockstar Heroine, Brooding Alpha, Guitar Lessons w/ Cute Kids, Personal Growth, Sacrificing for Love

Lucky PUCK

BOOK 7

Surprise Pregnancy, One Night Stand, Forbidden Romance, Love in the Workplace, Boss/Employee, Office Romance, Sneaky Dates, Instant Attraction, Age Gap, Mature Hero, Gentleman Alpha, Love After Divorce, Can't Keep Their Hands off Each Other, Career Milestones, Team General Manager, Team Nutritionist

Mr. HOCKEY

BOOK 8

Friends With Benefits, Instant Attraction, He Falls First, Brooding Alpha, Superhero Complex, Gentleman Alpha, Damsel in Distress, Knight in Shining Armor, Living up to Father's Legacy, Vegas Mafia Suspense, Comic Book Nerd, Wedding Planner Heroine, Band of Brothers, Finding Your Voice, Parent/Child Relationships

ClusterPUCK

BOOK 9

Age Gap, Secret Crush, Surprise Pregnancy, Shotgun
Wedding, Opposites Attract, The Owner's
Granddaughter, The Brooding Hockey Player, Forced
Proximity, Only 1 Bed, Career Milestones, Forbidden, Old
Family Friends, *Neanderthal* Hero, *Heiress* Heroine,
Parenthood, Beliefs, Growing Up, Manning Up, Facing
Your Demons, Family Legacy

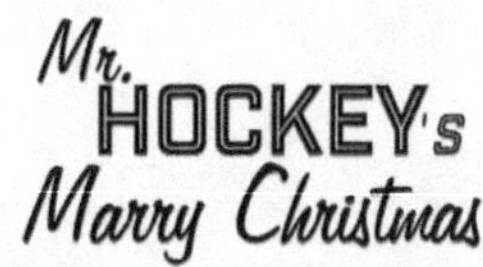
Mr. HOCKEY's Marry Christmas

BOOK 10

Christmas Marriage Proposal, No Third-Act Breakup,
Proposal Problems, Brooding Hockey Player Hero,
Buying a Home, Festive Holidays, Dear Santa Letter,
Gentleman Alpha, Building a Legacy, Comic Book Nerd,
Wedding Planner Heroine, Team Captain, Band of
Brothers, Family Relationships, OTT Romantic Gifts

about the author

BRIT DEMILLE is the alter ego of *NYT* Bestselling author, Raine Miller, having an absolute blast writing books quite different from what she writes as Raine.

Stories about sexy billionaires [millionaires make the cut too] who fall in instalove with young women who may or may not be virgins, and then go on to make adorable babies together are her favorite themes. In addition to the billionaires, hot hockey players are at the top of her list of favorite heroes, along with royals and ex-military bodyguards.

Most important when she writes a story is a happily ever after. But during the actual *writing* of the story, the most important thing is a cup of hot tea with a splash of milk (and don't forget the stash of cherry Jolly Ranchers). A dog or two will likely be in between her and the chair at any given moment, which is very handy, because they are the ones who approve everything she writes.

RAINE MILLER is a #2 *New York Times, USA Today,* and *Wall Street Journal* bestselling author since 2012. Before that, she spent two decades teaching kiddos to read—something she's most proud of. These days, writing steamy romance books pretty much fills up the hours...for which she keeps pinching herself to make absolutely sure she's not dreaming.

#Truth

She has a handsome husband, two amazing sons, and two very bouncy Italian greyhounds to keep her busy the rest of the time. Her boys know she writes romance books but gratefully they have zero interest in reading even a single one. *Thank. God.*

When she's not writing she's likely deep into a hockey game cheering on her beloved *VEGAS GOLDEN KNIGHTS* and dreaming up a new book. The greyhounds are likely to be in her lap while she writes the books or watches hockey—both dogs at the same time of course!

She loves to hear from readers and chat about the characters she's created.

You can connect with Raine on Facebook in her reader group, ***Raine Miller Romance Readers.*** She pops in to visit most days because it's a super happy place where romance awesomeness abounds day in and day out with the most amazing readers on earth.

> *My readers are the heart and soul of what keeps me writing the words.*

#Truth2

also by raine miller

The BLACKSTONE AFFAIR

NAKED, Part 1

ALL IN, Part 2

EYES WIDE OPEN, Part 3

RARE and PRECIOUS THINGS, Part 4

The ROTHVALE LEGACY

PRICELESS, I

MY LORD, II

BLACKSTONE DYNASTY

FILTHY RICH, I

FILTHY LIES, II

HOCKEY ROMANCE *as Brit DeMille*

CRUSHED, Vegas Crush #1

SIN SHOT, Vegas Crush #2

RED ROCKET, Vegas Crush #3

PUCK MONEY, Vegas Crush #4

SMOKESHOW, Vegas Crush #5

The KEEPER, Vegas Crush #6

LUCKY PUCK, Vegas Crush #7

Mr. HOCKEY, Vegas Crush #8

CLUSTERPUCK, Vegas Crush #9

Mr. HOCKEY's MARRY CHRISTMAS, Vegas Crush #10

CONTEMPORARY ROMANCE

CHERRY GIRL

HUSBAND MATERIAL

LOVELY PINK

HISTORICAL ROMANCE

The MUSE

The PASSION of DARIUS

The UNDOING of a LIBERTINE

Wedding Night Diaries

LORD BLACKWOOD'S VIRGIN

join raine mail

For my newsletter and information on upcoming books and events, you should definitely sign up for Raine Mail. Use the QR code below.

whispers *There's so many freebies in that thing.*

subscribe to Raine Mail

www.ingramcontent.com/pod-product-compliance
Lightning Source LLC
Chambersburg PA
CBHW030603170726
48283CB00002B/455